HOUSE
of
FRAGILE
DREAMS

Also by Anne Moose:

Arkansas Summer

HOUSE *of* FRAGILE DREAMS

ANNE MOOSE

MISSION VIEJO, CA

Published by ACT TWO, Mission Viejo, California
Cover design by Anne Moose
The painting, *"Me,"* by Colin Bootman, is used on the cover with permission of the artist.

For inquiries: annemoose.as@gmail.com

ISBN: 978-0-578-90068-1

For Peter, John, Olivia, & Paul.

CHAPTER ONE

SITTING COLD AND ALONE in a police interrogation room, I struggled to hold it together. I was desperate to talk to someone—to explain my actions to anyone who would listen—but hours passed and no one came. Glancing at the luminous red dot on the camera perched above the door, I wondered if I was being watched. I considered waving, or signaling for someone to *please* come talk to me, but decided to remain still, wanting to appear calm. But I wasn't calm, nor was I completely innocent.

I thought back over the last couple of weeks, and it was hard to fathom how quickly things had happened—and how much had happened. I shivered, then straightened my posture and took a gulp of air. *How much longer would I have to wait?*

CHAPTER TWO

IT WAS A FRIDAY night. I'd been to a going away dinner at a nearby restaurant, then returned to my small Long Beach office building to pick up a thumb drive I'd forgotten. I normally climbed the stairs—it being my habit to find exercise wherever possible—but it was late, and I was tired. The building had seemed deserted, so I was surprised, when the doors opened for the ride down, to see a tall black man in a t-shirt and jeans. I didn't recognize him, but I didn't want to appear fearful. On the contrary, I wanted him to notice my lack of hesitation—to see that I wasn't afraid. But as I entered the elevator, he looked quickly down at his sneakers, giving me little opportunity to offer a smile or visual cue of any kind. I did mumble a meager "Hi," and he nodded, but that was it.

Smiling to myself, I pushed the button for the first floor. The elevator descended, red lights above the door indicating, as we progressed, 4, 3… Before reaching 2 there was a major THUNK and we jerked to a stop. A moment later, there was a loud whirring sound and the lights went out, leaving us in total darkness.

My heart raced with a sudden adrenaline rush, and I'm ashamed to say that, for an instant, I wondered if the stranger next to me could somehow be responsible.

Out of the darkness I heard, "You gotta be kiddin' me."

I held my breath, waiting for the elevator to move. It didn't, and neither did the person standing next to me. "I can't believe this," I said, trying to sound calm. "I never take the elevator. I always take the stairs."

"You work in this building?"

"Until next week," I said, my fear now morphing into guilt at my gut reaction. "What about you?"

"No," he said, "I'm just here looking for my mother. She works late here some nights, but I guess she isn't working tonight."

I wondered which of the women I'd seen around the building might be his mother.

"Isn't there some kind of emergency button or something we should push?" he said.

"Hold on. We can use the flashlight on my phone." I felt around in my purse, then remembered hurling my phone in the car after listening to an obnoxious voicemail from my brother. I could picture it face-down on the passenger seat. "Oh no," I said. "I don't have my phone. Can we use yours?"

What came back was, "*Fuck.*"

"Seriously?"

"I dropped it on the cement this morning and had to take it to a repair place. *You believe that?* If I had it, I could've just called my mom and wouldn't be stuck here now."

Trying not to panic, I began feeling around on the elevator keypad. "I think I found the emergency button, but I'm not sure."

"Hold on," he said. "I have a lighter."

A moment later, the darkness was illuminated by an elongated flame, which he held close to where my finger was now poised to push what turned out to be the right button. "That's it," he said.

I pushed, but no alarm sounded.

I could now see the face of the man standing next to me. He was handsome, and though it feels shallow to admit it, his good looks helped calm my nerves.

"Do you think it did anything?" he asked.

"I hope so," I said. "But with this old building, nothing would surprise me."

"Push it again."

I did, and, like before, there was no indication that any kind of alarm had been raised. All we could do was hope that someone *somewhere* had seen our call for help. Maybe at a fire department or security company.

The flame disappeared and we were, once again, plunged into darkness. "This sucks," I heard. "I can't be stuck here."

"Someone will probably come rescue us," I said.

"Let's yell for help," he suggested. "Maybe someone else is still in the building."

"Good idea."

"HELP!" we both yelled in concert. "HELP!! We're stuck in here! Anybody, help!"

We yelled like that for maybe fifteen seconds, then waited for a response, but nothing came back. We yelled some more, then waited some more. Still nothing.

We stood in silence for a time, probably less than a minute, but the eerie quiet compounded the disorientation caused by the darkness. I pushed the emergency button a couple more times.

"I hope we're not gonna be stuck here all night," I said, trying to restore some sense of reality. "My name is Rachel, by the way." I figured if we were going to be trapped together, we might as well introduce ourselves.

"I'm Nate," he said. "And I can't be stuck here. I've got a son." He sounded kind of panicked.

We hollered some more, but eventually became hoarse, and it began to seem pointless. When we finally gave up, I could hear Nate's frustration boiling over next to me, expressed in a series of sighs and changes in his breathing. I could also smell that he was sweating heavily. Being without a speck of light, my other senses definitely kicked in. I could literally feel his state of mind.

My distress gave way to sympathy. "How old's your son?"

"Five. Name's Isaiah."

Now his tone was more genial, which spurred me on. "Where is he now?"

"With my sister, but she's expecting me to pick him up soon. She's a nurse and gets up at, like, four or something. I need to go get him before she goes to bed."

I wondered about the boy's mother, but didn't say anything. It sounded like she might not be in the picture.

"She's gonna be pissed as hell if I don't show up."

"You're stuck in an elevator. There's nothing you can do. She'll understand."

"Yeah, well, I guess so, but what's my son gonna think? I don't want him thinking something's happened to me."

I wanted to say something encouraging, but nothing came to mind. It was like the blackness surrounding us had seeped into my brain.

He chuckled sardonically and I could practically hear him shaking his head. "This is *so* messed up."

After that, we sat down with our backs against separate walls and fell into a silence that was punctuated only by an occasional heavy sigh or curse on his part. No one was coming to rescue us. That was clear.

Accepting that we might be in for a long night, I pulled my knees up to my chest and closed my eyes. I was silently admonishing myself for *not taking the stairs, like I always did,* when Nate spoke up.

"I just thought of something," he said. "I bet there's one of those trap doors in the ceiling. If so, maybe we can find a way outta here."

It seemed far-fetched, but I sensed his desperation and wanted to be supportive. "I guess we can take a look."

His lighter suddenly flamed on, and he stood up and held it up toward the ceiling. To my surprise, there did appear to be a moveable panel, but I couldn't imagine how he could possibly climb up to it. The elevator was too deep and wide for him to climb up using his legs, and I doubted he could pull himself up with his arms. The ceiling was too high. I tried to envision myself hoisting him up, but he was at least six feet tall and probably a hundred and sixty or seventy pounds. At five-six, there was no way I could do it.

The flame disappeared. "Take this and light it," Nate said, pressing the lighter into my hand.

As I flicked it back on, he stooped down and began untying one of his shoes. When he had it off, he stood back up and used it to push up the ceiling panel.

"It opens," he said triumphantly. "What if I boost you up there? There might be a ladder or some other way to climb out."

I knew damn well there was no way I was going to scale the walls of a pitch-black elevator shaft, but he sounded so hopeful that I wanted to at least feign a positive attitude. "I guess maybe I could take a look," I said, "but I seriously doubt there's any way to climb out."

"You never know," he said.

At that moment I was grateful for two things. First, I was wearing pants and a blouse I didn't care about. Second, I was light and reasonably agile. (At thirty-five, I prided myself on being fit.)

"Let me just take off my shoes," I said, determined to be a good sport. I handed him the lighter and removed my shoes, but my heart started beating so hard that I had to take a few moments to calm myself.

"I'm not asking you to do anything crazy," Nate said, seeming to sense my fear.

Holding the flame aloft as he worked on the panel, he looked older than I'd originally thought. I guessed mid-thirties. "I can get you up there, no problem," he said. "Then, just see what's there." He looked hopeful in the wavering light. "Can you do it?"

"I'm probably crazy, but okay," I said, and the look on his face really did make me want to try.

The lighter went out and he handed it to me. "Put this in your pocket."

I did, then asked, "So, how are we gonna do this?"

"I'm gonna just lift you up. Piece of cake. And don't worry, I won't let you fall."

"Okay," I said, trying to tamp down my fear.

I felt his hands on my waist. "Wait," I said, disoriented in the darkness. "I'm scared."

"You don't have to do anything you don't want to," he said. "It's totally up to you."

I stood quietly for several seconds, trying to summon courage. Then, impulsively, I said, "All right, let's do it."

"That's what I'm talkin' about," Nate said, and I felt buoyed by his enthusiasm.

His fingers tightened around my waist. "Now here we go. Just let me know if there's any kind of problem and I'll stop."

A moment later, I began rising, his large hands seeming to lift me without effort.

In total blackness, I felt my way to the opening in the ceiling and moved the panel all the way over. With Nate holding me steady, I placed first my hands, then my arms onto the top of the elevator. Once my arms were firmly placed, Nate pushed me further in, moving his hands briefly to my butt, then my legs as I made my way to safe purchase.

Cautiously, and with little grace, I managed to flip over into a sitting position. I had worried about how strong the roof of the elevator might be, but it felt reasonably solid. When I was situated, I heard, "You okay up there?"

I blew out a breath of relief. "I'm good. Now I just need to get the lighter."

Nate's voice rose up from the darkness. "Be careful."

I pulled the lighter from my pocket and, after a few tries, managed to get it lit.

"What's it look like up there?" Nate called.

Trying not to burn myself, I raised my arm and moved the flame slowly around, inspecting each of the four walls. I spotted the doors for the floor above us—probably about ten feet up—but saw no way of realistically climbing either up or down. "I'm sorry," I called back, "but I don't see a way out."

"You sure?"

"I'm sure," I said. "But I can see the doors for the third floor. If anybody's up there, maybe they'll hear us if we yell again. It'll probably be a lot louder if I yell from up here."

"Good idea," Nate said.

We screamed for help once again, and the elevator shaft did increase the volume of our cries, but, as before, they seemed to go unheard.

When we gave up, I was faced with the chilling prospect of dropping back down.

"Are you ready?" Nate asked when the time came to take the plunge. I was sitting with my legs dangling, and he had me as far as he could reach, which was about mid-calf.

The utter blackness was terrifying. "I'm not sure I can do this. Maybe I should stay up here."

"What if the power comes back on and the elevator starts moving? You might not want to be up there if that happens."

"Oh my God," I said, suddenly visualizing the elevator springing to life and going up. "Get me down from here—but please be careful."

"Don't worry, I got you," Nate said. "This is nothing. Just leave everything to me. Okay? You ready?"

"Ready as I'll ever be," I said. "On three, all right? You count."

"Okay. One...two...*three*."

At three, I slowly pushed my way out, feeling Nate's hands slide past my knees, over the outside of my thighs, around my hips and then to my waist, as he gently lowered me down.

"Wow," I said when I was firmly on my feet. "That was easier than I expected."

"I'm the man," Nate said, and, even in the dark, I was struck by his charm.

When he released me a moment later, we were back to square one. Trapped, with no end in sight. But something had changed that made the prospect a little less terrible, at least for me. Now we felt less like strangers and more like friends.

CHAPTER THREE

"I GUESS WE MIGHT as well sit down again," I said, now contemplating the very real possibility of an all-night wait. I lowered myself to the floor and felt my way to my stuff. I pushed my shoes over and rummaged through my purse for a package of life savers. *At least I could keep our breath fresh.*

Nate was sitting quietly against the wall to my left, and I wondered what he was thinking. "You want a lifesaver?" I asked, popping one into my mouth. "That's all I have in the way of food. I hope you had dinner."

"I'm fine," he said, and the way he said it made me picture him shaking his head.

"You know, this might not be an elevator thing," I offered. "It could be an outage in the neighborhood that won't last that long. There are probably guys out there working on it right now."

"I hope so, 'cause this is bullshit."

"I'm sorry."

"It's not your fault," he said. "And I'm sorry about my language. I'm just frustrated."

"What's your son like?" I asked, hoping he wouldn't mind the question.

"I can show you his picture. I have one in my wallet."

I heard him moving around, then the lighter came on and he scooted over next to me and handed me a little class photo. He held the flame so I could see it. "That was a couple of months ago."

I studied the picture, and little Isaiah, with bright eyes and a missing tooth, was as cute as they come. "He's adorable," I said, and I pictured him waiting for his dad, wondering why he was late.

"He's small for his age. But smart. Really smart."

Now I was looking at Nate, and I could see affection for his son written on his face.

"*Damn,*" he whispered under his breath, and his features suddenly transformed. "This was supposed to take, like, two seconds. I would have just called, but like I said, I messed up my phone."

He shook his head in frustration, the flame of the lighter reflected in his eyes. I felt bad for him, but also envied him, having such a beautiful little boy that he loved so much.

"Is Isaiah in Kindergarten?" I asked, trying to strike a more positive note.

"Just finished," he said. "He starts first grade in the fall."

I turned my gaze back to the picture and felt a familiar longing and wash of pain.

"I need to get him into a better school, though," Nate said, almost like he was talking to himself.

He reached for the photo and slipped it back into his wallet. A moment later, he let the lighter go out, but he didn't move back to the other wall where he'd been sitting before. He settled next to me against the wall facing the door.

"What kind of work do you do?" I asked.

"For now, I'm a mechanic," he said. "I got out of the military not too long ago, and that's what I did in the Army. Since I've been back, I've mainly been working for a buddy of mine who has a car shop. It's nothing regular, and the pay sucks, but I'm working on a degree in mechanical engineering, so pretty soon I'll be able to get an engineering job."

"I have a mechanic friend who's always looking for help," I said. "If you want to pick up some extra money, I can give you his number."

"Thanks," Nate said, "but I'm all right. We've been staying with my mom in Compton, and she isn't charging much rent, so I'm good for now."

As he was talking, I was thinking about the cottage standing vacant behind my house. There was an elementary school right up the street. I almost mentioned it, but put it aside. "You said, '*Since I've been back.*' Were you in Iraq?"

"Afghanistan. I was deployed over there twice."

"That must have been pretty intense," I said. "Although I assume, if you were a mechanic, you didn't have to fight. At least, I hope not."

"I mostly stayed on base and worked on Humvees," he said, "but I saw some pretty heavy stuff." There was an undeniable sadness in his voice, and I regretted my question.

"I was in a truck that got hit by an IED," he added after a few moments. "I got torn up pretty good, but some other guys got it much worse than me." He sighed, then added, "I don't really like talking about it too much. I'm trying to forget it, actually."

"I'm sorry," I said.

We sat in silence for a time, and I began picturing the horror he must have endured.

"I'm doing okay," he said finally, as if reading my mind. "I had a hard time for a while."

"I'm sorry for bringing it up."

"It's fine. They say it helps to talk, but I don't know."

"I'm a pretty good listener, and we might not be going anywhere for a while."

"You're good people," he said. "I could tell as soon as you got in the elevator. A lot of women would have done an about-face as soon as they saw me. You know, pretended like they forgot something in their office, or something like that. You didn't even hesitate. I don't see too much of that. I respect that."

"I'm sorry people behave that way," I said.

"Well, there are some knuckleheads running around out here that I'm afraid of myself. It's just unfortunate that every black man has to be thrown into the pot. Know what I mean?"

"I know exactly what you mean," I said. "My father was black."

"Get out of here," Nate said, and he sounded as pleased as he was surprised. "What, was he like a light-skinned guy? Because you don't look black."

"He was my stepfather, but he raised me."

"No kidding. Where'd you grow up? L.A.?"

"Here in Long Beach," I said. "He and my mom had a big and tall store. He was *really* tall."

"Basketball player?"

"Ever heard of Wilt Chamberlain?"

"Are you shitting me?" he cried, his voice raising an octave.

"Yeah, I'm shitting you," I laughed. "He wasn't a basketball player. But he was extremely tall. Big, too. Not fat, just, you know..."

"Big boned," Nate chuckled.

"Exactly." I smiled in the dark. "His name was William. He died of cancer a few years ago."

"I'm sorry," Nate said. "But you were raised by a black man, eh? That's pretty cool."

"I think so," I said. "He was a great father, and I definitely benefited from his perspective."

"I hear you."

I was getting ready to launch into a story about William when Nate said, "I hate changing the subject, but maybe we should try yelling again. I really have to get out of here."

I doubted it would do any good, but I kept the thought to myself. "I guess it can't hurt," I said.

Nate mumbled something under his breath, and the scent of his sweat filled the air. "I feel like such an idiot," he said bitterly.

The change in his voice surprised me. Before I could offer anything in response, he added, "Remember I told you I got hit by the IED? I don't have a normal bladder anymore. If I don't get out of here soon, I'm gonna burst."

I felt terrible and thought longingly of an almost-empty water bottle I'd pulled from my purse that afternoon. Suddenly, I had an inspiration. "I might have an idea," I said. "I have my phone charger and some hair stuff in a pretty sturdy Ziploc. Maybe you can use that."

"Nah," Nate said. "I couldn't do that."

"Are you sure?" I said. "It's a pretty big bag. Can I at least show it to you? I honestly wouldn't mind."

There was silence, and I could tell that Nate was thinking about it. "Seriously," I said. "It doesn't have to be a big deal."

He exhaled, then abruptly said, "Okay, let's see it. Do you want the lighter?" He sounded hopeful.

"I probably don't need it."

I opened my purse and found the bag. It was sturdy, and maybe big enough. I dumped out the charger and hair clips and handed the bag over, first tapping him to get his attention. I was going for his shoulder but hit his bicep. It was like a rock. No wonder he'd lifted me so effortlessly.

"What do you think?" I asked. "Will it work? It's the kind with a slider, so it's easy to close."

He flicked the lighter on. "This might be okay," he said. Now he was more than hopeful; he was relieved.

He turned and looked me straight in the eye. "You sure you're all right with this?" He shook his head and made a face. "It seems kind of…I don't know, *wrong*."

I smiled. "I can take it. Really."

"If you're sure," he said.

The lighter went out and he stood up and moved to a corner. "Here goes. This is pretty effing weird."

A few seconds later he started, and the salty smell of urine rose in the air. I felt terrible for him, because I knew he was embarrassed, but I could tell, even in the dark, that his need had been severe. I prayed the bag would hold.

"I don't know," he said when he was finally done. "It's pretty full. And hot." He laughed nervously. "I hope I can close it up." He chuckled some more. "This is so crazy. I can't believe I'm doing this."

Moments later, he had it sealed. "Okay, I think I got it, but I'm kind of afraid to put it down. I don't know if it's gonna burst or what."

"It'll probably be all right," I said. "Just as long as it's closed up tight."

Nate planted the bag in the corner, then illuminated it with the lighter. When he was satisfied it was stable, he let the flame go out and sat down next to me again. "What a difference," he said with exhilaration when he was settled. "Thanks for that. That was good thinking. *Whew*."

"No problem," I said.

Nate's breaths were long and deep, and I was alarmed to realize how distressed he must have been. I handed him a wet wipe that I pulled from a packet in my purse and he laughed. "You gotta love women and their purses."

"I've got everything in here but my phone," I said with regret.

"Where is your phone, by the way?" Nate asked. "Mine's in the shop. What's your excuse?"

"Just before I got here, I listened to a message from my brother and threw it. It's in my car."

"I guess whatever he said must have been pretty bad."

"It wasn't what he said. It was *the way* he said it."

We sat quietly for a while after that, and in the inky blackness, I started to feel like I was floating in space. Finally, out of the darkness, Nate asked, "So, what about you? You have any kids?"

"Nope, no kids." I hoped my matter-of-fact answer would close the subject for discussion.

"Married?"

"Divorced," I said, hating, as always, the failure that was implied by the admission.

"My wife and I got divorced," Nate said. "Then she died, unfortunately."

"*Oh nooo...*" I said, and it came out sounding like a moan. I tried to think of a more thoughtful response, but my mind went blank.

"You never did tell me what you do in that office up there," Nate said, obviously wanting to change the subject.

"I'm a writer," I said. "The group I've been working for is a non-profit, but they're moving up to Sacramento in about a week, so it won't be my office much longer."

"You relocating, too?"

"No. I just moved back here from the East Coast a couple of years ago. I have no desire to move again."

"New York?"

"Boston."

"So, what kind of writing do you do?"

"All different kinds, but, for these guys, I've mostly been helping with their website and working on grant applications. It's an organization that advocates for the disabled." Before I could say more, there was a loud *whoosh* and the lights abruptly came back on, making us both jump and squint in the bright light.

"Hallelujah!" Nate hollered. He sprang to his feet while I put on my shoes, then offered me his hand and pulled me up.

He nodded at the elevator buttons. "Would you like to do the honors?"

"Push away," I said.

Nate pushed a button and the elevator jerked to life, beginning a slow descent to the first floor. When we stopped with a jolt, the doors opened to a dimly lit lobby and strange feeling of anti-climax.

Nate and I looked at one another and smiled.

"What do you think I should do with that?" Nate asked, gesturing to the bag propped up in the corner. "I feel like an idiot. All I had to do was wait a few more minutes."

"It makes for a better story."

He laughed. "Maybe for you."

The doors to the elevator closed as we pondered the Ziploc. I raised my eyebrows. "We could leave it as a great unsolved mystery."

"Nah," Nate chuckled. "I couldn't do that." He pushed a button, and when the doors opened again, he cautiously lifted the bag and we both exited into the lobby. A moment later, he gingerly placed the specimen into a trash receptacle that was mercifully located only a few feet from the elevator door.

Now ready to go, Nate looked at me with an amused grin. "Gotta run," he said, "but it's been an honor."

Regretting that I'd probably never see him again, I pulled a business card from a pocket on the side of my purse and handed it to him. "If your sister gives you any grief about being late, tell her to call me and I'll set her straight."

He took the card and read it. "Rachel Hayes," he said. "Thanks."

I smiled and nodded. Then, before I could say anything more, he opened the door to the street, flashed one last smile, said, "Catch you later," and sprinted into the night.

CHAPTER FOUR

BACK HOME, I COULDN'T stop thinking about Nate and Isaiah. I tried to envision where they lived, but despite my proximity, I had very little experience in South L.A. Most of the images I conjured were from TV shows and movies. I thought again about my back cottage and wished I'd mentioned it to Nate. It seemed so perfect. There was a great elementary school just a block away.

The more I thought about it, the more I liked the idea. I was often lonely in my oversized house. I pictured Nate and Isaiah throwing a ball around the backyard, fooling around in the pool. I could think of a host of reasons Nate might not cooperate with my fantasy—one being the overwhelming whiteness of the neighborhood.

I considered William. He hadn't been uncomfortable in the slightest. On the contrary, nothing made him happier than to go out on a weekend and mow the front lawn, Marvin Gaye or Al Green blaring from the porch. At a burly six-foot-six, he knew he presented a spectacle, but he didn't care, and over time, he became the most beloved person on the block, famous for his boisterous laugh and backyard barbecues. He was known as *William Big and Tall*, or *Big William*, and when he died, practically the whole neighborhood came to the funeral. His sister Jane had comically observed that she hadn't seen so many white people crying "since the Kennedy assassination," and it really was a scene, with so many people—all shapes, colors, and sizes—weeping and blowing their noses.

I still struggled with the loss of both William and my mother, who, barely two years after William's passing, also died of cancer. I sometimes wondered at the wisdom of living in their house. As much as I loved it, it was too big for one person, and it was a constant reminder of the kind of life I'd failed to create for myself. It was also a massive bone of contention with my brother. After our mother died, I'd bought his share—at a price that was more than fair. But the house had since appreciated, so now he was claiming I'd robbed him. He and I had also inherited the big and tall store, which we sold for a handsome sum. But he'd managed to lose that money, and the money I paid him for the house. He wouldn't tell me how he'd lost it, but I figured it was something stupid, like a drunken weekend in Las Vegas. I did feel sorry for him—at first—but now I was sick of being a target for his rage.

For Dan, being angry was a way of life. He preached hatred against practically everyone, and, lately, had become so politically extreme and gun-obsessed that he was scary. I'd never seen him with a gun, but he often bragged that he had "an arsenal," and I believed him. He'd chosen on his own to stop talking to me, and I was thrilled for the hiatus. The message prompting me to hurl my phone was the first I'd heard from him in months.

The breaking point for Dan was a lawn sign I put up during the last presidential election. He made a big public show of pulling up the sign and thrashing my yard with it—all the while spewing expletives and phrases so predictable, they'd have been laughable in another context. But this was not another context. Dan's tantrum was both destructive and terrifying.

"You fucking libtard bitch!" he'd shouted as he ravaged and flailed, his eyes blazing. *"You know what you can do with this horse shit!"*

When he'd finally tired of laying waste to my mother's flower garden, he practically broke down my front door and threw the sign in my face, continuing with a tirade that was so loud and ugly, a neighbor called 911. By the time the police arrived, he was gone, but over the next few days, he left me messages that were totally unhinged.

He and I had never been close. He was ten when I was born, so the age difference between us was huge. According to my mother, he suffered terribly from the loss of our father, who died when I was just a toddler. As far as I was concerned, William was my father. To Dan, William was an interloper who'd stolen his mother, then pulled him up by the roots. My mother and William had tried endlessly to make Dan happy, but, over time, he became more and more troubled, eventually finding his way to people and ideas that fueled the bitterness inside of him.

Feeling melancholy and alone, I thought about a small cache of marijuana that someone had given my mother when she was sick. I wasn't a big pot smoker, but I sometimes enjoyed the creativity it evoked when I was by myself. I'd had some of my greatest inspirations when I was high—although, admittedly, I'd also had some of my worst. Ideas had a way of losing their luster once the drug wore off.

It was late, and I might have just opted to go to bed, but, instead, I filled the tub, pulled a joint from a little wooden box on my dresser, and proceeded to take a candle-lit bath. Ordinarily, a hot bath in flickering light was one of my greatest simple pleasures. That night, under the influence, it was much more.

I was inclined to conjuring, no doubt a symptom of the isolation I'd inflicted on myself since my divorce. That night, I conjured a conversation with Nate. I told him things in the bath that night, and in my imagining, he talked back. And though I was high, and it wasn't real, when I woke up the next morning, the luster of that interaction had *not* worn off, and I found myself wishing I'd offered him the cottage when I had the chance.

cs

I spent much of the next day finishing up a grant proposal I'd been working on. The deadline was looming, so I needed to put my nose to the grindstone, but I was constantly distracted by thoughts of Nate. Around two o'clock, I finally hit Send, which meant that, unless I got back a request for more changes, I was done—with both the grant application and the job contract.

I was in the process of wishing for the hundredth time that I'd gotten Nate's phone number, when my cell phone rang. I answered without paying attention to who was calling, and when I heard my name, my stomach lurched upon recognizing my brother's voice.

"I'm not interested in talking to you," I said before he could say anything more. "I've had enough."

I hated being so acerbic, but pretending we could have a civilized relationship seemed pointless. He'd caused me nothing but grief since my mother's death, and I knew by the tone of the message he'd left me that this time would be no different.

"I wouldn't call if I didn't have to," he said. "Unfortunately, I need to move into the cottage for a while."

This sent my adrenaline through the roof. "No way," I said. "I don't know what your story is, but there's no way you're moving in here." I took some deep breaths and tried to calm myself. "I'm sorry, Dan, but no."

"You can be sorry all you want," he hollered. "No matter what you say, that's my house, too, and I'm moving into the back."

I couldn't believe this was happening.

"First of all," I said as calmly as I could, "this is not *your house, too*. This is *my* house. I paid you five hundred thousand dollars in cash for your share of this house, so you have no claim on it whatsoever. *None*. And I refuse to fight with you about it anymore. I'm sorry about whatever's going on with you, but you're going to have to find somewhere else to stay."

He started to argue, but I cut him off. "I've rented the cottage, so even if I wanted to, I couldn't let you move in. It's not possible. I'm sorry."

I held my breath, praying he'd let it go, but, as always, he persisted. "What do you mean you rented the cottage? When did you do that?"

"It's none of your business when I did that," I said, then I tried to modulate my tone to sound less combative. "I'm sorry, but you've made it really clear that you and I can't have a relationship, so I need you to just live your life and leave me out of it."

I braced myself for what would come back, but there was silence on the other end.

"You have no one to blame but yourself," I said.

"*Fuck you*," he screamed, then he abruptly hung up, leaving me agitated and more than a little afraid.

ભ

After the phone call with Dan, I spent the rest of the day worrying that he'd show up and discover the cottage was empty. I knew he had no legal right to claim it, but I also knew that if he tried, I could be in for an extended nightmare. When I thought about offering the cottage to Nate, it seemed clear that now it was a bad idea. It wouldn't be right to put him in the middle of a battle.

I was lying on the couch in the living room, trying to read, but mostly feeling sorry for myself, when my cell phone rang. Relieved to see it wasn't Dan, I picked it up after the third ring.

"Hi, is this Rachel?"

I immediately sat up, recognizing Nate's voice. "Yes, this is Rachel. Is this who I think it is?"

"I don't know. Who do you think it is?"

27

"I think it's someone I would recognize even in the dark."

"Well, I guess you would," he said. "How are you doing? It looks like you made it home all right after our little adventure."

"I did," I said. "But what about you? Did your sister give you a hard time for being late?"

"She was all right once I explained everything."

A child's voice in the background made me smile. "Is that Isaiah I hear?"

"You remembered his name." He sounded pleased.

"Of course," I said. "I love kids. And I've actually been thinking about you and Isaiah."

"Really? What have you been thinking?"

"You know..." I said, nervous about what to say. "I was hoping you weren't in trouble, and that Isaiah wasn't too worried." I wanted to mention the cottage but bit my tongue.

"Like I said, everything turned out fine, but the reason I'm calling is I'm wondering about that mechanic you mentioned. I just talked to my buddy, and he doesn't have any work for me right now, so I thought maybe I could get your guy's number after all. If you don't mind."

"Of course I don't mind," I said. "Hold on and I'll find his number. His name's Jeff."

I went into my phone's contacts and recited the number. "If you want," I added, "I can call him and find out if he still needs someone."

"That'd be great. Thanks."

I hung up and called Jeff. He didn't answer, but I left a long message, talking Nate up, and playing up the veteran angle. When I called Nate back, I was going to ask him if he wanted to meet for coffee, but before I had a chance, he thanked me and said he had to run. Then, suddenly, he was gone.

A short time later, I got a message on Match.com from a guy I'd agreed to meet for dinner that night. I'd forgotten all about it. He was writing to double-check on the place and time. Not in the mood, I considered telling him something had come up, but I'd made the commitment, so decided to bite the bullet and confirm, hoping he wouldn't be just one more horny divorcé looking for a quick hookup.

CHAPTER FIVE

LOCKING THE FRONT DOOR on my way out that evening, I was happy I'd had the foresight to change the locks after my last blow-up with Dan. As I drove off, I kept an eye out for his truck. I knew he wasn't above waiting for me to leave, then snooping around to see if what I'd told him about the cottage was true. Just before leaving the house, I'd gone out and locked the gate that led to the backyard. I hoped this would keep him out but knew if he really wanted to get back there, he'd find a way in. I wished I had a dog. A big German Shepherd, or Pitbull.

With traffic, it was a forty-minute drive to where I'd agreed to meet Craig, and all the way I scolded myself for persisting with online dating. I had entered into it with great reluctance at the prodding of a friend, and so far, it had done nothing but confirm my suspicion that all the good men are taken by the age of thirty.

As I was parking the car, my thoughts turned to Nate, and I wondered if he'd talked to Jeff. I hoped so, and also hoped he'd call to let me know. I was just shaking my head at the monkey wrench Dan had thrown into my cottage idea when I noticed Craig watching me from the curb. I recognized him from his picture. I waved at him through the window, then got out of the car, telling myself, as I did, to keep an open mind.

Nicely dressed in a blue button-down shirt and suit pants, he definitely looked like a decent guy. According to his profile and what I'd managed to glean from a few emails (he wasn't a "phone guy"), he was forty-one, divorced with no kids, a lawyer, and politically liberal. He was also good looking with an impressive head of hair, which didn't hurt—although I tended to be wary of overly-attractive men.

"That was some pretty fancy parking," Craig said as I was stepping out of the car.

"You liked that, did you? I'm pretty famous for my parallel parking."

"Definitely impressive." He smiled, then pointed up the street to where a small group of trendy-looking people were milling around on the sidewalk. "The restaurant's just up there. Good thing I made a reservation."

As we headed up the block, a growing optimism replaced my dread, and I vowed to stay positive.

The restaurant we entered featured walls of Indonesian artwork and was bisected by a dramatic tropical fish tank that made the atmosphere luminous. Craig announced our arrival to a regally-dressed *maître d'*, and we were immediately led to a table near the back. A moment later, a busser arrived to give us menus and pour each of us a glass of water.

When he was gone, Craig lit up. "You look great. I love your long hair. A lot of guys go for blondes, but I've always been partial to brown hair. Yours is beautiful." He leaned forward. "You wouldn't believe how often women post misleading photos of themselves."

I was braced for a diatribe on overweight women who post old photos, but, instead, he followed up with, "Do you do a lot of online dating?"

"Not really," I said. The last thing I wanted was another conversation about bad dates and failed relationships, so I left it there, hoping he'd take the hint. He did.

"So, tell me, Rachel," he said with a gleam in his eye, "what's been happening with you?"

"Well, I got trapped in an elevator last night," I said impulsively.

"No kidding," he said, sounding intrigued. "Where? How long were you trapped?"

I started to tell the story, but before I got more than a couple of sentences in, he stopped me. "Wait. So, in the middle of the night, you got into an elevator with a strange man?"

"Well, it wasn't exactly the middle of the night."

"Still," he said. "You were taking a pretty big chance, don't you think?"

"I wasn't worried," I said. "It was fine."

"What did he look like? Old guy, young guy?"

Here we go, I said to myself, silently rooting for a response I could live with. "He was a black man in his thirties," I said matter-of-factly.

He paused and seemed to be calculating. "You look like you expect me to say something offensive."

"I'm just answering the question," I assured him.

He smiled and looked down at the table, obviously wanting to be careful about what he said next. "I can't imagine there wasn't at least some part of you that was nervous getting into that elevator."

"I wasn't nervous at all, and my father was black, so it's a sensitive subject," I said.

He gave me a quizzical look.

"Stepfather. But he raised me, so for all intents and purposes, my father."

"That's interesting," he said. "What was it like having a black father?"

It was tempting to answer the question honestly. To explain that William had implanted an awareness in me that set me apart from almost every other white person I knew. That when most girls I grew up with were reading Jane Austen, I was devouring James Baldwin, Maya Angelou, Richard Wright. That I sometimes felt like a spy in a group of white people. But, as always, I chose to answer the question by focusing on William and not the complicated contours of my psyche.

"It was wonderful," I said. "He was a great father and a really fascinating person, actually. I miss him every day."

We were interrupted by a waiter named "Raymond" who wanted to take our drink orders. We each selected a wine, then promised to be ready to order dinner when he came back. Afterwards, we turned our attention to our menus, although we stole occasional glances at one another. One of the times we exchanged a smile, and I wondered what he was thinking. I wasn't sure yet what to make of him, but there was no denying he was a cut above my previous computer-generated dates.

When the waiter came back with our drinks, we both ordered the same delectable-sounding duck dish. I was suddenly ravenous. All I'd eaten all day was an apple and a bowl of cereal.

෬

"You were going to tell me about your father," Craig said after the waiter departed with our orders.

"Okay," I said, and I felt the familiar mixture of love and pride that always filled me whenever I talked about him. "Well, he was originally from Philadelphia. Philly, as he would say. He was raised mostly by his grandparents. His mother died when he was very young, and his father ran off right after—although he came back into the picture later in his life."

I paused while a pretty young woman lit a small candle on our table. "He went to Vietnam right after high school, but he eventually got kicked out of the Army and spent time in the brig for punching a superior officer." I took a sip of my wine. "According to the way he told the story, the officer was berating some young kid who was traumatized after an ambush in which a lot of soldiers in his platoon were killed. William said something to the guy—you know, told him to leave the kid alone. The officer told him to shut up and called him the n-word, so William punched him." I smiled at the picture that came to mind. "I know it doesn't sound funny, but he had a great way of telling the story. Seeing that guy hit the floor was the highlight of his military career."

Craig was looking at me with obvious interest, if not affection. "How many years ago did he die?"

"Almost four," I said. "And I could go on and on about him. He really was an amazing person. He spoke a bunch of languages, owned a business, was involved in a lot of community stuff. Loved to cook, loved to tell stories, could build *anything*."

"What about your mom? What was she like?"

I looked away for a moment and my attention was drawn to an intricately carved mask that appeared to depict some type of goddess. In the dim light, and with swirling colors from the fish tank casting light and shadows over it, it looked otherworldly.

"She was unusual," I answered, turning back to Craig. "At least compared to all the other moms I knew. She was kind of a perennial flower child, I guess you might say, but she could definitely be business-like when she had to. She helped William run the clothing store he owned. He had a big and tall store, and she did all the books, all the tax stuff." I smiled at the thought of her. "She was multifaceted, to say the least."

I ran my finger around the rim of my wineglass. "She kind of prided herself on being unconventional. But she was really intelligent, really creative, extremely kind. She loved flowers and had an incredible passion for gardening. You wouldn't believe her garden. But she also did a lot of volunteer work, like making sandwiches at rescue missions, building houses with Habitat for Humanity—stuff like that. She and William both. There was a youth club they supported..."

I looked down at Craig's hands, which were folded on the other side of the table. "She was diagnosed with lung cancer right after William died. And she didn't smoke. It was totally out of the blue. *Horrible.* But she just refused to do chemotherapy."

I paused, struggling with a knot in my throat. "William did both chemotherapy and radiation before he died, and it ruined what little time he had left. After seeing what he went through, she didn't want any of it."

I looked back at the mask, trying to suppress the emotions that always accompanied memories of my mother's sickness and subsequent death. I had begged her to undergo treatment, but she wouldn't listen.

"I'm sorry about your mom," Craig said. "I bet she was beautiful."

Before I could respond, our server arrived with two plates of duck artistically arranged over some type of exotic rice and spicy vegetables. I was happy for the opportunity to move the conversation away from my mother. "I'm really hungry," I said, eyeing the food with relish. I picked up my fork and took a bite. "Oh my God, this is good."

After my third probably unladylike bite, I came up for air. "So, what about you? What's your family like?"

Craig glanced down at his plate and raised an eyebrow. "This is the best duck I've ever had," he said. "I'm going to have to remember this place." He picked up his wineglass and took a drink. "My family, huh?"

"You don't have to talk about it if you don't want to."

"I don't mind," he said, "but there's not much to tell, really. My family's nowhere near as interesting as yours."

Just then my cell phone rang.

"Sorry," I said. I pulled my phone from my purse to silence it and noticed it was Dan. I rejected the call, but I must have looked annoyed because Craig asked me if something was wrong.

"No," I said. "It's just my brother."

"You didn't mention you had a brother," Craig said. "Is it just the two of you, or are there other siblings?"

"No, just us."

"And is he also from your biological father, or is William his father?"

"No, he's from my real father. He's a lot older than I am."

"And what's he like? Are you close?"

I took a bite of rice and vegetables and thought about how to answer. I didn't want to think about Dan, much less talk about him. After swallowing, I picked up my napkin and wiped my mouth. "Definitely not close," I said.

"Does he live here in the L.A. area?"

"I'm not exactly sure where he is now," I said. "We're on opposite sides of pretty much any spectrum you can think of, so, frankly, the less we see each other, the better." I squinted my eyes. "I know that sounds bad."

"No, I know what you're saying," Craig said. "Politics, right?"

"That's not all of it, but it's a big part, I guess."

He gave me a reassuring look. "Politics has been ruining a lot of families lately. And friendships."

He grabbed a bottle of hot sauce from next to the wall and pulled off the top. "I have friends I don't talk to anymore." He shook the sauce over his rice, then screwed the top back on and set the bottle down. He took a bite and made a face. "Now, that's hot." He swallowed, then smiled. "Anyway, suffice it to say I understand about people falling out these days."

As if on cue, my phone rang again. "I'm sorry," I said. "I should have turned it off." I looked at who was calling and this time it was my next-door neighbor.

"Uh-oh," I said, having a bad feeling. "I'd better take this. I'll make it quick." I pressed the green phone icon. "Hi Nancy. I'm in a restaurant. What's going on?"

"I'm sorry to bother you," she said, "but I thought you should know your brother has been milling around your place for about the last forty-five minutes or so. Greg went out and talked to him, and he was asking a lot of questions about the cottage and seemed pretty upset. Did you tell him there was someone living back there? Because if you did, Greg might have screwed up."

I shot Craig a worried look. "Is he still there?"

"Yup," Nancy said. "His truck is parked in the driveway, and Greg thinks he might be drinking. He said he could smell beer on his breath."

I sighed heavily and wondered what I was in for when I got home. "Thanks, Nancy," I said. "And don't worry about the cottage. I did tell Dan I rented it, but Greg had no way of knowing."

"Are you going to be all right?" Nancy asked. "Do you want us to do anything?"

"I don't know what you can really do," I said. "Not unless you see him trying to break into the house, or something like that. But, even then, I don't know if it's a good idea to involve the police. Maybe you can just keep an eye on him and call me if you see him doing anything crazy."

"Okay," Nancy said, "and I'm sorry to have to deliver this news. I remember the havoc he caused the last time he was around."

"Thanks," I said, then I hung up and turned my attention to Craig, who was looking at me with concern.

"What's going on?" he asked. "Is everything okay?"

I sighed and rolled my eyes. "I haven't seen my brother in months, but right now he's sitting in my driveway. Drinking. That was my next-door neighbor. The last time she saw him he was destroying my front yard, so she's not a big fan."

I shook my head and took a bite of duck. "He wants to move in with me—or, rather, into a little in-law unit I have behind my house. I've told him no, but it looks like he's going to press it."

Craig looked alarmed. "Is he a violent guy?"

"I don't know," I said. "And I really don't even want to talk about it."

The waiter approached our table but Craig waved him away. "I don't remember if I told you this," he said, "but

39

I'm a prosecutor, so I know a little bit about disturbed men. Is your brother an alcoholic?"

"I'm not sure," I said. "He might be. But you're a prosecutor? I can't believe I didn't know that."

"I'm a Deputy District Attorney."

"Really? What kind of cases do you prosecute?"

"All kinds, but mostly violent crimes, like murder, armed robbery, rape. I do some drug cases but not petty stuff."

"Wow," I said. "For some reason I was thinking you were a tax lawyer or something like that."

"Nope, sorry, I'm not one of the rich ones. But getting back to your brother, if you want me to follow you back to your house when we leave here, I'll be happy to. Just to make sure everything looks kosher."

"Thanks," I said. "Let me eat some more and think about it."

We finished dinner, and I really *didn't* want to talk about Dan, so I directed most of the conversation to Craig's definitely interesting career as a Deputy DA.

By the time we left the restaurant I was feeling surprisingly good about Craig, but I didn't want to drag him into my conflict, so I turned down his offer to follow me home. Instead, I promised to send him a text when I knew I was safe.

CHAPTER SIX

DRIVING HOME, I WENT back and forth over how to handle Dan. It felt wrong to turn him away, but I also understood who he was. I'd be crazy to sign up for more of his shit, and, with Dan, there was always more shit. I recalled some of the terrible things he'd said to my mother before she died, and the memories made my temples pound.

Even then, even while taking abuse, she'd defended him. She blamed herself for Dan's malignance, believing she'd made a mistake marrying William while Dan was still at home. I disagreed. William had brought nothing but love and good humor into our household, despite the challenges posed by Dan. If my brother couldn't see it, it was because there was something broken inside of him that nothing could repair.

Over the years, psychologists had labeled him with a variety of personality disorders, but my mother had refused to accept their diagnoses, believing fervently that he would eventually come around. She'd tried everything she could think of to mend his spirit—sailing lessons, outdoor adventures, magic camp. She and William both had tried to interest him in sports. But nothing ever worked. He remained stubbornly on tilt, and he never acknowledged or appreciated their efforts on his behalf. If anything, he felt oppressed by their persistent attempts to fix him.

Despite everything, my mother never gave up hope, no matter how much grief Dan caused. And he caused a lot of grief. Between problems at school, drinking and drug problems, brushes with the law, and violent shows of temper that started in his late teens, Dan cast a constant pall over all our lives.

I knew what William would say about my current predicament. *"Don't let that boy ruin your life. He'll make it a living hell if you let him."*

William often spoke to me in my head. He'd been a big dispenser of wisdom when he was alive, and dying had done little to slow him down. I knew my penchant for imaginary conversations was odd, but William was good company, and his counsel was better than anything I'd ever heard from a psychologist or friend. As I was nearing home, he also chimed in on my impulse to offer the cottage to Nate.

"Before you do anything, make sure you examine your motives. You might think this man and especially that little boy are going to fill some hole in your life. If that's what you're thinking, it might not be wise to do it. It needs to be about them and not you. If it's about you, it's probably a bad idea."

I contemplated my motives, and they were such a tangle of different things, I couldn't be sure what I was really thinking deep down. It was true that when I envisioned Nate and Isaiah living in my backyard, I couldn't help seeing myself as some part of the picture, but I truly did want it for them. I had an empty apartment in one of the safest, most beautiful neighborhoods in Long Beach—where Isaiah could attend an excellent school. Nate had said himself he wanted to get Isaiah into a better school. Wouldn't it be nice to make the offer? It would. I believed that. But, of course, Dan was now screwing it up, just like he screwed everything up.

ɷ

The instant I saw Dan's truck, my resolve about how to deal with him wavered. I knew what I *wanted* to do, but it was hard to turn my back on him completely, especially knowing what my mother would want. I would not let him move in. On that I was firm. But maybe I could give him some money, or help him find a place to live, if that's what he needed. At the very least, I would try to remain calm and not be drawn into a battle.

Dan was in the driveway, so I parked in front of the house. I waited for him to emerge from his truck, but he didn't move. I got out of my car and approached him, thinking maybe he was asleep. He was. With his head back and mouth wide open, he looked like a fish on a hook. I expected to see him surrounded by empty beer cans, but I saw only one, which was a relief—although there were some duffel bags in the cab with him. For all I knew, they were filled with empties. In any case, I decided not to wake him and quietly entered my house, hoping I'd get lucky and he'd stay in the truck all night.

Once I was inside, I debated whether to text Craig, or wait. Anything could still happen. I decided to go ahead. What could he really do, anyway? I texted him: "Home safe. So far so good."

I immediately got back a thumbs up emoji, followed by: "Had a great night. Talk to you soon."

Just seconds after reading his message, I heard three sharp knocks on the front door. I wasn't going to get lucky after all. I took some deep breaths and tried to brace myself for whatever was coming.

Dan pounded some more, and now he was calling my name.

Starting for the door, I could hear my mother's voice. *"Be patient with your brother, Rachel, he needs you."*

I pulled open the door and Dan immediately rushed in, not waiting to be invited. "It's about time," he complained. "I've been out there for hours."

"I was out for dinner," I said, reminding myself to control my temper.

He headed for the kitchen, first craning his neck to peer into the living room—looking for what, I don't know. I figured he'd go straight to the refrigerator, and he did. "What have you got to eat?" he demanded. "I'm starving."

"Go ahead and make yourself a sandwich," I said. "You know where to find everything."

He began pulling items from the refrigerator, and I couldn't help but feel pity for him. He had several day's growth of beard and looked like he'd slept in his clothes for a week. I wondered if he'd been sleeping in his truck.

"Do you want to take a shower?" I asked, noticing that he also smelled bad. "If you want to, you can take a shower and I'll make you a sandwich. I can also wash your clothes if you want me to. I can give you a robe to wear until they're dry."

"Can I have some of this?" he asked, holding up an open bottle of wine.

"Help yourself," I said, resigned now to him spending at least one night. I wasn't crazy about him drinking, but I didn't want to argue with him, either. "Just don't drink all of it, if you don't mind," I added. "That's my last bottle of white."

I pulled two wine glasses from a cupboard and put them on the island in the center of the kitchen. "Pour me one, too," I said. "But then, seriously, go take a shower. You stink."

He gave me a sour look, then poured a huge glass for himself, not bothering with the one for me. Afterwards, he headed for the hallway.

"Use the downstairs shower," I called after him. "There are clean towels in there, and if you throw your clothes outside the door, I'll put them in the washer and get you a robe."

"*Fine!*" he hollered back, then he treated me to, "Man, do I have to take a vicious shit." Seconds later, I heard the bathroom door bang shut.

I poured myself a glass of wine and sank into a chair by the kitchen table. I knew I was being too nice, but I wanted to at least *try* to be a good sister. Hearing the squeal of the shower turning on, I chuckled nervously and shook my head. Then I raised my glass and took a drink of wine, praying things wouldn't go to hell, but knowing they probably would.

CB

Around eleven o'clock, Dan finally emerged from the bathroom, now clean shaven, with his dark hair combed back and still wet. His outgrown haircut was heading towards a mullet, and he had a noticeable beer belly, but with our father's olive skin and light-brown eyes, he wasn't bad looking when he wasn't wearing a sneer. "You look almost civilized," I said as he arrived barefoot in the kitchen, carrying his empty wineglass. My robe was short on him, reminding me that my mother had sometimes called him Chicken Legs. The description still fit.

He sat down at the table in front of the sandwich I'd made him and immediately began eating.

"So, what's going on?" I asked. "What happened?"

He swallowed a big bite, then picked up his empty glass. "Can I have more wine?"

I pulled the wine from the refrigerator and filled half his glass, then sat down across the table from him. "So, come on," I said, "what happened?"

I knew he'd never tell me what happened to his money. That was a taboo subject. But the last I'd heard, he'd at least had a job. He was some kind of mid-level manager at a Home Depot.

His face took on a pained expression, and I could see how hard it was for him to come to me in defeat.

"Did you lose your job?"

"No, I didn't lose my job," he said. "*I quit.* And I know what you're gonna say, so don't say it." He picked a piece of lettuce out of his teeth. "I did have another job lined up

46

before I quit, but it fell through at the last minute, so now I'm screwed."

"Have you filed for unemployment?"

"I can't get unemployment because I quit," he answered, his voice rising. "You only get unemployment if you're laid off, which is fucked up, but that's the way it works."

"Well, have you talked to Home Depot? Maybe they'll let you come back."

"There's no way I'm going crawling back to *Homo Depot*," he said with contempt.

"I thought you liked that job," I said. "What happened?"

"I don't want to talk about it. Let's just say I needed to get the fuck out of there."

"How long's it been since you quit?"

"I don't know," he said. "A few weeks."

He took a bite of the sandwich, then went on with his mouth still full. "I'm gonna find something, don't worry. I might even go to Idaho. I'm sick of fucking California. But I moved out of my apartment, so I need to stay here for a while until I figure out what to do."

He swallowed and then burped. "Your neighbor said no one's living in the back. What you told me was *bullshit*."

My heart started to race, and I wasn't sure what to do. I knew, without a doubt, that if I let him move in, it would be impossible to get him out, and he'd make my life a living hell. It's what he did. Mother or no mother, I had to hold my ground.

With William backing me up, I came back with a lie. "I've already promised it to someone else. I'm sorry."

I could see he was ready to erupt, so I quickly added, "I can give you some money to help you get by for a while. Maybe you can use it to move."

I held my breath, silently rejoicing at the prospect of Idaho. He didn't say anything, but his expression remained hostile.

Reluctantly, I added some leaves to the olive branch. "You can sleep in the guest room tonight, and maybe another night or so, but you need to find somewhere else to stay after that. I'm sorry."

"Oh, it's the *guest room* now is it?"

"Look, Dan," I said, "I don't know what else to tell to you."

His face was turning red, and I realized I really was afraid of him, which made me even more determined to stand my ground. Veins were starting to pop out and pulse on the side of his head.

"Please," I added. "You and I both know that you living here won't work."

"Won't work for who?" he shouted, spraying spittle-laced mayonnaise across the table. "I'd be just fine living out back! I'm not gonna cramp your perfect little leftie lifestyle."

He wiped his mouth with the back of his hand and glared at me. "If Mom were here, she'd think you were a selfish bitch! You know damn well I'm entitled to part of this house. You fucking robbed me."

Now I regretted I'd offered him anything, but I was determined not to engage in a screaming match.

"I'm not going to fight with you about the house anymore," I said as unemotionally as I could. "I'm finished with that. And after the phone messages you left me, I should be finished with you, too."

I stood up. "Since you're here, you can stay the night. But tomorrow, you need to leave. Move to Idaho. I think that's the perfect place for you."

I turned and headed for the door, my heart racing. "I'm going to bed. If you want to watch TV or whatever, that's fine. Just keep it low."

Not waiting for a response, I left the kitchen and went upstairs to my room. I braced myself for some kind of scary aftermath, but the only sound I heard was the television. Thankful for, at least, that, I locked my door and went to bed. But I couldn't sleep or stop my mind from spinning. I laid awake most of the night, worried about the cottage and praying for Idaho.

CHAPTER SEVEN

WHEN I GOT UP the next morning and checked my phone, I found a text message from Nancy. Not surprisingly, she wanted to know how it had gone with Dan. I responded: "Jury is out. Check back in a few hours."

I looked out the window, hoping that, by some miracle, Dan's truck would be gone, but it was still there, like an unwelcome monument to trouble.

I looked at the clock. It was just a little after eight. Dan was probably still asleep. I hated that I'd now have to tiptoe around my own house, dreading what would happen when he woke up. I'd struggled most of the night over what to do but still had no solid idea. As usual where Dan was concerned, I felt paralyzed by the push-pull of anger and guilt, but as I entered the kitchen and headed for the coffee maker, there was one thing about which I was certain: Dan would not move into the cottage.

With my mother whispering in my ear, I prepared to make breakfast, but as I was grating cheese and chopping onions, I devised a plan to garnish his eggs with another pitch for Idaho. At this point, I considered Idaho my greatest hope for salvation.

Dan didn't emerge from his room until well after ten o'clock, which gave me plenty of time to both shower and do a little research on the "potato state." By the time he finally lumbered into the kitchen around ten-thirty, I was ready for him.

"Sit down," I said, pointing to the kitchen table. "I'll get you some coffee, and I'm making you an omelet."

I knew he was skeptical of my hospitality, but he was never one to turn down free food, so he pulled out a chair and plopped himself down at the table. "Thanks," he said grudgingly.

I put a cup of coffee in front of him and he picked it up. "You don't have to cook for me, you know," he said. "I can take care of myself."

He took a drink of coffee and nodded to where I was now pouring eggs into a small frying pan. "You women are all alike," he said. "You start in with the cooking when no one is even asking, then end up complaining that you do all the work."

I ignored the remark, refusing to be baited into an argument. Instead, I put two pieces of bread into the toaster, then used a spatula to spread the egg evenly in the pan before adding cheese, ham, onions, tomato, and avocado. A minute later, I sprinkled finely chopped parsley over a perfectly cooked omelet before sliding it onto a plate. With my brother watching like an ungrateful hawk, I pulled the toast from the toaster, buttered it, then delivered the food to the table, still intent on keeping the peace.

As he began digging in, I perched myself on a stool and pondered how to casually raise topics like the cost of living in Boise and natural beauty of Coeur d'Alene. I hadn't yet decided how to start when my cell phone rang from the counter by the stove. Getting up to glance at the number, I realized, in an instant, that it was Nate.

"I'll be back in a minute," I said, then I picked up the phone and headed out of the kitchen. As I was leaving, Dan mumbled something under his breath. I couldn't make it out, but it sounded snarky, which was no surprise. When I reached the top of the stairs, I answered the call with nervous anticipation. "Hi Nate," I said, now entering my room.

"Hey," he said back. "Did I catch you at a good time?"

I closed the door and flopped down on my bed. "Sure, what's up? Did you speak to Jeff?"

"Yeah. I saw him at his shop this morning. It looks like something's gonna happen with that, so I just wanted to call and thank you."

There was a short silence, and I felt the overwhelming urge to bring up the cottage. I knew it was hasty, but faced with the terrifying prospect of my brother moving in, I decided on the spur of the moment to take the leap. "I have a question for you," I said.

"All right." he said. "Shoot."

I heard some voices and laughter in the background. "Is that Isaiah I hear?"

"That's him," he said. "I'm out in the yard and he's playing with one of the neighbor kids. Was that the question?"

"No," I said, suddenly filled with uncertainty. "So, okay, before I ask you, I just want to say that if you aren't interested, I totally understand. I've been thinking about something, and maybe it's off the wall, but I want to know what you think about it."

"Okay," Nate said. He sounded intrigued.

I glanced over at the door and lowered my voice. "Remember when you told me you were hoping to get Isaiah into a better school?"

"Uh, I guess so," he said.

"Well, I live in a great school district, and I have a little unit on my property that you might like. There's an elementary school right up the street, and I wouldn't need you to pay rent right away. I know you're probably trying to save money. Also, I have a pool, but if it's a problem..."

"Wait, wait," Nate was saying on the other end.

I stopped what must have sounded like a ramble and felt suddenly foolish.

"So, what...you're saying you have some kind of apartment or something?"

Realizing that I needed to back up, I took a breath and explained everything more carefully, this time emphasizing the quiet neighborhood and school up the street. When I was done, he seemed interested but leery.

"This is a lot to take in," he said. "I need to think about it, and probably find out more. Like where you are, and I don't know..."

"There are some complications I should probably tell you about," I interrupted. I wanted to come clean about my brother but wasn't sure what to tell him.

"Complications?"

"Well, up until yesterday it was a whole different story," I said.

Nate hollered for Isaiah to stop doing something. It sounded like he may have been playing with a dog. "Sorry," he said. "I have to stay on my toes with little man over here."

"No problem," I said, smiling at the image that popped into my head. "So, look," I went on, "I know this all sounds a little weird and out of the blue, but if you're interested in finding out more, and about the complications and everything, maybe we can meet and talk about it. Do you think maybe we could get together today?"

"I don't know about today," he said. "I promised Isaiah I'd take him to the playground, and later on I need to do some work on the house for my mom. She's got a plumbing problem in her bathroom I told her I'd take a look at. I also need to go to the hardware store. Then, tonight, she's making a special dinner to celebrate my birthday."

"Today's your birthday?" I asked.

"It is."

"Happy birthday," I said.

"Well, thank you," he said. "It is a happy birthday."

"How old?" I asked.

"This is thirty-two."

"I don't suppose you'd like some company at the playground?" I said. "I'd love to meet Isaiah. But, since it's your birthday, it might not be the best day..."

"No, no, it's okay. That actually sounds good," he said. A moment later, he told me where to meet him, and when, and we said goodbye, leaving me two hours to figure things out with Dan before heading out.

ଓ

When I arrived back at the kitchen, Dan was gone and his plate was sitting, unrinsed, in the sink. I walked to the guest room and knocked on the door.

"Hold on," he said. "I need a minute."

I could hear him rustling around and wondered what he was doing. "Well, when you're ready, I'll be in the kitchen," I said. "I want to talk to you."

I went back to the kitchen and started to do the dishes. When Dan walked in a minute later, he was wearing cargo shorts and a t-shirt that read "FNN: Fake News Network." He was trying to get a rise out of me, but I wasn't going to take the bait.

"I need to talk to you," I said, nodding to the kitchen table. "Can you sit down?"

He sat down and gave me a look so contemptuous it made me rethink what I was going to offer him. "Do you have any aspirin?" he said. "I've got a monster fucking headache."

I pulled a container of Tylenol from a cupboard and handed it to him with a glass of water.

He took two Tylenols and a gulp of water, then glared at me. "So, okay, what?" he demanded. His voice was so angry it pushed me off balance.

"Why are you looking at me like that?" I said. "I don't understand you. I just made you a nice breakfast, and if you give me a minute, you'll see I'm going to offer to help you." I sat down at the table and looked him straight in the eyes. "What have I ever done to make you hate me so much?"

He simply looked back at me in stony silence.

"Look," I said, "I'm sorry I'm not letting you stay, but it's your own fault."

He clenched his jaw and continued his icy stare.

I tamped down my anger. "I've been thinking, and I'm prepared to give you some money to help you move to Idaho or wherever and get a fresh start. I did a search on the Internet, and there are some Home Depots in and around Boise..."

"*Fuck Home Depot!*"

"Fine," I said, "Fuck Home Depot. The point is, I'm willing to give you some money. I think Idaho sounds like a great idea, but do whatever you want. Just please, no more terrorizing me, because, frankly, I don't need it and I don't deserve it."

He contorted his face. "I've never *terrorized* you."

"Are you kidding me?" I said. "Do you recall leaving me a message calling me a *fucking cunt?* Trashing the front yard? Pounding on the door and going so crazy my neighbors called the police? Threatening me over who I *voted* for?" I stopped to take a breath. "The last time we talked, you called me a *greedy fucking whore.*"

"You *are* a greedy fucking whore."

"*That's it,*" I shouted, no longer containing my temper. "I was going to give you ten thousand dollars, but now you can forget it." I pulled a check from my back pocket, held it up so he could see it, then tore it into pieces in front of him.

"What do you think?" I added, my blood now boiling. "I have money to burn? Buying this house, I spent every penny from the store. I've had to take out a mortgage to pay the taxes and keep it up. I can't help it if you pissed your inheritance away in some idiotic drug deal gone wrong, or whatever it was. This is *my* house. I bought it, I take care of it, and now I want you to leave and not come back. Go to fucking Idaho and leave me in peace. I'm done."

Looking like a snake ready to strike, Dan responded with his standard fallback. "Fuck you!"

I stood up and marched to his room, which, not surprisingly, was a complete mess, with the bed torn up, clothes and towels everywhere, and duffel bags strewn all over the floor. I picked up a duffel bag, carried it to the front of the house, opened the door, and threw it onto the porch. Then I went back to retrieve the others. When I got back to the room, Dan was there, and, judging by the color of his face, he was violently angry. "Get the fuck out of here!" he shouted. "I don't want you touching my stuff."

"Yeah, well, I don't want your stuff in my house," I said. "You have five minutes to get it out of here."

"Or what?" he demanded.

I held my breath and struggled with my emotions. "Please," I said finally. "You being here is not good for either of us. I'll write you another check if you'll please just go. And I think you need to get some therapy or something. Your behavior is not normal."

His face remained fixed in a look of abject hatred, and I had no doubt that he really did have some type of mental problem. But I was equally certain that I couldn't help him. All I could do, at this point, was help myself.

I glanced over at one of the duffel bags partway open on the floor and was alarmed to see what appeared to be the barrel of a large gun. When I looked back at Dan, it was clear he'd followed my gaze and seen my reaction. "If that's what I think it is, I want it out of here this instant," I said, "or I will definitely call the police."

"I'm leaving," Dan said. Then he zipped up the bag and hauled it, along with another one that looked suspiciously heavy, out of the room. "I will take that check, though," he called back over his shoulder.

He returned shortly and proceeded to load the rest of his bags into his truck while I wrote him another check. It was painful, but I considered it worth it to have him out of my life—hopefully for good, although I knew I probably wouldn't be that lucky.

When he and all his stuff were in his truck, I handed him the check. "Please use this wisely," I said, feeling my mother watching over my shoulder. "And, seriously, Dan, I really do think you need to get some help. There's no shame in it."

He snatched the enveloped, turned the key, and revved the engine hard. "You're wasting your breath," he said, then he laid scratch out of the driveway and sped off down the street, leaving me feeling ridiculous and cursing myself for giving him so much money. Moments later, Nancy appeared at her side door, uncharacteristically put together in a pant suit and silk blouse. She walked over to commiserate. "Looks like that went well," she said.

"How can you tell?" I shook my head and had to laugh.

"Think he'll be back?"

"I don't know. He's talking about moving out of California, but we'll see."

"We're going out to a funeral, but after that, we're here if you need us," Nancy said. She placed her hand on my back. "You know that, right?"

"I know," I said. "And I'm sorry I've been so antisocial. I don't know what's wrong with me."

"You're fine," she said. "And I hope he does leave the state. The farther away the better."

CHAPTER EIGHT

AN HOUR LATER, I was on my way to meet Nate at a park I'd never been to before. My phone buzzed while I was parking the car, and I was relieved to see it wasn't my brother. It was Craig with this message: "Hope all is well. Will call soon to schedule another date. Looking forward to it."

I texted him back: "Sounds good."

I thought about Craig as I was walking to the playground. I'd been so preoccupied with my brother, and now Nate, I'd barely had time to process the time I'd spent with him. He seemed okay, although I'd learned from experience not to place too much stock on one or two dates. For a lot of men, online dating was nothing but a merry-go-round. Someone like Craig could probably have a different woman every night if he wanted to. He did seem interesting, though, so I figured I'd go out with him again and see what happened.

When I arrived at the playground, I instantly recognized Nate. He was sitting on a bench with his legs crossed and eyes trained on the elaborate play area spread out in front of him. In a white baseball cap and sunglasses, he looked totally relaxed.

"Hey there," he said brightly when I arrived.

I planted myself next to him. "Hey there to you, too."

Wasting no time, I turned to see if I could find Isaiah among the throng of kids scrambling over the colorful array of climbing, swinging, and sliding structures. After a few moments, I spotted him running up, then sliding down a long curvy slide. He was wearing what appeared to be some type of Halloween costume. When I turned back to Nate, I could tell by the smile that widened across his face that I'd identified the right boy.

"He's obsessed with superheroes," he said. "If we'd let him, he'd probably sleep in a cape."

I looked back at the play area, and now Isaiah was whizzing—red cape flying behind him—toward a large dome-shaped set of climbing bars. On his way, he turned to flash his father a gigantic grin. He looked so jubilant that I actually choked up by the pure joyfulness of the scene. With the sun shining, the sky blue, and gleeful squeals and laughter all around, I was flooded with a feeling I almost didn't recognize. Happiness.

Isaiah waved at his father from the top of the bars, and Nate waved back. Seconds later, the little superhero climbed down and bounded across the rubberized surface to another structure, this time a set of swings.

Nate beamed. "He'll definitely sleep tonight."

"He's the cutest thing I've ever seen," I said.

"So now what's all this you were talking about on the phone?" Nate asked, his eyes still glued to Isaiah. He was now swinging on a large tire, watching Nate to make sure he was still looking.

I opened my purse and pulled out my sunglasses, then took a deep breath, put on the glasses, and began my pitch. I described the cottage and yard, then went on to emphasize the elementary school just up the street. I made it clear I wasn't making the offer because I needed the rent, explaining, "You wouldn't have to pay me anything—at least not right away. It just seems like it might be a perfect fit." I wrapped up by describing the wildcard posed by my brother, which I wasn't sure how to assess. "He may be gone for good, or he could show up tomorrow," I said. "There's no way of knowing."

Nate had been listening intently while simultaneously smiling and waving at Isaiah, who was now back on his feet, zooming and bounding like a tiny caped gazelle. Nate was just getting ready to respond when Isaiah changed course, then ran over and leaped onto his lap. "Did you see me, Daddy?"

Damp with perspiration and smelling salty, he commenced to chatter and fidget as I observed in rapt silence. When he finally began to wind down, Nate straightened a velcro tab on his cape, then picked him up and planted him in front of me for a formal introduction. "I want you to meet someone, Isaiah," he said. "This is Rachel. She's the lady who got stuck in the elevator with me."

Isaiah's face lit up, and I could see where a new tooth was now growing into the gap I'd seen in his picture. "You went on top of the elevator," he said with wide eyes.

"I did," I said, pleased that, apparently, he was impressed.

"And it was *really* dark," he pronounced with a dramatic flair.

"Yes, it was," I said, "but I wasn't scared, because your daddy was there, too, and I knew he would protect me."

He beamed with pride. "Daddy's strong, and I'm strong, too." He flexed his skinny arms and made small fists.

I reached out. "Okay if I feel?"

He nodded, then I felt the muscle in one of his arms as he grimaced and flexed extra hard.

"Wow," I said. "You *are* strong."

He shot Nate a quick grin, then swiveled around and looked back at the playground.

"Wanna play some more?" Nate asked.

Isaiah nodded, then said goodbye before charging off in the direction of the tallest slide.

"That is one adorable little person," I said as I watched him climb up the ladder.

"Thanks," Nate said. "I don't disagree." He nodded and waved to Isaiah, then turned to me with an easy smile. "I'm not sure what to tell you about your place," he said. "It's a lot to think about." He adjusted the cap on his head. "No matter what I decide, you're definitely nice to offer."

He turned back to survey the playground and locate Isaiah before going on. He exhaled. "I do have reservations," he said, "and it's not just your brother. There's some other stuff I need to think about."

I debated whether to ask him to explain, or leave it. For the moment I let it go, hoping he'd elaborate. When he didn't, I pulled out my phone. "This is not at all to pressure you," I said, "but I brought some pictures. Wanna take a look?"

"Yeah, okay," he said. "I am kind of curious."

I pulled up some photos I'd taken that morning, then handed him the phone. "Here are a few."

He waved to Isaiah, then took off his sunglasses and looked down at the phone.

"*Damn*," he said when he saw the first picture. It was the outside of the cottage with the patio and pool in the foreground. He studied the photo for a good ten seconds, then slowly swiped his way through the living room, kitchen, bathroom, and two small bedrooms, one on the ground floor and the other in a loft above the living room. All of the rooms were furnished, and I wondered if I should mention that he was free to take or leave any of the furniture he liked.

I remained silent and watched his face as he examined the pictures, glancing up between each to check on Isaiah, who was now back on the tire swing, his cape a swirling red beacon.

When he came to the end, he handed me the phone and put his sunglasses back on. "It's a great place," he said with a nod of sincerity. "I don't want to come across as ungrateful, but like I said, I need to think about it."

I was unsure what to say, and I began to wonder what he was thinking. Isaiah was waving from the swing, and I waved back, feeling suddenly foolish.

Eyes on the playground, Nate spoke up. "I don't know if it's a good idea to take Isaiah to a neighborhood I'll probably never be able to afford," he said. "What's it gonna be like when we move and end up living in a completely different type of area? A different school..." He shook his head. "As tempting as it is, I think it might be a bad idea."

Disappointment rose inside of me, and I was ashamed to realize how much I'd wanted it for myself.

Battling back a desire to persuade him, I thought about a nephew of William's who'd once spent a week with us when he was twelve. He was from a poor section of Philadelphia, and when he saw our house, he was awe-struck. I was initially uncomfortable over our relative opulence, but William offered a different perspective. *"There's no reason the boy shouldn't see how we live,"* he'd said. *"He needs to understand that if he works hard in school and sets high goals for himself, he can live well, too. Don't you be embarrassed by our house. His mother sent him here to see this house."* His name was Robert, and when William died, he'd arrived at the funeral in a beautiful three-piece suit, fresh out of Cornell Business School.

"I understand," I said finally. I was going to change the subject and ask him about Jeff, but he started talking at the same time. "You go," I said when he hesitated.

"I was just gonna say that if you want to offer the place to someone else—you know, before I decide—it's fine. It sounds like, maybe because of your brother, you might want to get someone moved in there pretty quick." He removed his sunglasses, cleaned them on his blue Nike t-shirt, and then put them back on.

"There's no big rush," I said. "I won't rent it to anyone else." I thought about my brother and hoped he was on his way to Idaho.

"I also need to consider my mom," Nate said, now seeming to be thinking out loud. He smiled and shook his head. "She complains sometimes, but I know she likes having us there. *Most of the time.*" He laughed, as if some funny thought or memory had suddenly come to mind.

"You can take your time deciding," I said. "And you're welcome to come by if you want to see the place."

I could tell by the look on his face that this piqued his interest. "You should," I said. "You should come by. It'll give you a chance to see the neighborhood and check out the school up the street."

He squinted, signaling uncertainty.

"I'm sorry. I'm not trying to give you the hard sell," I said. A moment later Isaiah arrived back for another rough and tumble on the bench, this one involving some extended tickling that sent him into hysterics.

Shortly after things wound down, I took a picture of the two of them. Then, not wanting to overstay my welcome, I wished Nate a happy birthday, said goodbye to Isaiah, and headed back to my car, promising, before I left, to send Nate both the photo and my address, in case he wanted to come by or check it out on Google.

ଔ

The first thing I did when I got home was pull up the picture. I had expected it to be good, but it was so much better than good that I was initially stunned by the image, which had an almost magical essence. My phone always amazed me with the quality of its pictures, but this photograph—apart from positively glowing with the electric blues and greens of the surrounding grass and sky— captured the rich colors and joyous spirit of father and son so vividly that I had a hard time taking my eyes off it. I initially regretted that I hadn't asked Nate to remove his sunglasses, but after staring at the photograph for several minutes, I decided it was perfect, the undeniable focus being the shining eyes of one of the most adorable children I'd ever seen.

I debated whether to send the photo to Nate right away, or wait until he'd had more time to think about our meeting. I ended up sending it, hoping he'd be as pleased as I was by the vibrant portrait. Along with the photograph, I texted him my address, wished him another "Happy Birthday," and told him I hoped to see him again soon. I warned myself not to expect an immediate response, but before I even finished the thought, I got a text back: "Thanks. Will be in touch."

Over the remainder of the day, I probably revisited that picture no less than ten times, fixated on a vision to which I had no business becoming attached. I knew very little about Nate and suspected my ardor for Isaiah was unhealthy, and yet I couldn't stop thinking about them.

CHAPTER NINE

I WAS BRACED FOR a long period of waiting and wondering, but around noon the next day, Nate surprised me with a text: "Nice seeing you yesterday. When can I come see your place? What the hell..."

I responded: "2:00 would be fine, but any day or time is okay. Just let me know what works for you."

I got a text back right away saying he would come at two, which sent me into a frenzy of preparations that mainly involved cleaning my kitchen and attempting to make myself look good without seeming like I was trying. By the time he arrived, I was nervous but ready.

When I looked through the peephole, which was my habit before opening the door, he was surveying the yard, which, under the shade of a towering maple, was a glory of blooming shrubs and flowers my mother had meticulously labeled with names like *Hydrangea Macrophylla* and *Rhododendron Simiarum*. I had not inherited my mother's gift for gardening. These days, both the front and back yards were the dominion of an energetic gardener named Arturo. But I took pride in her botanical legacy, and now it was at peak splendor.

I pulled open the door and Nate greeted me with a simple but pleasant, "Hey." He looked sporty in a white t-shirt, white leather tennis shoes, and black trainers with a white stripe on the side of each leg.

"Hey," I said back, then I beckoned him in, suddenly struck with the same discomfort I'd felt when William's nephew had first visited.

I had done a fair amount of redecorating since my mother's death, both to tone the place down and dispense, to the extent that I could, with the sense I was living in a shrine. But despite my eclectic decor, there was no denying the vaulted ceilings, large windows, and wide expansive rooms. The simple truth was I was living in a three-thousand square foot house that I'd done absolutely nothing to earn or deserve, and I'd never felt it more acutely than now, with Nate standing in the tiled entryway. Nevertheless, I put on my happiest face, said, "Come on in," and shepherded him into the living room, where French doors offered a view of the backyard. I opened one of the doors and Nate followed me onto the patio.

"Wow," he said, surveying the yard. Besides having a tiled patio, pool, and cottage, it expanded over a sizable lawn surrounded by a lush mixture of tall trees, tropical plants, and flowering vines. Large ferns and elephant ear philodendron created a jungle-like atmosphere toward the back. Bougainvillea on the far left added a wall of shocking pink.

"It's actually kind of embarrassing," I said.

"Why would you be embarrassed?"

"I don't know," I said, trying to think how to explain. "I'm sure it sounds trite, but I guess I feel uncomfortable having so much when so many people have so little."

"I hear you," Nate said. "It is pretty trippy, though. It's like you have your own private little paradise."

"I moved in after my divorce, when my mom was sick and needed someone to take care of her," I said. "After she died, I just couldn't face leaving, so I bought out my brother and stayed. I don't know if I'll be here forever, but, for the moment, I can't seem to let it go."

"I don't blame you," Nate said. "I wouldn't want to let it go either." He was gazing up into a huge ficus tree behind the cottage that was interlaced with purple morning glories. I argued constantly with Arturo about those morning glories, which, in his book, were weeds.

I swept my eyes across the yard, which held so many childhood memories. I'd spent entire summers in the pool, and my mother and William had hosted literally hundreds of barbecues, large and small, from *Chez William*, which is what they'd called the patio, with its large built-in grill and tiled bar.

I laughed out loud.

"What?" Nate asked.

"I was just thinking about William's cannonballs," I said. "He used to holler, '*Here comes the Cannonball Express!*,' then he'd run and do a cannonball, and anyone within ten feet of the pool would get drenched. It was like being in the front row of the killer whale show at Sea World."

We both laughed.

"It was pretty hilarious," I added. "If he did one off the diving board, we'd lose half the water in the pool."

I turned to Nate and we shared another chuckle. "My parents put their heart and soul into this place. The yard was nothing like this when we moved in. They did all the landscaping, planted every plant, built the patio, built the cottage. William's famous line was, 'Ain't *no* place I'd rather be,' and he meant it."

Nostalgia washed over me and I struggled with a knot in my throat. "His fingerprints are all over this place. He and my brother even helped dig the pool."

I visualized my brother, when he was maybe sixteen, his face flushed red, covered with sweat and dirt. That summer my mother had hoped he'd finally bond with William and come out of his shell, but despite what she'd described as "positive signs," it didn't happen.

Nate was now studying the cottage. With an ivy-covered roof, small porch, and curtained windows on both sides of a carved wooden door, it resembled something from a storybook.

"They built it for guests," I said. "Mostly relatives from back east. Some didn't have much money, so it was a way for them to have a nice vacation that didn't cost too much."

"I can see why your brother wants to move in," Nate said.

"Yeah, well, if he were a normal brother, it wouldn't be a problem."

"If you don't mind me asking, how come he's so broke? You said you bought him out of this place. That had to be a pretty big chunk of money."

"It was a huge chunk of money," I said, tamping down a familiar anger. "I have no idea how he managed to lose it all. When I question him about it, he raves about *'getting screwed'* and *'bad investments,'* but he refuses to tell me what actually happened. I have a feeling he gambled it away, but I'll probably never know." I shook my head. "It makes me crazy when I think about it."

"I'm sorry, I shouldn't've asked," Nate said.

"I don't mind the question. I just don't have an answer." I nodded at the cottage. "Ready to take a look?"

"Sure," Nate said, then he followed me around the pool and stepped up onto the porch while I retrieved a key from underneath a potted plant. "I see it's pretty high security," he said with a look of amusement.

"Well, I don't always use the same pot," I said, meeting his smile. I handed him the key. "Here you go. Go on in."

He opened the door and we went inside. I lifted the blinds on the front windows to let in the sun. "Nice," Nate said, surveying the living and dining areas of the main room. Light-colored furniture and bamboo floors made it seem spacious. To the left, a small kitchen was separated by a bar of blue Mexican tile that matched the tilework in pool. On the right, a set of stairs led up to the loft.

I pointed to a hallway straight back. "You can check out the master bedroom and bathroom if you want."

Nate headed to the hall and poked his head into the bathroom before entering the bedroom, which contained a queen-sized bed and two matching chests of drawers. "There's a pretty decent-sized closet," I said from the doorway. Nate was silent, and his expression was difficult to read.

"What do you think?" I asked.

"I don't know what to think," he said. "It's all beautiful, and definitely tempting, there's no doubt about that." He was staring at a framed photograph of the Santa Monica pier that one of William's cousins had taken. "I'll tell you what, though," he added, turning his gaze to me. "Whatever I decide, I want you to know I consider you some kind of angel for offering."

"It's not a big deal," I said, "and you don't have to decide right away. At least now you know what the place is like." I nodded at the ceiling. "Want to see the bedroom in the loft?"

"Why not?" he said, then he followed me back into the living room, where I stopped and gestured to the stairs. "You can go up. I'll wait down here."

Nate strode up the stairs and was quiet for a few moments before trotting back down. "It's definitely nice," he said, glancing around the room. He nodded out the window. "Isaiah would go crazy over the backyard."

"When I was in high school, I gave swimming lessons to kids in the neighborhood," I said. "I'm certified and everything. So if he needs swimming lessons..."

"He'd definitely need some swimming lessons," Nate said. He pursed his lips. "Like I said, you're incredible, and the place is great, but I need some time to digest all this." He squinted his eyes. "I hope you don't think I'm jerking you around."

"No. Not at all. You can take all the time you want."

Nate was looking out the window again, and I wondered what he was thinking. "I know it's not that late," I said, "but would you like a beer? You can't fully appreciate the yard without sitting on the patio and drinking a beer."

Nate looked pleased. "I could drink a beer—if you'll have one, too."

"Of course," I said.

I closed the blinds and locked the place up, then Nate and I walked back around the pool and into the house. On the way to the kitchen, Nate stopped to examine the mantle over the fireplace, attracted by a handful of family photographs. He swept his eyes over the photos, then settled on a picture of William and my mother standing on an ornate bridge in Paris. "Great pictures," he said. "And you weren't kidding about William being big. What was he? Six-six, six seven?"

"Six-six."

"Your mom was pretty—like you," Nate said, and I felt myself blush.

He focused next on a picture of a big family barbecue William had hosted shortly after I started college. In the front row, my mother and I stood out among fifty or sixty smiling people, all shapes, sizes, and ages—mostly black, but not all. Dan was nowhere to be seen. He'd been out of the house for more than a decade by then.

"That was a family reunion," I said, as Nate studied the photo. "Most of these people are either related to William, or married to someone related to William."

"It looks like a nice group."

"It was," I said. "One of William's cousins who's big on genealogy rounded everyone up. It was a wonderful party." I picked up the picture and pointed to a tall woman standing in the back. "This is William's sister. She came all the way from Florida. She's gone now, too." I pointed out several other stand-outs in the group, then placed the photograph back on the mantle. "What about your dad?" I asked. "Is he still alive?"

"That's a sad story," he said. "I probably need at least a couple of beers to tell that one."

I didn't know what to say, so I remained silent as he turned his eyes back to my parents on the *Pont Alexandre* bridge. We lingered like that for a time, me wondering about his father, and Nate lost in thoughts of his own. When we moved to the kitchen, Nate perused a small shelf of cookbooks and I opened two beers. I handed him one, and he raised it with a smile. "Cheers," he said, then we clinked bottles and both took a drink.

As Nate lifted the bottle to his mouth, I couldn't help noticing the muscle in his arm and silky gloss of his skin, beautiful against his white t-shirt. "It's good," he said, nodding at the beer. He turned back to the cookbooks. "You like to cook?"

"I don't do anything fancy when it's just me," I said. "But when I have someone to cook for, yeah, I enjoy cooking. What about you?"

"I cook a little bit," he said, and he brightened in a way that took me by surprise. "I'm best on the grill, but I do all right in the kitchen." He tipped his bottle at the books. "I'm not big on recipes. I'm more of a *seat-of-the-pants* type guy."

"Well, if you and Isaiah come live here, you'll have to treat me to some of your seat-of-the-pants cooking," I said, wishing now more than ever that it would happen.

"Promise," he said, and the look in his eyes gave me butterflies.

CHAPTER TEN

WE HAD GONE BACK outside and were into our second beers when Nate reintroduced the subject of his father. "My old man shot himself in the head," he said out of the blue.

I must have had a startled look on my face, because afterwards he said, "I'm sorry. I was having a thought and that just kinda popped out."

"You don't have to apologize," I said. "But I'm so sorry. That had to be horrible for you and your family."

"It was pretty terrible," he said. His voice was even, but his eyes betrayed a deep sadness. I wondered why his father had done it but figured he'd offer the information if he wanted to talk about it.

"What was the thought you were having?" I asked.

"I don't know, just how funny life is. How you don't know from one day to the next what might happen. Life can take some strange twists and turns."

He took a pull of his beer, looking both strikingly handsome and crushingly sad. "My father had some really bad luck. *Seriously* bad luck, and he just couldn't see a way out, I guess."

He stopped, and I could tell by a quiver in his jaw that he needed a moment to collect himself. The air was hot, and a veneer of sweat was visible on his forehead, which was now furrowed by whatever was going on inside of him. "I'm sure I don't have to tell you that life can be hard on a black man," he said finally. He raised his chin and looked out over the expanse of the yard. "Even William. He had all this, but I bet it wasn't always easy." He looked at me and shrugged. "Or maybe it was. I don't know. Maybe he was lucky."

He put his beer on the table next to his chair. "I joined the military right after he did it," he said. "I was in college when it happened, and it messed me up so bad, I had to drop out. I guess I figured if I joined the Army, it would give me an outlet for all my anger."

I was trying to work out how his marriage and Isaiah figured into the timeline, and, as if reading my mind, he answered the question. "Isaiah's mom got pregnant right after my first deployment."

I had questions there, too, but remembering his wife had also died tragically, I stayed silent while he reached for his beer and finished it off.

As if sent to lighten the mood, two squirrels bounded across the lawn, raced up a tree, then leaped onto the cottage roof in an acrobatic display that made Nate laugh. "We have a lot of squirrels in this neighborhood," I said. "They used to drive William crazy, because they can be destructive, but my mom and I always loved them."

"I can see why," Nate said, still watching as they flew back onto the tree, then flitted in and between branches before racing back down and disappearing into another yard.

I was sorry I'd broken Nate's train of thought with my comment and hoped he'd go back to talking about joining the Army, but he didn't. Instead, his face settled into a smile and he silently gazed up into the trees. I wondered if he might have gotten a bit of a buzz from the two beers.

"Are you hungry?" I asked finally, thinking about some food I could bring out.

I could tell by a sudden change in his expression that he was torn, and probably confused about what I had in mind. I was offering him a place to live, but was that all I was offering? Even I wasn't quite sure. All I knew at the moment was that I didn't want him to leave.

He regarded me solemnly. "Can I ask you something?"

"Sure."

"Why me?" he said. "Of all the people you could have asked to move in here, why did you choose me?"

Before I could even think about how to answer, my brother materialized from around the side of the house. He'd come in through the backyard gate. I'd unlocked it earlier for the pool guy.

"I've been knocking, but you weren't answering," he stated casually, as if his appearance were the most natural thing in the world.

I was initially so surprised I was speechless, and I could tell by the look on Nate's face that he had no idea who he was looking at. "Nate, this is my brother Dan," I said finally. I tried to keep my tone civil, although I was both furious and bitterly disappointed.

"Who's this?" Dan asked with a snide expression. "Your boyfriend?"

"What are you doing here?" I demanded.

"I need to get into the house," he said. "I have a real estate guy out front who needs to get in and take a look around. I'm gonna have an appraisal."

"What are you talking about?" I said.

"I need to know how much the place is worth, because I'm suing you for the money you owe me."

Anger rose inside me like lava, and I struggled to remain composed. "You need to leave right now," I said. "And there's no way I'm letting anyone come in, so you can forget about it."

"Fine," he said. "But you'll be hearing from my lawyer." He smiled sarcastically. "Nice meeting you, *Nate*." With a maddening look of satisfaction, he then spun around and disappeared around the side of the house, leaving me wondering if it was too late to stop payment on the check I'd stupidly given him.

I turned to Nate, "I'll be right back."

I ran to the gate, opened it, and watched as Dan leaned into a car window, talking to a man with a short beard. I contemplated confronting whoever it was, but I didn't want to cause a scene, so I closed and locked the gate and returned to where Nate was now standing next to his chair with a questioning look on his face.

"I'm sorry about that," I said. "But now you can see what I'm up against. I wouldn't blame you if you wanted nothing to do with any of this."

I took a deep breath, trying to quash my anger. "He's such an asshole. And that appraisal stuff was bullshit. He did that just to fuck with me."

Nate looked sympathetic, but, not surprisingly, he announced it was time for him to get going. "I'm sorry," he said. "I know I'm bailing on you at a bad time, but I really do need to get back."

I did my best to hide my disappointment. I wanted to answer his question, *Why him?* I also wanted to avoid the panic I knew would hit me once I was alone. Unfortunately, there was nothing I could do. Nate was up and ready to go. After he made a quick trip to the bathroom, I walked him out to his car. Thankfully, Dan and the supposed "real estate guy" were gone.

Before getting in, Nate stopped and turned to me. "I'll let you know soon what I decide. And, seriously, thank you."

For an awkward moment I wondered if I should move in for a hug. Judging by his body language, I think he felt the same uncertainty. But neither of us made the move, so no hug. Instead, we shared an embarrassed smile, said good-bye, then each turned our own way—Nate to his car, and me back to the house.

CHAPTER ELEVEN

ONCE INSIDE, THE FIRST thing I did was call my bank and inquire about the check. I knew there was little chance Dan hadn't already cashed it, but I figured it was worth a try. He had, of course, cashed it, leaving me to wonder if I'd given him the resources he'd now use to sue me. I hoped he was bluffing, but I had no way of knowing for sure what he was up to. For the time being, I told myself the best thing to do was remain calm. If I allowed him to upset me, I was letting him win whatever twisted game he was trying to play.

The last thing I wanted was to be in any kind of war with Dan, but it looked like I might have no choice. I thought about calling the lawyer who'd handled our estate but decided to wait. There was no need to panic yet. Instead, I opted for a bath, which was my standard refuge whenever things were going wrong.

As I was running the water, I turned on the television in my bedroom, but what I saw was so maddening, I snapped it off. I wasn't one to turn a blind eye to politics or current events, but in the interest of my mental health, I resolved to take a break from the news. If the country was determined to go to hell, there was nothing I could do to stop it.

Before stepping into the tub, I noticed the partially-smoked joint sitting in a clay dish by the bathroom sink, where I'd left it. I decided to have just a little bit. *What the hell*, I thought, *I didn't have to go anywhere.*

I lit the joint, settled into the bath, then took in two long slow hits before tamping it back out in the dish, which I'd set on the side of the tub. By the time I released the second stream of smoke, I already felt better. I managed to languish for a time in a reasonably serene state, but, inevitably, my mind became active, and I began thinking about a short story I'd been writing in fits and starts about a woman whose marriage had been devastated by the loss of a child. I'd been contemplating turning it into a novel, but now it struck me as laughably unoriginal.

I regarded my body in the dim light—literally contemplated my navel—and couldn't help feeling a familiar sense of waste. I loved my body and wanted, more than anything, to find someone to share its secrets. But I was repelled by the modern-day practice of casual hookups.

I examined the smooth taut skin of my abdomen and was astonished, as always, by the absence of even the tiniest hint that it had once stretched to cover what looked like an enormous, perfectly round balloon. It was as though I'd imagined the months of feeling a child growing and moving inside of me, of marveling at the changes in my body— the plumping of my breasts, the widening of my hips, the mysterious brown line that bisected my ever-expanding belly.

I wished I could forget the pregnancy I'd welcomed so fully and experienced with such awe and wonder, but I also resented my body for its callous perfection—its seeming denial of the stillbirth that had ended my dream of motherhood, and almost my life. Some days I wished it had taken my life.

"So much for serenity," I said out loud.

I was on the verge of conjuring William for a pep talk when my phone rang. Thinking it might be Nate, I stood up, wrapped myself in a towel, and went to my bedroom to see who was calling. By the time I arrived, the ringing had stopped, but I could see that the caller was Craig. I checked to see if he'd left a message, and he had. There was also a message from my brother, who'd apparently called while I was running the bath. I had no desire to hear Dan's message, but I listened to Craig's, and it was the standard, "Let's get together, give me a call back." I didn't feel up to a conversation, so I returned to the tub, this time with a book that I hoped would keep my mind off both Dan and my perfect stomach.

⌇

The next morning, I was tempted to delete Dan's voicemail, but I knew I had to face the music, so I braced myself and played it. What I heard was not what I expected. I had to listen to it several times to understand what he was saying, because he was drunk, and it also sounded like he might have been crying, although it seemed forced. The gist of his message was that he hated himself, he knew he was a fuck-up, and I could keep my precious house. He didn't say he was sorry. The word *sorry* was not in his vocabulary. His last words before hanging up were, "I know what you think, and you're right. I'm just a fucking loser."

As strange as it sounds, I would almost have preferred more threats and name-calling. At least then I might have had the recourse of a restraining order. I knew him well enough to know that he was almost certainly trying to play me. I was known for my tender heart, and he knew how to use it to get what he wanted. *I'd just given him ten thousand dollars.* But nothing ever satisfied him where I was concerned. He enjoyed tormenting me. I wasn't sure what he was after. Maybe it was more money, but I had a feeling it wasn't that simple. Dan's disaffection was complex. In any case, I suspected his surrender was spurious, and was determined not to lower my guard.

Shortly after I listened to Dan's message, Nate called, and I could tell just by the way he said hello that he was going to deliver bad news.

"I'm afraid I'm going to have to pass on your place," he said, and there was genuine regret in his voice. "As tempting as it is, there are a bunch of reasons why. I'm staying with my mom, and she helps with Isaiah quite a bit. That's one thing. And, you know, we already talked about some of the other things."

"I understand," I said, trying not to let on how disappointed I was. I wanted to tell him I'd be happy to help with Isaiah, but I didn't want to push. The next thing I knew, he thanked me again and said good-bye. Then, just like that, my little fantasy was gone.

As usual when I felt myself slipping into a place of self-pity, I reminded myself that, by comparison to most lives on the planet, mine was a mountain of blessings. *What right had I to feel sorry for myself?* And, besides, fantasies had a way of giving way to reality. *Right?* If Nate and Isaiah moved in, who knew what kind of unexpected consequences might occur? I didn't really know Nate, after all. He was probably a completely different person than I imagined. I had most likely dodged a bullet, I told myself. And yet I couldn't shake my disappointment, especially where Isaiah was concerned. I'd grown attached to the idea of a sweet little boy scampering around the yard. Too attached, I had no doubt. But, still, I was stung by the loss and crushed that I might never see Nate again.

I wondered how much Dan and his little impromptu visit had influenced Nate's decision. My guess was *a lot.* And he knew nothing of Dan's "arsenal." I was ashamed to recall that when I'd told Nate about Dan at the playground, I'd neglected to mentioned his guns. I knew they'd be a show-stopper.

Dan and his weapons made me furious. People loved to talk about "the right to bear arms," but what about the people forced to live in fear of those *"arms?"* I thought about the most recent mass shooting. Scores of people mowed down by a nut with an automatic weapon. And why? Because it was more important for lunatics to have arsenals than for the rest of us to be safe?

I flashed on an altercation my husband had once had during a short period we lived in Texas. It ended with our neighbor pulling a gun. Over loud music! In Texas, being fearful of people with guns was an all-the-time thing. *Don't piss anyone off, because you never knew who was packing.* Now I was afraid of my own brother.

Telling myself I needed to think about something else, I remembered that I still hadn't contacted Craig. I listened to his message again and realized I might be blowing it—he was an interesting guy and seemed nice. I sent him a text: "Sorry I didn't reply sooner. When you have time, call or text and let's talk about getting together."

Since it was a weekday, and he had an important job, I didn't expect to hear back right away, but almost immediately, he texted me this: "Want to have dinner tonight?"

Pleased by his enthusiasm, I texted him back. Five minutes later, we had a date to meet for sushi at a place not far from the Los Angeles Courthouse.

CHAPTER TWELVE

LATER THAT AFTERNOON, I was working on my laptop when Craig called. "I'm finished earlier than I expected," he said. "Do you think maybe we can change our plans."

"What did you have in mind?"

"How about I cook you dinner?" he said. "I eat out pretty much every night these days, and I'm tired of restaurant food."

"Where do you live?"

"I have a little apartment in Echo Park," he said. "It's actually a pretty big mess, but I think, given a little lead time, I can make it reasonably presentable."

"What about coming here and I'll cook?" I suggested, preferring to meet him alone for the first time on my own turf. "That'll save you the hassle of cleaning and me the hassle of battling traffic."

"Works for me."

I was relieved. "Is there anything you don't eat?"

"I'm pretty easy," he said. "I'm gluten tolerant, I'm not sure I even know what *vegan* means, and with the exception of tongue, which I think is a texture thing, I can't think of anything I won't eat if someone else is cooking."

"Okay," I said with a laugh. "So, I'm cooking, and no tongue." Then I gave him my address and told him to come around seven.

By the time seven o'clock rolled around, I was not only ready for him but looking forward to his arrival. I was just in the bathroom fooling around with my hair when I heard the doorbell.

"This is quite a house," Craig said when I pulled open the front door. "I love these old Spanish style homes. And the trees, and your flower garden... Wow."

"I can't take any credit," I said. "My mom was the original green thumb. Now I have a gardener who takes care of everything. I need to go more drought-tolerant at some point, but I haven't been able to bring myself to do it yet."

"It'll be a shame," he said.

"Come on in and I'll show you around."

He stepped inside and was visibly impressed as he passed the living room and then followed me into the kitchen. I pulled a couple of wine glasses from a cupboard while he planted himself on a stool next to the granite island.

"My parents had the kitchen remodeled right before William got sick," I said.

"It's beautiful," Craig said, looking around to take it all in. He rubbed his hand over the gray and black granite. "This place must be worth a fortune."

"California's pretty crazy," I said, not wanting to dwell on it. I held up a glass. "I'm going to have wine, but would you rather have a beer?"

"I'll take a beer," Craig said.

I poured myself a glass of cabernet, then pulled a beer from the refrigerator, opened it, and handed it to Craig, who was now standing next to me, looking at a picture of my parents in a magnetic frame.

He gestured to the photo with his bottle. "I was right about your mom," he said, raising his eyebrows. "And I see what you mean about your step-father being big. What did you say his name was?"

"William."

Craig held up his beer. "To William," he said. "And your good lookin' mom."

In the light of the kitchen, I could see that his thick hair had flecks of gray. I also noticed his eyes were an unusual color. Neither brown nor green. *Hazel*, I guess, would be the word, but a version I'd never seen before. He'd obviously gone home before driving over, because he was dressed more like a cowboy than a lawyer, with jeans, a blue and green plaid shirt with the sleeves rolled up, and not exactly cowboy boots, but leather boots that were well worn.

"Like 'em?" he asked, noticing me looking at his feet.

"I do," I said. "They definitely look like they could tell some stories."

"That they could," he said. He flashed a smile and took a drink of his beer.

"Come on outside," I said. "I'll show you the back."

Instead of taking him through the living room, we went out a side door into an area of the yard that was partially visible from the kitchen, the most prominent feature of which was a large vegetable garden surrounded by a sturdy wood and chicken wire enclosure.

"Great garden," Craig said, inspecting my leafy medley of large and small tomatoes, peas, squash, lettuce, and other assorted vegetables and herbs.

"I know I sound like a broken record, but, again, I can't take credit. I have an arrangement with my gardener, Arturo. He does most of the work and takes whatever he wants for his family. It's an incredible deal for me, and it's amazing how much food this produces. I could never eat all of it myself."

"What's the story with the chicken wire?" Craig asked. "Do you get animals back here?"

"It's mostly for squirrels," I said. "They were a big problem last year. This year Arturo's not taking any shit."

Craig laughed. "Okay if I pick a tomato?"

"Pick as many as you want," I said, raising my wine.

Craig unlatched a small gate, stepped inside, and picked a cherry tomato. After wiping it on his shirt, he popped it into his mouth, then bit down with a look of exaggerated pleasure.

"Aren't they good?" I said. "This was all Arturo's idea. He has four kids, and sometimes they come over and help. His brother-in-law built the enclosure."

Craig ate another tomato and tossed one to me. "You have to be careful," I said, "because they squirt." I ate the tomato and, as always, was astonished by the richness of its flavor. No store-bought tomato ever tasted so good. "It's kind of fun when Arturo brings his kids over," I said. "They like helping because I let 'em use the pool." I nodded out past the side of the house. "Come on and I'll show you the rest."

Craig latched up the gate and then followed me as I walked toward the backyard. "Wow," he said when the whole thing was in view.

"That's what everyone says," I said.

"You can't take credit, right?"

"You got it."

"Your gardener doesn't take care of the front and this whole area back here by himself?" It was more of a statement than a question.

"He has a guy who helps him occasionally, but mostly it's just him. He's pretty amazing."

"I'll say," Craig said, seeming especially dazzled by the pink bougainvillea dominating the whole left side.

He followed me to the patio where we both sat down. "Nice," he said, nodding at the pool. "I love the tilework."

"William and my mother did most of it themselves," I said. "They even went to Mexico to buy the tile."

"Do you swim?"

"I don't do laps anymore, but I still jump in on occasion. These days I mostly just sit next to it. It's kind of a waste, I guess, but I like having it. There's something about being near water." I took a sip of wine and leaned back in my chair. It had been a hot day, but now it was cooling off, and the air was scented by a trellis of jasmine to the left of the patio doors.

"So, tell me what happened with your brother the other night," Craig said. He looked over at the cottage. "That's obviously the in-law unit you mentioned."

I told him the whole story, including seeing the gun in Dan's bag. When I was finished, he appeared alarmed about the gun.

"So, you haven't heard from him since he left you the voicemail?"

"Nothing so far," I said. "But, look, I don't really want to dwell on my brother. I'm sick of thinking about him. Maybe, instead, you can tell me about the case you were working on today."

"There's not much to tell," he said. "We were set to go to court, but the defendant ended up accepting a plea agreement."

"What was the charge?"

"Second-degree murder," he said matter-of-factly. "Seventeen-year-old kid shot another kid about the same age." A look somewhere between sadness and disgust settled on his face. "It was a gang thing."

I pictured the young shooter, his life wasted. Another young man dead. And for what? "What's the kid like?" I asked. "The one who took the plea."

"I don't know," he said. "Kind of what you might expect, I guess. Black. Raised by a single mother. It's sad. He just threw his life away."

"What about the boy who was killed?"

"Suspected drug dealer. Eighteen, but already with a record as long as my arm."

93

"What's going to happen to the other one?"

"He'll do fifteen years, maybe less if he stays out of trouble."

"Do you know why he did it?"

"Do you really want to get into it?"

"I'm kind of interested."

"All right," Craig said. "So, we aren't really sure about motive, but we know it was gang-related. In the end, he confessed, so it doesn't really matter."

"But don't you have to confess in order to take a plea agreement? It's my understanding that innocent people sometimes accept plea agreements because they risk much longer sentences if they go to trial. And, let's face it, if you're poor and black and have a court-appointed lawyer, what are the chances you won't get convicted?"

I'm not sure if Craig was amused or irritated. He may have been a little of both, judging by the way he was looking at me.

I raised my eyebrows. "Don't prosecutors do everything they can to avoid going to court, including threatening *really* harsh sentences if people refuse to take a plea?"

"Trust me," Craig said, "I'd never prosecute someone if I didn't think he was guilty. Two witnesses positively identified him, and he had a weak alibi."

"So, he had an alibi?"

"His mother and brother alibied him, but it's not uncommon for family members to lie in cases like this. And the brother has a record."

"So, you're saying if a kid is home with his family, that can't be considered an alibi?"

"It's an alibi, but, like I said, it's weak." Craig shook his head in amusement. "I think maybe you should have become a lawyer."

"I kind of wish I had. I came close."

"You're still young. What's stopping you?"

"I don't know," I said. "It feels like it may be too late. I have been thinking about it, though. I actually took the LSAT quite a few years ago. I was all set to apply to law school, but then I let my husband talk me out of it."

I smiled and stood up. "As much as I hate to change the subject, I think it's probably time to cook. Do you like lamb?"

"Love it," Craig said, then he followed me back to the kitchen, where I cooked, he sat and drank beer, and we eventually bonded over a mutual love of Brussels sprouts sautéed in butter and garlic.

ఇ

By the time we finished dinner and were ready for dessert, I was feeling pretty good about Craig. We'd had an interesting conversation, mainly about politics and movies. We managed to mostly avoid discussing past relationships, although I did learn that Craig's divorce was amicable, which seemed like a good sign.

We were out on the patio eating vanilla ice cream and raspberries when he asked me point blank about my marriage, which, up till then, I'd avoided discussing.

"So, I get the feeling you don't like talking about your ex-husband," he said.

I shrugged. "I can talk about him, I guess. What do you want to know?"

"It's not like I have any specific questions," he said. "It just seems like your marriage is a sore subject. Like you seriously don't want to talk about it, which makes me wonder if you're over it."

"I'm over it," I said. "We've been divorced for two years now, and I've probably been over it for longer than that."

"So, you were the one who ended it?"

"Well, I'd say he ended it when he got involved with one of his coworkers, but, strictly speaking, I was the one who filed for divorce."

"I'm sorry," Craig said. "That had to be hard."

I shrugged and wondered how much else to tell him. "It wasn't great," I said finally, "but, to be honest, it wasn't only the affair." I paused to take a calming breath. "I had a baby that died in a stillbirth. Full term. And I know it's a cliché, but after it happened, things were never the same."

I could tell by the look on Craig's face that he didn't know what to say. No one ever did—even to the point where some people avoided me for months after it happened.

"It's okay," I said, trying to help him out. "I'm not going to say I'm necessarily over that, but I don't dwell on it, and I'm mostly fine. It's just one of those things."

"I'm so sorry," Craig said, and there was compassion in his eyes.

"I guess it's why I avoid talking about my marriage. It's not my favorite thing to think about."

Although I knew it was abrupt, I stood up and reached for his now-empty bowl. "I'll take these into the kitchen," I said, then I retreated into the house to pull myself together and ponder what might come next, now that we'd finished dessert and it was getting late. I was feeling reasonably attracted to Craig, and I could see he was attracted to me, but I wanted to keep things from getting too physical too fast. Being in my house made it tricky. I hoped I could get him out the door without any awkwardness.

I was in the middle of rinsing our bowls in the sink when I heard Craig come up behind me. Silently, he placed his hands on my hips. I didn't move and held my breath. I knew that what happened next would set the expectation for what would, or would not, follow.

It had been a long time since I'd been with a man, and I was wary. I didn't want a causal thing. I wanted to explain this to him, but suddenly his hands were tightening on my hips and he was turning me.

He looked into my eyes, then leaned in and kissed me. First softly, then with more urgency. Soon he was moving his hands over my body and pressing so close, I could feel his excitement. It was clear where *he* thought things were going. It would have been easy to surrender. Part of me was tempted, but I wasn't comfortable, wasn't ready.

We paused to look at one another, and his eyes were searching. I could tell by his expression that he sensed my uneasiness. "Is this not okay?" he whispered.

I was relieved he was asking. "I like taking things kind of slowly," I said.

"What are you afraid of?"

"I'm not afraid," I said. "It's just the way I am."

"Let me show you who I am," he whispered. "Let me make love to you."

"I don't know."

"You know," he said. He kissed me gently. Then again, still lightly. "You're a beautiful woman. I'm a man. It's the most natural thing in the world."

He resumed kissing me, his hands now moving to more sensitive parts of my body. I pushed lightly against his chest, intending to pause things long enough to think, but my push was met with resistance. I applied more pressure, but he was as immovable as a wall, causing me to increase my effort to the point where there was no doubt what I wanted.

"What's wrong?" he asked, finally releasing me with a look of surprise. He seemed agitated.

"You're scaring me," I said, stepping back.

He stepped closer. "There's nothing to be afraid of. I like you. I thought the feeling was mutual." He didn't seem exactly threatening, and he did look handsome in the dim light of the kitchen, but now I was uncomfortable and more than a little confused. For a few seconds there, he'd seemed menacing. I might have been over-reacting, but I wasn't sure.

"I'm sorry," I said. "I'm just someone who needs more time."

"Message received," he said, raising his hands in the air. "I'm not going to force myself on you."

He stepped backwards and mumbled something about needing to get up early. Then, with an abruptness that made it clear he was upset, he headed for the front door, leaving me doubting I'd ever see him again, and pretty sure I didn't want to.

ଓ

That night I couldn't sleep. So many things were rattling around my brain: the terrible end to my evening with Craig; my disappointment with Nate; my brother; law school, and whether it really was too late. I resisted thinking about my mother, whom I knew would be overbearing on the subject of Dan. I had no such resistance to William. As always, he provided solace on all fronts, advising me to stand firm with Dan, forget Craig, and pursue becoming a lawyer, if that's what I wanted. *"It's not too late,"* he insisted. *"All the reading and writing you've done, you could do law school with your hands tied."*

William had often expressed regret that he hadn't become a lawyer—a degree in law being, in his estimation, the best weapon against injustices that gnawed at him constantly, despite his own success and comfort. He'd once met Thurgood Marshall at an NAACP convention, and it affected him profoundly. A photograph of that meeting had been one of William's most prized possessions. Elegantly framed, it now graced the wall of my bedroom. It was probably valuable, since the photographer was Gordon Parks. To me it was priceless, but also a reminder of another one of my failings. And it was ironic, because I'd given up law on the theory that it would leave me too little time for children.

CHAPTER THIRTEEN

WHEN I OPENED MY eyes the next morning, I couldn't help wondering how things might have panned out if I'd been less resistant to Craig. Maybe I'd over-reacted. I recalled William from the night before: *"If he were on the up and up, he'd have understood and not run off like a jackass."* I was inclined to agree but couldn't help second guessing myself, which was my tendency.

I decided to put Craig out of my mind and contemplate law school. Maybe, at the very least, my ill-fated evening would be the spur I needed to revisit that possibility. I wondered if there were a statute of limitations on the LSAT. Did my score still stand, or would I have to take it again? I resolved to do some Googling and find out.

Around eleven o'clock, I was in the kitchen reading over an English Muffin when I got an unexpected text from Nate. His message was simple: "Have time to talk?"

I texted back: "Sure. Should we meet, or talk on the phone?"

I hoped he'd want to meet and wondered if he were having second thoughts about the cottage. It also occurred to me that he might ask me out.

As I waited for the next text to pop in, I tried not to have any expectations. I was tired of being disappointed. I was just looking out the window at a squirrel trying to chew his way into the garden when my phone rang. Seeing it was Nate, I picked it up. "Hi there," I said.

"Hey," he said back. "Is this a good time?"

"Sure. It's great to hear from you. How are you?"

"I'm all right," he said, but something in his voice hinted he wasn't. "I was thinking about what you said in the elevator the other night. About being a good listener." He paused. "I was wondering if maybe we could get together and talk." He laughed nervously. "It's no big thing. I'm fine. But I could use someone to talk to if you're willing."

"Of course I'm willing," I said. "Do you want to come over here? Or I can meet you somewhere close to where you are, if that's better."

"I can come over there," he said. "I could use the change of scenery."

"That'd be great," I said. "And you can come any time. I'll be here all day."

"I can be there in a couple of hours. Would that work?"

"That would be perfect," I said, and my first thought after hanging up was, *Thank God I didn't spend the night with Craig.*

 CB

Two hours later, almost to the minute, Nate arrived, seeming the opposite of how he'd sounded on the phone. He looked cheerful in a turquoise v-neck t-shirt and jeans, his sunglasses perched on top of his head. I was dressed similarly but in shorts, and my hair, freshly washed, was down and slightly untamed.

"Looks like you got the memo on today's color scheme," I said, gesturing to our clothes.

Nate laughed. "You look good."

Unlike our last goodbye, there was no awkwardness over whether or not to hug. Nate leaned in for a warm one. He smelled like soap, and I could tell by the way he squeezed me that his warmth was sincere. When we separated, I led him into the kitchen.

"What can I get you?" I asked. "I have sparkling water, ice tea, orange juice..."

"I'm fine," he said, removing his sunglasses and placing them on the island.

I gave him a look and smiled.

"Okay," he said, "I'll take some orange juice. Thanks."

While I pulled a bottle of juice from the refrigerator, he stepped over to the window by the kitchen table. A moment later Arturo materialized and acknowledged Nate through the glass. Nate nodded back.

I poured two glasses of juice, put the bottle back in the refrigerator, then walked over to the window and waved to Arturo, who lifted a hand and smiled under the brim of his straw hat. I handed a glass to Nate. "I was going to suggest we go out and sit in the yard, but any minute now he's going to start up with the mower, so until he's finished, we can sit in the other room."

Nate followed me into the living room, where the sun shining in through the glass doors was causing reflections from the pool to flicker across the walls and ceiling in undulating waves of light. It was a wondrous effect that only happened at a certain time of day.

"This is a great room," Nate said. "I love the crazy light."

"It does this for about an hour or two every day, unless it's cloudy," I said. "It's one of my favorite things about the house."

I led Nate across the room to where most of my furniture was arranged on top of a huge Middle Eastern rug that my mother and William had shipped back from Morocco. It was one of the few items of theirs I'd kept in the space. I sat down on the couch and Nate settled into a love seat to my right. Both were within reach of a large wooden coffee table.

Nate leaned forward and put his juice down on a coaster. Sitting back, he grabbed a pillow and placed it on his lap. "You're probably wondering why I'm here."

"You said you wanted someone to talk to," I said. "I'm happy you called." I placed my own glass on the table, then nestled into the corner of the couch, my bare feet tucked underneath me.

Nate sighed and shook his head like he was thinking about something in particular. "Sometimes it's just nice to get away, you know."

He paused for a time, and I didn't want to push , so I sat quietly until he was ready to go on. After a few moments, he said, "Ever since I've been back, you know, since I left the Army, I've had so much to deal with. Work, school, trying to be a good father. Dealing with, you know, losing my wife, with her parents, my mother, all the crazy stuff in the neighborhood—all the shit in my head from the war. It's just a lot, you know." He rubbed his hand over his short cropped hair. "On top of everything, coming back from where I've been, I don't see things the same way I used to, and it's hard for people to understand that."

"I can imagine," I said, and I could see by the expression on his face that he was holding in a lot of powerful feelings. "How close are you to being finished with school?"

"I'm heading into my last set of finals now, and then I'm done," he said. "Then I'm hoping to get out from under some of this stuff. But, in the meantime, some of the noise I have to deal with is starting to get to me."

He cocked his head and cast his eyes at the waves of light glimmering on the beamed ceiling. "That's a trip," he said.

"My mom used to call it *water world*. She liked to come in here and meditate or do yoga when it was like this." I smiled at the memory of her downward dogging on a mat she used to lay out in the center of the room.

Nate was looking at *me* now, seeming to be studying my face. His own face was handsome in the shimmering air, and I was struck, as always, by the beauty of his eyes. Isaiah had the same dark eyes and heavy lashes.

"I want you to know that if you change your mind about the cottage, it's here for you," I said. "Even if you just want to use it as a place to study, or get away when you need to." I nodded solemnly. "Really."

"Thanks," he said, "but I'll be all right. To be honest, as much as I'm complaining about the pressure and everything, I know I can do what I need to do on my own. And it's a good lesson for Isaiah. He needs to see you have to work hard for things."

He stared down at the pillow in his lap, then back up at me. "Me coming to see you today, it's not about your place."

He squeezed the pillow and exhaled. "One of the hardest things about being back here, you know, after being in the war and seeing what I saw over there, is it's made me have a lot less patience with people here. Know what I mean? It's like, things don't have to be so...*I don't know.*" He shook his head. "Some people, they're just lost, you know, and it's a damn shame."

He looked away and seemed to be wrestling with something. He turned back. "One of the hardest things is I never wanted to have kids outside of marriage." His face was filled with regret. "I don't remember if I told you this, but before my wife died, we got divorced. But it was her, you know. I didn't want it. If it were up to me, I woulda never left. I don't care how hard it was. I woulda stayed."

He tightened his lips and shook his head. "My family was not perfect. My father struggled with all kinds of demons. But he was there. He stayed."

He paused and fiddled with the fringe on the pillow in his lap. "I want things to be solid for Isaiah, too, you know. And with *no demons, no bullshit.* I want him to have a good life. A happy childhood." His gaze shifted back to me, and I had the impulse to reach out and touch him, but I didn't.

"You're a fantastic father," I said. "I've seen you with Isaiah. I don't know what you're worried about. You're doing all the right things. Pretty soon you'll graduate and get a great job, and everything'll be easier."

"I know. And, trust me," Nate said, "I'm not normally this screwed up. Some stuff happened this morning..."

Before he could finish, we were startled by two sharp knocks on the patio door. It was Arturo signaling for me to come out and talk to him. I wanted to tell him I was in the middle of something, but he was insistent.

Annoyed by the interruption but not wanting to be rude, I apologized to Nate, then got up and went to the door and opened it. "Hi Arturo," I said. "What's going on? Is something wrong?"

"I'm sorry to bother you," he said, glancing in at Nate. "But I need to show you something." His demeanor was uncharacteristically serious.

"Now's not the best time. Can I come out in a few minutes?"

"It's all right," Nate said, standing up. "It'll give me a chance to use the bathroom."

"Okay," I said, now resigned. "I'll be right back."

As Nate left the room, I followed Arturo across the patio and out into the yard, wondering what could be so urgent. I guessed the squirrels had finally managed to break into his garden, but instead of heading around the side of the house, he led me to the back of the yard, behind and to the left of the cottage. My mother had called this part of the yard "The Jurassic Zone," because the elephant ear philodendrons, palms, and other exotic plants she'd planted back there had rapidly grown into what looked like a tropical forest.

Arturo stopped at the edge of the lawn and pointed to the dark soil at the border of the Jurassic area. "See there?" he said. "Footprints."

Sure enough, a couple of large footprints were clearly visible in the damp earth. "Can you tell if these are new, or if they've maybe been here for a while?" I asked.

"I think new," Arturo said, his features furrowed under the shadow of his hat. He shrugged his shoulders, then parted waxy green leaves to provide a view into the space that, in another ten feet, backed up to a brick wall. "Come see," he said.

I followed him straight back, treading carefully in my bare feet, which felt every root and variation in the soil. "See there?" he said, pointing to more footprints. "And there." He nodded to the wall, where smears of dirt were indicators that someone with muddy feet had probably scaled it. "What do you think?" he asked. "Kids?" He was no doubt remembering one summer when some teenagers had come in and used the pool when no one was home.

I shook my head. "I don't know."

"I don't know, too," he said, "but I don't like it."

"Maybe I'll talk to the police about keeping an eye out," I said. "In the meantime, don't worry about it."

He looked at me sideways as if to say he *was* going to worry about it, then led me back onto the lawn and returned to his mower.

CHAPTER FOURTEEN

WHEN I STEPPED BACK inside, Nate was standing in front of one of my bookcases, a book in hand. "You have a lot of books by black authors," he said. "Did you inherit these, or are they yours?"

"They're a mixture," I said. "But most are mine."

He was holding *The Warmth of Other Suns*, by Isabel Wilkerson. "Have you read this one?"

"Yeah. That's a wonderful book. Have you read it?"

"No, but I'd like to once I get finished with school."

"You're welcome to borrow it."

"Thanks. I think I will, if you don't mind." He nodded back at the bookshelf. "Have you read all these?"

"Most of them."

He reached for a well-worn book of poems by Langston Hughes. "I know this one," he said, a lilt of nostalgia in his voice. "My mom used to read this to us when we were kids. I could probably still recite a few of these by heart."

"Me too," I said, loving that we had something so precious in common.

He opened the book and immediately broke into a smile. "Wow, 'The Dream Keeper.' I haven't thought about this in probably twenty-five years." He began slowly turning pages. "Oh *man*, does this take me back. 'Winter Moon'...'April Rain Song'...Here's a nice one: 'Quiet Girl.' Remember that one?"

I nodded.

His smile widened. "I would liken you to a night without stars..."

I felt myself blush. A moment later, he closed the book and rubbed his palm over the cover with quiet reverence. The curve of his lips sent a wave through me.

"You can borrow that one, too, if you want," I said. "It would be a nice one to read to Isaiah."

"No, I couldn't," he said. "Not this one. But thanks." He returned the book to the shelf, then we went back to where we'd been sitting before Arturo interrupted us.

"I'm sorry about the gardener," I said after we got settled.

"It's fine," Nate said.

Before I could respond, the doorbell rang. *"What now?"* I said. I stood up. "I'm sorry. I'll be right back."

Pulling open the door, I fully expected to see Arturo with something new for me to worry about. What I saw, instead, was a middle-aged delivery guy holding a dozen long-stem red roses in a glass vase. I knew instantly they were from Craig, and though I guessed he was offering an apology, I would rather have seen almost anyone at my door. Now Nate would think I had a boyfriend.

I took the flowers, said, "Thank you," then hustled them as quickly as I could into the laundry room adjacent to the kitchen. Anxious to get back to Nate, I didn't bother to check the card. I just stuck them on top of the dryer and closed the door behind me.

"Looks like you have an admirer," Nate said when I returned to the living room and sat back down.

"It's a little embarrassing," I blurted out.

"Why should you be embarrassed?"

"They aren't what you might be thinking."

"What do you think I'm thinking?"

"Never mind," I said, feeling like an idiot. I looked down at my lap, then raised my head to see Nate staring at me. The look in his eyes was hard to read.

"I wish I'd met you a year from now, instead of now," he said. "Then maybe I could be the guy sending the flowers."

In that moment I had the urge to tell him so many things. I flashed on the conversation I'd imagined in the bath the night we met. Even then I'd had the instinct to open up to him. And I knew why. I understood my need to reach out to black men. But I didn't want to make a fool of myself by coming on too strong.

I smiled and tried to tamp down my nerves. "As far as I'm concerned, there's no difference between now and a year from now. You don't have to prove anything to me."

Nate had a solemn look on his face. "You want to know the main reason I turned down your offer?"

I nodded.

"I don't want to be the guy living in the back because you feel sorry for him. I don't want to be that, period, but I especially don't want to be that with someone like you."

"Someone like me?"

"Someone I'd rather meet when I'm on my feet."

He gave me a look. "You know what I mean." His brow was creased and his eyes shone with intensity. "The guy sitting here now—I can promise you, this won't be me for long."

Now his hand was at the top of his head and he was rubbing his hair. "I guess coming here today was a bad idea if I wanted you to see me as some kind of together guy. I just had a bad day, you know." He gazed straight into my eyes, unlocking a vault of emotions I'd been keeping at bay. I waited a few beats and took in a long breath before answering.

"You don't have to worry about how I see you," I said. "What I see is a strong, intelligent man who's working hard to make a good life for himself and his son. I don't feel sorry for you, or have any reason to look down on you. I'm sorry if I made you feel that way."

I gestured with my hand around the room. "I didn't do anything for any of this. I didn't earn it, or work for it, or build it. And I'm no great success. Look what *you've* done. You risked your life in Afghanistan, working on complex machines and dealing with God only knows what kind of stuff that I honestly can't even imagine. You're on the precipice of an engineering degree requiring classes most people wouldn't even consider taking. *I know what it takes to get that degree.* You have a child who's one of the most adorable little humans I've ever seen. You're kind and hardworking and, on top of it all—I'm just going to say it—

you're a stunningly beautiful man. You've got everything going for you."

Nate smiled and looked down. When he looked back up, the expression on his face was so raw and honest, I felt it in my stomach. He started to say something, then stopped.

"What?" I said. "What were you going to say?"

He clenched his jaw, then let out a long controlled sigh. "It's what I was gonna tell you before the gardener showed up."

"What is it?" I said. "What's wrong?"

"My ex-wife's parents are trying to get partial custody of Isaiah."

I was confused. "Grandparents don't have any right to custody, do they?"

"I didn't think so, but this morning I found out they're petitioning for it." He paused, and there was fear in his eyes. "They're Jehovah's Witnesses, and some lawyer in their church is egging 'em on." He tilted his head and frowned. "I don't mind them being in his life. They're his grandparents. But they're going too far. He's *my* son."

Just then, his phone rang. "Sorry," he said, showing annoyance at yet another interruption. He pulled the phone from his pocket and looked at it, then muttered, "*Damn.*" He stood up. "I need to take this. Okay if I take it in the kitchen?"

"Of course," I said, then I watched as he placed the phone to his ear and strode out of the room, answering "Hey" as he went. When he returned a couple of minutes later, it was obvious from both his posture and the sunglasses hanging from the neck of his shirt that he had to leave.

I got up. "I hope everything's okay."

"It's nothing I can't handle," he said, "but I have to go. I wish I didn't have to."

"Me too," I said.

"I'm sorry about bringing my shit to you like this, then running," Nate said. "You must think I'm..."

"Stop," I said, "*Nate*. I think we've established what I think of you." I smiled and tried to hold my face still as I looked into his eyes.

We were close to one another, and an undeniable current sparked between us. With light still flickering overhead and the hum of Arturo's mower filling the air, Nate stepped closer, and a physical wave rose inside of me. A moment later, he leaned down and kissed me. It was a soft kiss, and he followed up with a longer one that took my breath away.

"You make it pretty hard to leave," Nate said, running a hand over my hair.

I laughed. "I make it hard?"

He smiled, and I filled up with a longing I was certain was mutual.

"I didn't even ask you about your brother," Nate said, taking my hand.

"I'll tell you about it when you come back. You are coming back?"

"Soon as I can," he said. Then he gave me one more soulful kiss before disappearing out the door, leaving me wondering who'd called and already yearning to see him again.

CHAPTER FIFTEEN

AFTER SPENDING THE BETTER part of an hour lolling uselessly in my room, staring at the picture from the playground, I moved my lolling to the patio, where I alternated between thinking about Nate, stressing about my brother, and communing with William.

I'd never told anyone about my "conversations" with William, or how strongly I still felt his presence in the house. His omnipresence never troubled me. I didn't feel spied on, or judged. He was simply there when I needed him. The gist of his wisdom on this occasion was, *"Be patient. Don't worry. Just go about your business and let things unfold."*

Taking his advice to heart, I headed into the house to retrieve a book. But instead of grabbing the book, I impulsively took a detour into my office and turned on my laptop. I had been wondering what it was like where Nate and Isaiah lived, so I pulled up Google and typed *Compton* with the intention of taking a tour of the area. In all the years I'd lived in Southern California, and for all my enlightened rhetoric, the truth was I'd never set foot in Compton—at least not as an adult. I'd been there a few times with William when I was a child.

I zoomed into the Google map, grabbed the little man icon, and swooped it down until I had a street-level view of a residential neighborhood of small homes, the most striking characteristics of which were bar-covered doors and windows and spiky metal fences in front of practically every structure.

I commenced clicking my way up streets and around corners and soon realized it really was a mixed bag. Some of the neighborhoods I saw looked no different from many areas of Southern California, with palm trees, well-kept homes, and tidy yards. Others spoke undeniably of poverty. But none of what I discovered was as bleak as I'd imagined. I was in the process of wondering where Nate was going to school—he hadn't said—when I heard some knocks on the door and then the doorbell.

Hoping it was Nate, I closed my browser and headed downstairs, taking a quick detour into the bathroom for a swish of mouthwash just in case. When I arrived at the front door and looked through the peephole, I was delighted to see it *was* Nate, with Isaiah fast asleep over his shoulder. Thrilled, and with my pulse quickening, I pulled open the door.

"I'm sorry I didn't call," Nate said, a stressed expression on his face. "I was in the car..."

"You don't have to apologize," I said. "I'm happy to see you. Come on in."

I moved out of the way so he could step in, then closed the door behind him.

I smiled at Nate, then focused on Isaiah, still asleep and looking angelic. "Should we put him down in the bedroom? I have a guest room just up the hall."

"He always falls asleep in the car," Nate said, shifting Isaiah in his arms. "He's out cold."

"Come on, I'll show you," I said, starting for the bedroom. Nate followed me into the room and placed Isaiah gently on the bed, then paused to see if he'd awaken. He stirred but didn't wake. Looking back and forth between father and son, I don't know which vision made me happier. "He's so sweet," I whispered.

Nate smiled, then nodded at the doorway and followed me out of the room, leaving the door partially open. "He might be scared if he wakes up and doesn't know where he is, so I need to make sure I can hear him if he calls me."

I gestured toward the living room and headed for the couch. "I'm sorry to just show up unannounced like this," Nate said, settling next to me.

"You don't have to apologize," I said, taking his hands. "I've been hoping you'd come back and wondering what happened. Is everything okay?"

Nate looked tired and emotionally spent. "It's my sister," he said. "Not the nurse. I have another one. Chandra." He shook his head. "To be honest, I don't feel like getting into it. It's a whole long thing. But she's at my mom's now, and it's chaos over there. She's hysterical, her husband's been banging on the door... I had to get Isaiah out of the house." He rubbed his head in an expression of quiet frustration. "It's like I told you. I need to get myself up and out of there, but I hate landing on you like this."

"It's okay," I said, "Really. I'm happy to see you."

He managed a weary smile. "I have a pretty important exam tomorrow," he said. "I was wondering if I could study here for a while, and maybe you could help me look after Isaiah. I'd take him to my sister's, but..."

"Nate. Stop. I'm glad you brought Isaiah, and of course you can study here. You don't have to explain anything." I looked into his eyes. "Seriously."

He froze for a moment, and I thought he might kiss me, but, instead, he just looked at me as though pondering some deep question.

"Have you had any dinner?" I asked, wishing I knew what he was thinking.

"No, but I don't expect you to..."

"*Please*," I said, squeezing his hands. "Let me feed you. You study, I'll keep my ears open in case Isaiah wakes up, and everything'll be fine."

The relief written on Nate's face was palpable. I was offering him so little, and yet the appreciation expressed in his eyes was immense. It made me feel both strangely sad and filled up with gratitude of my own. I was just so damn happy to be needed.

"Okay," Nate said. "Thank you." He smiled and visibly relaxed. "I just need to go get my laptop and some books out of my car."

I leaned over and kissed him with as much affection as I could muster in a three-second kiss. Then he went out and collected his things, and I headed for the kitchen, elated to have someone to cook for after so many months alone.

ભ

While I began preparing a simple dinner from what I had in the refrigerator and out in the yard, Nate worked in my living room, surrounded by books and papers filled with what, to me, looked like hieroglyphics.

"Most of engineering is math," he explained when he noticed me looking at the book open in front of him.

"I'm impressed," I said, reading the chapter title. "I don't even know what *thermodynamics* means."

"It has to do with heat energy."

I smiled. "Like I said, I'm impressed."

"Well, don't be too impressed until you see how I do on my exam tomorrow."

"You're gonna kill it," I said.

"Oh yeah?" he said, reaching out and pulling me down onto the couch next to him. "What makes you so sure?"

"I just know," I said, cuddling up close, then leaning over for a kiss.

"I won't interrupt you for too long," I said when we took a break to smile at one another. "I just wanted to see how you're doing. Dinner won't be ready for a bit."

"You can interrupt me any time," he said, pulling me back for another kiss.

A moment later a tentative voice chimed from up the hall. *"Daddy?"*

Nate's face brightened. "I hear you, Isaiah." He stood up and headed for the guest room, calling again as he went, "I'm coming to get you, little man. Hold on."

After a minute, the two of them returned, Nate wearing a fatherly grin and a sleepy-looking Isaiah snuggled firmly in his arms. "Do you remember Rachel?" Nate asked, rubbing Isaiah's back. "You met her at the playground. Remember?"

Isaiah nodded, then pressed his face into Nate's armpit. Nate chuckled. "He's acting like he's shy, but just wait."

Isaiah made a little grunting sound and continued to bury his face into Nate, but a moment later he broke out into a peal of laughter as Nate tickled him in the side.

"There he is," Nate said, kissing his cheek. "Wanna get down?"

Isaiah shook his head.

"Hungry?"

He nodded.

"Want some dinner?"

Another nod.

"Do you like chicken and mashed potatoes?" I asked.

Isaiah turned to Nate as if putting the question to him. "You can answer," Nate said.

Isaiah buried his face again, but I could tell by a stifled grin that he was pleased to be the center of attention.

"I also have some tomatoes and vegetables from my garden," I said. "I might need some more tomatoes. Do you think you could help me pick some?"

This appeared to pique Isaiah's interest; he raised his head with a look of curiosity blooming across his face. He was wearing red shorts and a Sponge Bob t-shirt, and the vision he and Nate presented was a heart-warmer.

"Do you like chocolate milk?" I asked.

Isaiah looked at Nate with wide eyes, his eyebrows comically raised.

"You want some chocolate milk?" Nate asked.

Isaiah nodded enthusiastically, then squirmed to get down.

"Would you like to come to the kitchen with me?" I asked after Nate had set him gently on his feet.

Isaiah looked up at his father.

"Go ahead," Nate said, giving Isaiah's head a little jostle. "I'll keep studying, and you can have some chocolate milk and help Rachel out in the garden."

Nate and I shared a smile, then I took Isaiah's hand and led him into the kitchen, where I lifted him onto a stool in front of the island counter.

While I prepared the chocolate milk, Isaiah surveyed the kitchen, seeming to process every inch of his surroundings in fine detail. By the time I placed the glass of milk in front of him, his attention was solidly focused on the picture of William and my mother on the refrigerator. I thought about explaining the photo, but before I could decide what to say about it, his attention had moved to the window.

"The vegetable garden is right outside there," I said, nodding to where he was looking. "In a minute, we'll go out and you can pick some tomatoes. And maybe some carrots. Do you like carrots?"

He squinted as if thinking, then gave a thoughtful nod. "I didn't like 'em when I was little, but I do now." He picked up the chocolate milk with two hands and took a gulp. Now sporting a milk mustache, he turned back to the refrigerator and focused on the picture of my parents. I had no doubt he was curious about William.

I walked over to the refrigerator and pointed to the photograph. "This is my mother and father," I said.

"Do they live here, too?" he asked.

The subject of death loomed uncomfortably. Since Isaiah's mother was dead, I suddenly wished I'd ignored his attention to the photo. The last thing I wanted was to delve into the topic of lost parents.

"No, I live here by myself," I answered.

Isaiah took a quick look around, then settled his gaze on a copper pot of steaming potatoes sputtering atop my stove. He looked back at me, and I thought he was going to say something about the potatoes. Instead, he surprised me by asking, "Are you rich?"

Trying to think how to answer, I stepped back to the stove and turned the gas off under the potatoes, which were now soft enough to mash. Next to the potatoes, chicken breasts rubbed with herbs and olive oil were waiting to simmer. I picked up a fork and moved them around in the oil, although I hadn't yet turned on the heat. I was stalling, not knowing how to answer. "I guess I'm kind of rich," I said finally, hoping that would satisfy him and be the end of the subject.

Isaiah looked like he was thinking, and I couldn't help wondering how a child so young parses the world, or people, in terms of differences in material wealth. The question struck at the very heart of the uneasiness that defined my life.

I was braced for another question about my parents, or being rich, but Isaiah changed the subject. Putting down his cup, he looked over at the window and said, "Can we see the vegetables now?" Relieved, I nodded, then helped him down from the stool, grabbed a big plastic bowl, and led him out the side door.

Once we were outside in the garden, discovering surprises in the leafy enclosure provided exactly the happy communion I was hoping for. Isaiah was especially enamored of the carrots, squealing with delight each time a squat and determined pull rewarded him with the appearance of another earth-covered wonder to shake, inspect, then toss in the bowl. With every successful uprooting, I conspicuously marveled at his strength.

"Let me feel that arm again," I said after he managed to pull up a long "double" that resembled two spindly legs. He flexed so I could feel, then beamed with pride before squatting to muscle out another one.

When we'd filled the bowl to the brim with carrots, tomatoes, and sweet peas, Isaiah became interested in looking at the rest of the yard. The pool was out of view, but he could see that there was a much larger area to explore. "Can I go there?" he asked, pointing to the lawn and visible trees. It must have looked to him like a park.

"Sure," I said. "I'll give you a tour." I lifted him over the threshold of the enclosure and latched the gate. I had intended to take his hand, but the instant he was out, he ran off in the direction of the backyard, excited to see what was there. He stopped when he got to the edge of the house and had a view of the whole backyard. When I caught up to him, he pointed to the pool. "Is that yours?"

I nodded.

"Everything is?" he asked, now surveying the lawn, patio, and cottage. There was awe in his voice.

"I'm afraid so," I said, understanding that irony was lost on a five-year-old.

He stared at the far end of the yard for a few moments, then turned toward the cottage and pointed. "Who lives there?"

"No one lives there at the moment," I said. "It's a place where people can stay if they're visiting."

He was quiet, and again I wondered what was going on in his head. "Can I see?" he asked.

"You mean see inside the cottage?"

He nodded, and I felt a hint of panic. I didn't want Nate to think I was trying to sell him on the idea of moving in.

"Maybe later," I said. "We should probably go back inside and wash the carrots for dinner. Also, I need to mash the potatoes. Would you like to help me mash the potatoes? It takes some muscle."

Isaiah grinned. "I think I could do it."

I returned the smile, relieved at the change of subject. He turned his attention once again to the lawn, focusing on the Jurassic Zone at the far end. "Wanna race me to the other side before we start mashing?" I asked. "I've seen you run, and I know you're fast."

He raised his eyebrows, wide-eyed—a look I now recognized as a trademark. "*Ready, set, go!*" he cried, then he bolted across the lawn and was so cute and enthusiastic, I almost forgot it was a race. When I finally took off myself, I made sure not to catch up until he'd already arrived at the other side and declared victory.

"Oh my gosh, you *are* fast!" I said as I pulled up next to him. I collapsed to my knees and was suddenly reminded of the footprints Arturo had shown me earlier in the day. I knew they were probably Dan's, but put them out of my mind, preferring to focus on Isaiah. With bright eyes and his mismatched new tooth, he looked so adorable that I wanted to squeeze him.

"What's that?" he asked, pointing to a garden gnome William had given my mother one year for her birthday. With a white beard and pointy red cap, he was partially hidden by foliage, just past the border of the grass.

"That's a gnome," I said. "It's kind of like an elf, or friendly troll."

Isaiah appeared to be processing. Then, seeming satisfied, he asked, "Wanna race back?"

"Okay," I said, "but this time I might need a head start."

"You can have a head start," he agreed, and I had to chuckle at the vision he presented, with his little red shorts, and Sponge Bob ogling me from his t-shirt.

"Just a little one," I said. I crouched down into the ready position and cried, "Ready, set, *go!*"

I sprinted off, careful not to get so far ahead that he couldn't overtake me. In a few moments, he zoomed past, flashing a grin as he raced to the finish line.

Arriving at his heels, I was met with a high five, then a hug that I would have paid good money for. Afterwards, I announced, "It's time to start mashing. Ready to give it a go?"

Isaiah nodded eagerly, and Sponge Bob appeared to concur.

CHAPTER SIXTEEN

WHEN WE FINISHED DINNER, Nate announced that it was time to start thinking about heading home. We were in the kitchen, and I was standing in front of the sink, putting dishes in the dishwasher.

"You guys are welcome to stay here tonight," I said impulsively. "You can stay in the guest room, or even sleep in the cottage if you want to." I felt myself blush and held my breath, waiting to see how Nate would react.

"I don't know," he said, but I could see he was thinking about it.

"I wanna stay in the little house!" Isaiah cried with a bounce of excitement.

Nate looked at me with raised eyebrows.

"I'm sorry," I said. "I didn't mean to cause a problem."

He rubbed his head. "We didn't bring anything for an overnight stay. We don't even have a toothbrush."

"Well, I'm not trying to talk you into anything," I said, "but I'm sure I have a couple of toothbrushes you could use. I have a drawer full of stuff I get every time I go to the dentist." I decided to go for broke. "I even have some of my old books in a room upstairs, so if he's interested, I can read Isaiah a bedtime story."

Isaiah did the trademark look, then followed up with an earnest, *"Please, Daddy."*

I was heartened by Isaiah but worried I was getting carried away, so I looked at Nate and back-pedaled. "How about Isaiah and I do a bedtime story, you do a little more studying, and then you can take him home after?"

"I wanna sleep in the little house," Isaiah whined.

"I'm sorry," I said to Nate. "I should have asked you out of earshot."

"It's all right," he said, and he didn't seem upset. On the contrary, he was looking back at me with tenderness.

He smiled down at Isaiah. "Why don't you guys go pick out a story, I'll do some more studying, and I'll think about it. I'm also gonna call your grandma and see how things are going over at the house." He put his hand on top of Isaiah's head. "Sound okay?"

"Okay," Isaiah agreed, then he turned to me with a look of anticipation.

"Ready to pick out a book?" I asked.

He nodded.

"All right, let's do it," I said, then I took him by the hand and led him upstairs into what had once been Dan's bedroom but was now a storehouse of boxes and miscellaneous items that I hadn't yet figured out what to do with.

I opened the closet door and pulled out a large box my mother had given me when she thought a grandchild was imminent. It contained scores of books she'd saved from my childhood, some that I could probably still recite by heart. *Frog and Toad are Friends, The Sneetches, Goodnight Moon, A Child's Garden of Verses, Horton Hears a Who...*

As I pulled up the sides of the box, the musty but familiar smell that arose from inside induced emotions inside of me that were so powerful, I had to stop for a moment and fight back tears. It was the loss of my child, and not childhood memories, that suddenly hit me like a great wave. I should have known better than to breach the closet, but now it was too late.

Feeling my color rise, I took a couple of slow, deep breaths, then pulled out a stack of books and laid them onto the floor next to where Isaiah was now sitting on his knees. As he eagerly surveyed the options, I made an effort to pull myself and my emotions together. I called William to mind and let his deep voice soothe me. *"You're all right,"* he said, like he always said when I needed him. *"Just keep breathing."*

Isaiah picked out three books—one he knew, and two he didn't—then followed me back down to the guest room, where we climbed onto the bed and settled side-by-side to begin reading. By the time we got started, I was steady and Isaiah was anxious to dive in to *Aesop's Fables*, which, he informed me, was one of his grandma's favorite books.

As we read, I couldn't help noticing the sweet scent of Isaiah's skin and warmth emanating from his skinny little body. We were in the middle of *The Ant and the Grasshopper* when Nate finally tapped on the door and joined us on the bed, picking Isaiah up and depositing him onto his lap.

"Look," Isaiah said, pointing with excitement to the cover of the book he was holding. *"Aesop's Fables."*

"I see that," Nate said, then he turned to smile at me with approval. We locked eyes, and I realized in that instant that this simple scene represented almost everything I wanted most in life. I savored the moment, praying it was the beginning of something that would last.

"You read, Daddy," Isaiah said, pointing to the page where we'd stopped. He adjusted himself in Nate's lap, then broke into a sweet smile of satisfaction. It was clear this was a familiar and much loved ritual.

"Okay," Nate said, giving Isaiah's leg a squeeze. Seconds later, he commenced reading, not stopping until Isaiah was asleep and I was suddenly wondering what would happen next. "He's down for the count," Nate whispered.

He closed the book, then placed it on the bedside table next to a small clock. It read 8:59. He glanced down at his sleeping son, then turned to me with a searching look, as though unsure what to say. I was unsure myself, so I met his gaze with a smile that I hoped would buy me some time. Before I found inspiration, Nate broke the ice. "I hate to say it, but I should probably get him back to the house."

"I'm sorry I was so pushy earlier," I said.

"You don't have anything to be sorry about," he said. "You've been great. You saved my life tonight, but we really shouldn't stay over. I've got my exam tomorrow, and I need to get Isaiah back so my mom can look after him while I'm gone."

I must have looked embarrassed, or disappointed. "Don't get me wrong," he said. "I'd love to stay, but I really shouldn't. And, anyway, I'm afraid we need to have a conversation before we take things any further."

"What is it?" I asked, trying to sound casual. "Is this a conversation we can have now?" I didn't like pressing, but I wanted to know right away if there was some deal-breaking issue that would ruin what, just moments ago, had seemed so promising.

I studied his face, and he appeared to be debating with himself. "If you're going to break my heart, I'd rather get it over with as soon as possible," I said. I tried to keep my tone light, but my voice trembled and fear was probably written on my face. I was never good at hiding my feelings.

Nate sighed. "Let's put Isaiah down and go into the other room. We can talk now if you want to."

☙

Isaiah was tucked in, and Nate and I sat looking at one another on the couch in the living room. Nate took my hands, hesitant to hit me with whatever it was that was coming. "What is it? You can talk to me," I said.

I detected fear in his eyes. I'd seen the same look in my husband's eyes when he told me another woman was pregnant with his child. "Seriously," I said. "What is it?"

He sighed. "There's no easy way to tell you this, so I'm just going to tell you." He took a deep breath and looked genuinely scared—of what I couldn't imagine. "You remember I told you I was injured in Afghanistan?" he said.

I nodded.

"I guess because I had friends who died, or were hurt much worse than me, I don't like doing the 'poor me' thing, but I was actually hurt pretty bad. Especially my bladder. It's why I had to pee so bad in the elevator, and why I use the bathroom a lot." He paused for a moment, seeming to rally courage. "There was also damage to, you know, other areas. That, and some of the surgery I had…"

He sighed and lowered his voice. "It's hard saying it." His forehead was furrowed and his lips trembled. "It affected my ability to have an erection."

He went silent, and the expression on his face was so pained that it broke my heart. "Nate," I said. "I'm sorry to hear this, but it doesn't change anything for me. Not at all."

"You're saying that now," he said, "But…"

"*No*," I interrupted, "I mean it. It doesn't matter."

I squeezed his hands and tried as hard as I could to communicate with my eyes how sincerely I meant what I was saying. "Look," I said, softening. "It's obviously early, and there's no telling how far you and I might go, but I can assure you that what you just told me will not be a problem on my side. Unless it means you aren't interested in any kind of physical relationship, but that's not what you're saying, is it?"

"Of course not," he said.

"Then believe me," I said. "We'll work around it."

I was going to go on, but he stopped me with a "Shhhhh," then pulled me into his arms and held me tight. "We can talk later," he whispered. "For now, I just want to hold you."

og

We sat entwined for some time before either of us spoke again. I was hesitant to break the silence—not knowing what Nate was thinking or feeling—but eventually the quiet began to feel awkward. I was just summoning the courage to speak up when Nate beat me to it. "I maybe shouldn't've dropped that on you like that," he said. "It's just hard to find the right time."

"I'm glad you told me," I said. "And you can trust me when I tell you *it doesn't matter.*"

"Can I show you something?"

"Sure," I said.

He moved me over on the couch and pulled up the bottom of his t-shirt.

I hadn't actually pictured the injuries he'd described, but if I had, I'd never have imagined the level of damage now staring me in the face. The skin covering most of Nate's abdomen was so badly scarred that I was shocked by the sheer horror of what he must have suffered. He had both long and short scars going every which way and a significant area that had been burned. There was more I couldn't see, but I saw enough to understand that he'd been horribly injured. Because Nate's skin was dark and his cuts were even darker, and shiny, there was a surprising beauty to some of it.

I traced one of the long scars lightly with my finger. "Does it hurt?" I asked, looking up into his eyes.

"No," he said. "The nerves are all screwy now, so when you touch me one place, I actually feel it someplace else. It's weird. But it doesn't hurt anymore. It just looks bad."

His dark eyes glistened, and his lips broke into a sad smile. "I can deal with the scars, it's the other stuff that's hard to handle."

I looked back down at his scored skin and, once again, ran my finger along one of his scars. "You know, there's something I need to tell you, too," I said. I sat back and he pulled his shirt back down.

My throat started to constrict, and I took a long deep breath, afraid I wouldn't be able to talk. Nate was looking at me expectantly, with no idea what was coming.

"When I was married, I had a baby that was stillborn," I said. "A boy." I paused to take another breath and stifle the urge to cry. "Afterwards, I got a pretty serious infection. I was in the hospital for quite a while and ended up having a couple of surgeries. I didn't have a hysterectomy or anything like that, but as a result of everything, I'm no longer able to get pregnant."

Nate's eyes filled with compassion, then he pulled me back into his arms and held me close.

"You realize we haven't even been on a single date yet," I said after a few moments.

Nate loosened his grip and tilted his head so he could see my face. "Wanna catch a movie once I get these tests behind me?"

This made both of us laugh, then we went back to quietly holding one another, understanding that we'd skipped the dating part and gone straight to falling in love.

CHAPTER SEVENTEEN

NATE DID EVENTUALLY GO home. I understood him needing to leave, and it gave me time to process the quantum leap we'd somehow taken in the course of a single evening. We hadn't talked much more. We'd simply enjoyed the feeling of closeness that came over us like a drug. When Nate was gone, the feeling remained. I know it stuck on his side, too, because he sent me a romantic text as soon as he arrived home.

It wasn't until an hour or so later that Dan was back in my thoughts. At first I resisted, not wanting to spoil what felt like a watershed day. But I went into the laundry room to grab a clean towel for a bath and saw the roses I'd stashed on top of the dryer. I plucked the card, curious to see what Craig had said, and was shocked by what I found.

Roses are red,
Violets are blue,
Life is a bitch,
And so are you.

There was no name, but I found it impossible to believe Craig had sent this message. It had to be Dan. William used to buy my mother and me roses for our birthdays and other special occasions, so I figured the rose thing was about that. As for the message, it was classic Dan.

I thought about the footprints in the backyard. Was he lurking around out there somewhere? Had he gone into the cottage? I looked at the vase of roses and felt like smashing it. It was so typical of Dan to do something mean-spirited like this.

I grabbed the flowers, took them out to the trash can by the garage, and threw them in with force, wishing, in the process, that I'd turned on the backyard lights before going out. After putting the lid back on the can, I stood still, listening, but everything was quiet. I silently cursed Dan for making me feel unsafe in my own backyard.

Despite my discomfort, I decided to check the cottage for any signs Dan had been there. First, I went into the house and turned on the backyard lights. When I went back outside and looked for the key on the porch, it was gone. I recalled my remark to Nate about switching pots. *Had I put it under a different one?* I looked under another pot and found it. I was certain I'd placed it under the first one but put it out of my mind for the moment and focused, instead, on entering the cottage.

At first glance, everything appeared normal. I went into the kitchen, looked around, and saw nothing out of place. I opened the refrigerator. Nothing suspicious there. Next, I headed for the hall and inspected the bathroom, then the back bedroom. Everything still looked fine. I was starting for the front door, happy and ready to leave, when I remembered the loft. Glancing over at the stairs, I noticed a small something on the floor. When I walked over to check it out, I discovered it was a flat fleck of dirt that someone had tracked in. "Shit," I said out loud, thinking about the footprints in the yard.

I went up the stairs, but there was no sign Dan had slept in the bed, or disturbed anything that I could see. I switched on a lamp and looked around. The loft didn't have a closet, but it did have a small chest of drawers. I pulled open the top drawer and it contained only a set of sheets and some towels. I inspected the other drawers, and they looked fine, too. Remembering Dan liked to sleep with the window open, I checked the window, but it was both closed and locked.

Sitting down on the bed, I thought about whether there could be another explanation for the soil on the floor. Unfortunately, I couldn't think of any. Dan had almost certainly been there.

I stood up, snapped off the lamp, and headed back down the stairs, annoyed but relieved that whatever Dan might have been up to, he was gone now, with nothing left behind but a spot of dirt.

CHAPTER EIGHTEEN

THE NEXT MORNING I called my security company and made arrangements for them to come out and extend the house's alarm system to include the cottage. By eleven o'clock, I'd also heard from Nate. His test had gone well, and he was spending the rest of the day working for Jeff. He seemed enthusiastic about the extra money. He was even more enthusiastic when I suggested he come over after he got off. We considered a more formal "date," but decided we'd be happier in my house eating takeout from Nate's favorite Chinese restaurant. Isaiah was going to spend the night with his cousins at Nate's sister's house, so it was a good opportunity for us to be alone.

I had spent most of the previous night unable to sleep, fantasizing about a life I could picture with clarity and worrying that my hopes were unrealistic. I knew myself well enough to know I could adapt to a life that posed challenges, but there was no telling how deep Nate's scars might go, or how they'd play out in the long run. As far as his physical limitations were concerned, I had no trouble envisioning a satisfying situation from my side. I envisioned with relish much of the night.

It was late afternoon, and I was trying to decide what to wear for my evening with Nate, when I heard the buzz of an incoming text. Hoping it was Nate, I reached for my phone and was surprised to see it was Craig. It had only been a couple of days since his inglorious departure from my kitchen, but it felt like eons. His message read: "Have been wondering how you're doing. I hope I'm not on your bad list."

I began writing a reply that would politely but firmly shut him down, but I erased it, deciding to wait until the next day to respond. Nate was on his way, and I didn't want to think about anything but him.

I was all but trembling with anticipation when he finally arrived, and I could see by the look on his face that he was shaky himself. In a matter of just a few days, we'd catapulted our relationship into a zone with all kinds of unspoken expectations, so it wasn't surprising we were nervous.

"Come on in," I said as he stepped into the house. "I'm happy to see you."

"I'm happy to see you, too," Nate said, moving in close for a kiss.

"Are you nervous?" I asked when we parted to smile at one another.

"Terrified," he said, his smile broadening.

Mine widened, too. "Come on back and we can start on a nice bottle of wine I have."

He followed me into the kitchen, placed a large bag of takeout on the island counter, then parked himself on a stool while I went to the cupboard.

"Is wine okay?" I asked, "or would you rather have beer?"

"Wine's fine," he said.

I grabbed two glasses, then held up the bottle for his approval. "Looks great," he said, so I poured two glasses, then handed him one.

"Cheers," I said, sitting down next to him and raising my glass. I could tell by the way he was looking at me that he was exactly where he wanted to be.

"Cheers to you," he said, then he took a drink, holding a smile even as he swallowed.

"So how was it at Jeff's?" I asked.

"It was good," Nate said.

"And your test was good?"

"Test was good." He looked amused, and I knew what he was thinking. I was nervous and it was coming out as small talk.

I could feel myself blushing and didn't know what to say, so I leaned over and we kissed. Afterwards I said, "Shall we sit outside for a while before we eat?"

"Sure," Nate said, "but first I need to make a pit stop." He seemed embarrassed, but I waved it off.

"Go on, you know where it is. I'll wait for you outside."

When he was on his way back to the patio, he stopped in the living room and appeared to be studying the picture of my parents on the bridge in Paris. I went back inside and stood next to him.

"Sorry," he said. "I got side-tracked."

"That's okay," I said. "I love that picture."

"I didn't say anything the other day, but I have a photo of my parents almost exactly like this," he said. "Same bridge and everything."

A couple of minutes earlier he'd seemed playful. Now he looked serious. "My mother's big dream was to go to Paris," he said. "For years she saved for a trip. Talked about it all the time. Planned it all out. Then, finally, about a year before my father died, she got her wish. Two weeks in a hotel with a view of the Eiffel Tower." There was sadness in his voice, and I thought he was going to go on, but, instead, he nodded toward the patio and we went out and sat down by the pool.

"My father's dream was to have his own business," Nate said after we got settled. "He majored in business and engineering at Cal State LA." He paused to take a drink of wine, then seemed to get lost in a thought or memory.

"Eventually, he did it," he said finally. "He had a little shop that machined parts for the aerospace industry. He did pretty well, too, although I never remember him ever being relaxed. He was *always* stressed. To hear him tell it, he was constantly having to prove himself—you know, because he was black. He felt like he was never in the club, you know. But, even so, he did okay. We were never what you would call well-to-do, but we had a nice house and everything. The house I'm staying at now isn't where I grew up. I grew up in Torrance."

He sighed, and I could tell by the pained look in his eyes that he was going to tell me about his father's suicide. "He was stressed and all, but everything was reasonably good until his company got audited and he found out that the guy who'd been doing his books for, like, twenty years, had been stealing from him. He also found out that, because of that guy, his company owed a huge amount in back taxes and penalties."

He shook his head and his eyes turned bitter. "When the IRS found out about the trip to Paris, they tried to make out like my parents were living some kind of lavish lifestyle, but nothing could have been further from the truth. None of the stuff they accused him of was true. But trying to clear himself, and trying to pay off his back taxes—all of that destroyed my father and drained every cent my parents had. They lost the house. *Everything.* He finally couldn't take the pressure and humiliation anymore."

Nate's jaw trembled and he looked at me apologetically. "I'm sorry," he said, "I guess I just want you to know what you're dealing with here. Me and my family, we've been through some stuff."

"You don't have to be sorry," I said. "I've been through some pretty serious stuff myself."

I leaned over, took his face in my hands, and kissed him as tenderly as I could. We kept kissing, and I could feel his emotions rising. Mine were rising, too.

I had debated about what to wear, and finally decided on a light dress that had been one of my husband's favorites. Now, as things were heating up, I was suddenly conscious of how little lay between Nate and what was underneath.

He placed his hand on my thigh and looked into my eyes. "This okay?" he whispered.

I nodded, and my pulse quickened.

We kissed some more, now with more intensity, and Nate's hand moved further up. "Still okay?" he asked, once again pausing to look into my eyes.

I laughed. "Are you kidding? If I were strong enough, I'd be carrying you up the stairs right now."

Looking both pleased and surprised, Nate stood up and lifted me into his arms. "Point the way."

ℭℨ

None of what I'd envisioned the night before came close to equaling what came next. First off, with the help of a pill, the issue Nate had described in my living room was not completely true—amazing him as much as it did me. Equally surprising was the skill, tenderness, and imagination he brought to each new phase of our lovemaking. With all the various things we tried and the depth of feeling that infused each moment, I felt almost as if I were experiencing sex for the first time. By the time we finally gave in to hunger and brought the Chinese food up to my bed, I was both exhausted and happy. Nate looked pretty happy himself.

"You definitely undersold yourself," I said with a smile after swallowing a big bite of chow mein.

"Well, I've got a long way to go," he said, "but it's reassuring to see things moving in the right direction." He was eating an egg roll. "The doctor said I might see some improvement with time. Let's hope it continues." He raised his eyebrows. "It helps to have such a sexy incentive." He picked up my hand and kissed it, then grinned and popped the rest of the egg roll into his mouth.

He was starting to dig in to a carton of sweet and sour pork when he noticed the photograph of William and Thurgood Marshall on my wall. He got up and walked over to where the picture was hanging. "Is this who I think it is?" he asked.

"Yup," I said. "That was an NAACP conference in Boston."

"Old William got around, huh?" Nate said, clearly impressed.

"He was pretty proud of that picture," I said. "Believe it or not, it was taken by Gordon Parks. You know Gordon Parks?"

"The photographer? Of course." He crimped his features into a look of astonishment. "*Damn.* Thurgood Marshall, Gordon Parks..."

He disappeared into the bathroom for a minute, then came back and studied the picture some more. With a sea of suited, bespectacled men in the background, it definitely had the look of history to it. But the stand-out feature, as always, was William's towering stature, made all the more powerful by the spirit that shined out of his eyes.

Nate came back and laid down next to me, propping his head up on his hand. "What are you thinking about?"

"You," I said. "And William." I looked back over at the picture. "I guess I was also thinking about applying to law school, which is something I might want to talk to you about at some point, but I don't know..."

"What do you mean you don't know? You'd be a great lawyer," Nate said. He hadn't even hesitated.

"You really think so?"

"I know so."

"How do you know?"

"I just know," he said. "It's obvious. It's also obvious you won't be in it for the money." He played with a strand of my hair. "I know your heart."

A feeling of well-being rose inside of me like a tide. "You have no idea what it means to me to hear you say that," I whispered. Afterwards, I settled into his arms and floated in a dreamy state of half-sleep, focused only on the scent of his skin and steady beat of his heart.

When I woke up the next morning, Nate was already showered and dressed. He was sweet, presenting me with both coffee and a generous helping of affection before finally apologizing and running off. And I could tell by the way he kissed me, and especially by the way he looked at me before leaving, that he'd be back as soon as he could.

ॐ

The days that followed could not have been more perfect if I'd scripted them myself. With finals coming up, Nate had to focus on studying, but each evening after Isaiah had gone to bed, he would drive to my house, study for a couple of hours, then put away his books and spend the rest of the night with me. In the morning, he'd rise, shower me with kisses, then leave while it was still dark to be home before Isaiah woke up.

During that time, we kept Isaiah out of the mix. Nate wanted to make sure things were "real" before letting him get too attached. I knew he was being wise, but I also knew

Nate and I were real. I'd never been more certain of anything in my life.

On one of those nights, Nate finally told me what happened to Isaiah's mother. "She had a broken ankle," he said bitterly. "*You believe that?* She was in a cast for a couple weeks and everything seemed fine, but then one night she started having pain. She was going to have it looked at in the morning, but before she had a chance to go in, she died of a blood clot in her lung."

We were lying face-to-face, and I could feel Nate's breath as he spoke. "We were already divorced at that point, but it hit me so hard. And poor Isaiah. And her parents. *Oh my God.* They'll never get over the loss." He rolled over onto his back and pulled me so close that I could feel his heart beating in his chest. "Because he was so young when it happened, Isaiah doesn't even really remember her anymore. We try to keep her memory alive. Her parents especially. They show him pictures, and talk about her watching over him from heaven and all of that, but I don't think he has any real memories. Which is sad, but maybe it's easier on him, I don't know."

I kissed Nate's neck and tried to communicate with touch what I lacked in words. He pulled me tighter and nuzzled the side of my head. "He gets plenty of love. He's all right. But when it first happened, I can't even tell you what it was like. Having to explain to him over and over again why his mother wasn't coming home...ever. It was horrible."

CHAPTER NINETEEN

AS THE DAYS PASSED, a future with Nate and Isaiah seemed more and more assured. The road ahead of me was so filled with promise, I was almost afraid to believe it. Then, sure enough, my vision was torpedoed.

According to what I was told on the phone, my brother had been in a terrible car accident. Thankfully, no one but him had been hurt, but he was now in the hospital suffering from a host of serious injuries. The person I talked to didn't come right out and say it, but it was implied that he may have been drunk driving. I also got the impression I'd been tracked down more out of concern for his hospital bills than his well-being. In short, Dan was in dire straits—medically, and very possibly financially and legally—and I was being pulled into the middle of it.

Driving to the hospital in bumper-to-bumper traffic, I wrestled with myself, pin-balling between anger, guilt, sympathy, and frustration. Shaking, and with my mother's voice ringing in my ears, I tried to channel my feelings in the direction of sympathy, but my own much louder voice was yelling that I was sick of being pulled into Dan's miserable orbit.

As soon as I got to the hospital, I was hit with a barrage of questions about Dan's health insurance. He had been unable to produce any proof of coverage, and it was clear he was racking up quite a bill. Not able to be of any help, I suggested they contact Home Depot to see if he was still covered by whatever he might have had there. I didn't say so, but I would have bet my life he was uninsured.

He was asleep when I entered his room and, according to a nurse on his floor, he'd been mostly unconscious since arriving at the hospital by ambulance. He'd apparently spent several hours in the ICU and only just been moved to a room. It was a double, with someone else on the other side of a closed curtain. I don't know what the other patient's story was, but I knew he was there by the presence of multiple noise-emitting devices.

Dan was also pretty elaborately hooked up, and his condition was worse than what I'd imagined. He had what was described to me as a "traumatic brain injury," multiple broken ribs, a collapsed lung, and his right arm was broken in two places and hanging in a sling. To say the least, he was in a bad way, and like it or not, I was all he had in the way of family. Figuring he was also short on friends, I felt an unexpected swell of compassion. It was true he was an obnoxious jerk who took pleasure in causing me grief, but seeing him so horribly injured, with his head bandaged and two black eyes, it was hard not to feel for him.

I sat down in a chair beside his bed and contemplated the cult of haters who'd used his insecurities to turn him into his own worst enemy. It made me both angry and sad, especially because it was so unnecessary. My mother and William had tried endlessly to help him, but his armor had been impenetrable.

I studied Dan's face, purple and swollen beyond recognition, and tried to recall a time when he was not troubled. I could muster a handful of memories in which he seemed happy, but not many. The most vivid was Dan on a ten-speed bicycle, circling the driveway of our old Pasadena house as my father was washing the car. I was probably not much more than two, and must have been in a playpen on the front lawn, because I remember watching from behind wooden bars as my father, in a loose-fitting green shirt and shorts, would occasionally turn the hose onto Dan, causing him to laugh and holler for him to stop. I don't know why this particular moment in time is crystallized in my memory, but it's one of my few recollections of my father, or of Dan seeming just like any other normal brother.

My only other recollections of Dan from those days are of him getting a guitar for Christmas, and then hearing him playing from behind a mysterious door for some time after. Eventually, the playing stopped, and I don't remember seeing the guitar again after we moved from Pasadena to Long Beach.

I have only the vaguest memory of Pasadena. A leather photo album is proof that a time before William existed, but, for the most part, that period of my life draws a blank. My mother and I looked at that album together before she died, and I confessed to feeling zero connection to the father in the photos. In truth, I felt only a grudging connection to Dan. He was a mere background character in the haze of my earliest years—a glum and slumping presence whose life had little overlap with mine, separated, as we were, by such a wide gulf of age and circumstance.

Behind the curtain next to me I heard what sounded like gasping, so I concentrated on listening, wondering if I needed to call a nurse. After a few moments, the gasping stopped. I peeked behind the curtain, feeling like I should see if he was all right, and the vision that met my eyes made me wince. The patient was an older man, emaciated, and not long for this world, by the looks of it. With a tube supplying oxygen through his nose, he was, at least, breathing, so I let go of the curtain, figuring that, with all he was hooked up to, an alarm would sound if he were in any immediate danger.

I loathed hospitals. Between my mother and William— not to mention my own medical nightmares—I'd spent more than my share of time immersed in the miseries that went along with being sick and helpless. Just the smell of a hospital now was enough to make me want to run. So, as I sat between Dan and the man behind the curtain, absorbing the grotesque atmospherics of their surroundings, I felt as sorry for myself as I did for Dan and his pitiful roommate. I thought about Nate and how beautifully things were blossoming between us, and I couldn't believe I was now sitting in what felt like a house of horrors. I did not want this.

I looked down at a bag of urine hanging from the side of Dan's bed and was reminded of Nate's pee bag adventure in the elevator. He'd handled that indignity with such good humor. Now here was Dan with a pee bag, and it was thanks to an adventure in drunk driving. I shook my head in disgust.

I was just thinking about texting Nate when my phone buzzed. I was put off to see it was Craig, with the message: "Need to talk to you about something. Is it a good time to call?"

I was staring at the message, contemplating how and if I should respond, when he sent me a second. This one made me sit up at attention: "It's about your brother. Please call ASAP."

I looked at Dan, bruised and broken, and wondered why on earth Craig would be texting me about him? I had no idea, but I knew it couldn't be good. I stood up and left the room, calling to a nurse at the nurse's station as I went, "I'll be back in a few minutes. I have to make a phone call."

I went out to a hallway that skirted the rooms on the outside of the building and dialed Craig's number. After only two rings, he answered, "Hello, this is Craig."

"Craig," I said, "It's Rachel. I got your message. What's this about?"

"Hi," he said. "Rachel." He hesitated. "Look, I know this is weird, but I'm working on something, and it appears as if your brother is involved. I wonder if I can talk to you about it."

"I'm at the hospital now," I said. "He's been in an accident."

"I know. It's how I made the connection between the two of you."

I was confused. "I don't understand."

"I can explain it to you, but it would be better if I told you in person."

Now I was both confused and annoyed. Was he using whatever this was to try to see me again? "Can't you just talk to me over the phone?" I asked.

"I'd prefer to meet. It will be purely professional, I promise. For the record, I'm sorry about what happened at your house. Really. No excuses. But, as I said, this will be purely professional."

"What's going on?" I asked. "This is so crazy."

"I know," he said. "It's a weird coincidence. But I'd rather not discuss it over the phone. I can come to the hospital and we can meet in the cafeteria if that works for you. You're at Long Beach Medical Center, right?"

I shook my head at the sheer strangeness of what I was hearing. "I guess it would be okay," I said, "but I don't know how much longer I'll be here. I'm not planning to stay all day."

"I'm not that far away," he said. "Can I meet you in the cafeteria in about half an hour?"

"All right," I agreed. Then we hung up, and I was left wondering what in the world Dan had gotten himself into.

ങ

Down in the cafeteria, I was breathing in the minty scent of my tea, feeling like a zombie, when I caught sight of Craig striding over. He looked all business in a dark suit and tie.

"I'm sorry I'm late," he said, pulling out a chair and sitting down across from me. "Traffic was terrible."

"It's fine," I said. I'd been waiting for forty minutes but suppressed my annoyance.

"How's your brother?"

"I don't know," I said. "Not great, I guess. He's still out of it, but I haven't talked to a doctor yet, so I'm not really sure. I gather he has some kind of traumatic brain injury, which doesn't sound too good, and he's got a bunch of other problems—some broken bones and a collapsed lung. But what's this about?"

Craig sighed. "Part of my job in the Special Crimes division I work for involves keeping track of domestic terrorist groups. You might not realize it, but California has one of the largest and most active populations of white nationalists in the country."

"Oh my God," I said, feeling his words in my stomach. "Are you saying my brother is a white nationalist terrorist?"

"I can't say anything definitive, but we know he's been buying guns from a group we've been monitoring that traffics in illegal weapons."

I thought about the gun I'd seen in Dan's bag and the other bags that were suspiciously heavy. "He's definitely into guns," I said. "It's one of the reasons I want to stay away from him."

Craig nodded as if this were something he already knew. "When he was brought into the ER, he was given a blood alcohol test. We were hoping that if we had him for a DUI, we could use it as leverage to get him to talk to us about the group we're interested in. Unfortunately, he passed the test by just a hair. And I mean *a hair*." He sat back in his chair. "It's good news for him, but not for us."

"So, what does all this mean? What are you saying?"

"I'm saying that we know your brother is involved with some pretty shady people. I can't say how deep his involvement is, but he's on our radar."

He paused and frowned. "When I realized, only just this morning, that he was your brother, I decided to talk to you for two reasons. First, and probably foremost, I want to warn you to be careful. I understand, because of his accident, and because of some of the things you told me the other night, you may come under some pressure to take care of him. If you end up doing that, I just want you to understand the situation."

My cheeks heated up and I felt sick. I'd been avoiding thinking about having to take him in—having to nurse him. I shook my head and took a deep breath, willing myself not to cry. Craig looked sympathetic.

"You said you wanted to talk to me for two reasons," I said. "What's the other one?"

He hesitated, looking nervous about whatever it was.

"It's okay, just tell me," I said.

He crimped his lips. "I don't want you to feel pressured by this," he said, "but, if you're willing, you may be able to help both him and us."

"Help how?"

"Well, if you do end up taking care of him, maybe you can keep an eye out for suspicious activity or behavior."

"Like what?"

"Maybe people coming around that don't seem quite right, suspicious phone calls, odd or secretive behavior that would indicate he's hiding something—that type of thing."

"How does that help him? Not that I have any burning desire to protect him. I'm just curious."

"Well, if we can find a way to convince him to cooperate with us, we might be able to give him immunity for anything he's involved in. So anything you might see that could give us some leverage..."

"So you think he's involved in criminal activity?"

"He's definitely been purchasing illegal firearms and ammunition."

"If you know these people are selling illegal guns, why don't you just arrest them?"

"I promise you, we will be making arrests. It's just a matter of waiting for the right time to get the most bang for our buck, so to speak."

"You said *terrorists*. What do you mean by that?"

"I can't really talk about it," Craig said. "What I can say is there are some extremist groups in the area that have become more and more active over the last few months—on the internet and with respect to illegal activities. One of them is the group your brother is associated with. Dan doesn't appear, at the moment, to be any kind of major player, but he's definitely involved, at least, tangentially. At the very least, he's been buying weapons."

"Why would he even need to buy them illegally?" I asked. "Can't you practically walk into any Walmart these days and buy a gun?"

"It's a little more complicated than that, but I understand your point," Craig said. "Unfortunately, your brother has been purchasing military weapons and ammunition.

All unregistered, and mostly stolen. And that's all I can really tell you. I've already told you more than I should."

I stared at Craig in amazement. I had known for years that Dan had an unhealthy relationship with guns, but this was so much worse than I'd ever imagined.

"I *really* don't want to have to take care of him," I said. "I can't even believe this is happening."

"I understand," Craig said. "But whatever happens, just keep your eyes open. And if you do see or hear anything you think we should know about, let me know. That's it. And, of course, don't tell him about any of this. The last thing I want is to put you in any kind of danger."

"What kind of danger? What are you talking about?"

"You're probably in no danger," Craig said. "But it doesn't hurt to be cautious. These are serious people your brother's been involved with. So just be aware. That's all."

I felt suddenly crushed by the weight of everything. And just when I was finding some happiness. "What if I want nothing to do with any of this?" I asked. "Do I have any legal obligation to do anything?"

Craig hadn't yet started to answer when I heard the buzz of an incoming text. Glancing at my phone on the table, I saw it was the alarm company. "Shit," I said, realizing someone was probably at my house wondering where I was. "I need to take care of this real quick."

Craig looked at his watch. "I need to run, anyway." He slid his chair back. "As far as your question is concerned, you don't have to do anything you don't want to." He stood up. "I'll be traveling for the next couple of days and won't be very accessible, but as soon as I get back, I'll be in touch and we can talk more. In the meantime, please leave me a message if you see or hear anything you think might be important."

He stared at me for a few seconds with a look that said *this is serious business*. Then he pushed his chair back in, thanked me for seeing him, and headed for the door, rushing like he was late for something important. As he strode off, I called the alarm company and apologized for standing them up. I also canceled the alarm, it being clear that, for the moment, I had much bigger things to worry about.

ය

It took me some time to fully process what I'd learned from Craig. Given Dan's recent trajectory, I wasn't really surprised, but I burned with anger, and I couldn't help but feel hurt for my parents. William had treated Dan with the patience of a saint—had bent over backwards to be kind to him. Now Dan was taking up with white supremacists? My stomach churned with disgust.

I thought long and hard about what to do next. I wanted to leave the hospital and never look back, but I wasn't able to do it. As much as I was sickened by what I'd learned from Craig, I flat-out wasn't capable of abandoning Dan when he had no one else. Or maybe I just needed to look him in the eye before slamming the door. In any case, I wasn't ready to slam the door just yet. Not while he was so broken.

When I did finally go back to his room, I found him being tended to by a stocky nurse I hadn't seen before. Dan now appeared to be awake, but he was clearly confused about where he was and what was happening.

The nurse looked up from the chest tube she'd been checking. "Are you a relative?" I detected a Southern twang.

"I'm his sister," I said.

Dan didn't seem to hear, or if he did, he didn't react. His eyes had been open—at least to the extent possible, swollen as they were. Now they dropped shut and he appeared to lapse back into sleep.

"How is he doing?" I asked. "Has he talked at all?"

"He's made a squeak or two, but that's about it," the nurse said. "We're giving him morphine, and with his head injury, it'll probably be a while before he comes around enough to talk."

"So, what's a while?" I asked. "Hours? Days?"

"It's hard to say. We'll just have to wait and see."

I looked back at Dan and now his eyes were open again. He turned his head in my direction, but his expression was blank and there was no sign he recognized me. I walked over to the chair next to his bed and sat down. "Dan, it's Rachel," I said. "Can you hear me?"

He stared at me through eyes that were little more than slits in misshapen purple mounds but said nothing. "You're in the hospital," I said. "You've been in a car accident."

His cracked lips parted slightly, and I thought he might try to talk, but he didn't. He just let out a slow moan, then, after a few seconds, closed his eyes again and went still.

The nurse changed his IV bag, which was hanging from a hook on a stainless steel stand. Afterwards, she wrote something on a clipboard attached to the end of his bed. When she was ready to leave, she took a squirt of hand sanitizer that was mounted by the door. She nodded to a white board on the wall. "If you leave your number, we'll call you when he comes around." She glanced back at Dan. "For now, I doubt he even knows you're here."

When she was gone, I went back and forth with myself about what to do. I finally picked up a marker and lifted it to the board. They somehow already had my number anyway, so why not? I scrawled my name and phone number in bright blue letters.

Driving home, my chest ached, and I spent the rest of the afternoon trying to ward off panic. I was nervous about talking to Nate, but I finally did call him. I told him about the accident but not what I'd learned from Craig. I would tell him everything eventually—but later, after I'd had more time to think.

CHAPTER TWENTY

I WAS HOPING IT would be at least a day before I was called back, but close to four o'clock, I got word from the hospital that Dan was starting to come around. He was apparently "combative and belligerent," and they wanted to know if I'd be willing to come help calm him down. They also wanted to speak to me about some test results that had come back.

Aggravated but resigned, I jumped in the car and drove back to the hospital in rush hour traffic. On the way I called Nate, and he was understanding. "You gotta do what you gotta do," he told me, and I reluctantly agreed— although I'd rather have been heading for a firing squad.

When I got to the hospital, I discovered Dan had been moved. He was now in a private room—no doubt the result of his bad behavior. When I finally located him, I found him cranked partially upright, feebly sipping water from a bended paper straw. The cup was being held by a small Latina nurse who, upon seeing me, put it down on a tray next to a standard-issue Jell-O and bowl of chicken bouillon. She greeted me with a hopeful smile.

"Are you Rachel?" she asked, nodding at my name on the white board. She moved the table from over the bed and began adjusting Dan's pillow.

"Yes, that's right," I said.

Dan still seemed pretty out of it, and now that the table was pushed away, I could see that his left hand was tied to the side rail of the bed. He looked over at me and his face was a battered mask of misery.

"Hi Dan," I said timidly, stepping to his bedside. Although one of his hands was in a sling and the other was tied down, I was fearful of how he might react. He didn't move, and his expression remained fixed.

"I'm going to page the doctor," the nurse said, appearing anxious to leave the room. She looked at Dan. "Maybe your sister can help you try to eat some soup, or maybe a little Jell-O." She used a too-loud voice, as though speaking to a child.

Dan didn't say anything. His lips were swollen and, for a moment, they quivered like he might try to speak, but he didn't. I could tell by the dazed look in his eyes that he was heavily drugged.

"We gave him some medication to settle him down," the nurse said. A small plastic name tag on her smock identified her as *Sonya*. "He's been pretty upset—saying he wants to leave. But we can't let him do that."

She smiled at Dan and upped the volume again. "You need to stay here so we can take care of you." She looked at me and whispered, "A doctor will come talk to you." Then she took a squirt of hand sanitizer and exited the room.

I sat down next to Dan's bed and wondered what to say. Much to my relief, after just a few seconds, he closed his eyes and appeared to drift off, leaving me feeling agitated over why they'd felt it necessary to call me. What could I do but sit and stare at him?

Studying Dan's pathetic countenance, I tried to conjure a feeling of warmth, but in a cold room that probably billed at a thousand dollars an hour, it was hard to see the situation through a compassionate lens. From where I sat, Dan had made this stinking bed, and I was being yanked into it whether I liked it or not.

I closed my eyes and focused on my breathing, trying to bring myself to a place of sympathy. I called my mother to mind, and I could practically hear her telling me to stop thinking about myself and start thinking about Dan.

Poor Dan, I thought bitterly. Dan, the armed-to-the-teeth white supremacist. I was glad my parents hadn't lived to see the day. They'd be horrified. *I was horrified.* And I knew in my bones that I'd have to take him in. What was the alternative if I didn't? A better person might have felt some kind of pity or sisterly concern, but all I could honestly feel was despair at how his mess was poised to screw up my life.

Suddenly William was telling me in his velvety voice, *"Calm down. Take things one step at a time. Everything will be all right."* I closed my eyes and tried to find comfort in feeling his presence, but I remained distraught. I missed William, and my mother, and having a normal life. I was tired of sickness and hospitals and loss. And, more than anything, I was tired of Dan.

‡

Thirty minutes after the nurse's departure, a doctor finally arrived. He was surprisingly young, appeared Middle Eastern, and smiled charmingly as he paused to use the hand sanitizer by the door. "I'm Dr. Hashemi," he said, stepping over and extending his hand. "You're the patient's sister?"

"That's right," I said, noticing his firm grip. "I'm Rachel."

He nodded amiably, then turned his gaze to Dan, who was still asleep. "So, I don't know how much you've been told," he began. "As you can see, your brother has sustained an injury to the head in addition to multiple broken bones and a pneumothorax. *Collapsed lung.*" He gestured to a medical apparatus hooked to the side of the bed. "I don't anticipate him needing the chest tube much longer. It'll probably come out tomorrow."

I had risen when the doctor entered the room, and now he motioned for me to sit back down. Adjusting both his glasses and his demeanor, he looked somber. "Because of the head injury we did an MRI of his brain, and I'm afraid we discovered a fairly large mass on his frontal lobe. It's what we call a *frontal meningioma.*"

I don't know what I expected in the way of test results, but it definitely wasn't this—although I shouldn't have been surprised. Cancer took my father, my mother, and William. It was one of the few constants in my life. Diagnosis; illness; death. *Lather; rinse; repeat.*

"He has a brain tumor?" I asked. I knew the answer, of course. I just didn't know what else to say.

"That's correct," the doctor said, "although it may not be as bad as it sounds. Most meningiomas are benign, and they tend to be slow-growing, so it's doubtful there's any imminent danger to his life. It could be malignant, however. There's no way of knowing without a biopsy. But, in any case, judging from what we can see, it appears to be operable."

A swirl of emotions now battled for purchase in my brain. I felt completely blindsided.

"Do you know if he's been having headaches?" the doctor asked. "Or maybe mood swings, or odd or uncharacteristic behavior? Patients with this condition can also sometimes suffer seizures, which might account for his accident."

I was struck with a sudden deluge of doubt and fear. "When you say slow-growing," I asked, "what do you mean? Do you mean over years?"

"It can vary widely," he said. "It's certainly possible to have a meningioma go undiagnosed for years. As I said, they tend to be slow-growing, and they can be asymptomatic for quite a long time."

My mother's voice was suddenly shrieking in my ears that this was the answer to Dan's disintegration. As for my own voice, I doubted it could be that simple. There were legions of Dans with no brain tumors who were simply hopped up on a steady diet of malignant propaganda.

"You and your brother will need to talk to a neurosurgeon about scheduling a biopsy," the doctor said. "And I'd recommend he get one as soon as possible."

He nodded to Dan, who was beginning to stir and moan. "I see they have him restrained. If he's been acting irrationally, it could be the tumor. Have you noticed any significant changes in his behavior lately?"

I let out a sardonic laugh, and I could tell by the doctor's expression that he understood my reaction. "So he has been acting strangely?"

"I don't know," I said. "He's had problems and been irrational as far back as I can remember, so it's hard to say." I paused to wonder if a tumor could account for Dan's attraction to armed extremism, but I doubted his malevolence was operable. I wasn't that lucky.

"I'm pretty sure he doesn't have health insurance," I said. "Does that mean they won't treat him?"

"You'll have to work that out with the hospital," Dr. Hashemi said. "But, in the meantime, you need to discuss his options with a neurosurgeon and schedule a biopsy. Someone from neurology should be in for a consult probably tomorrow."

With his eyes still closed, Dan let out a groan.

"It looks like he may be coming around," the doctor said. "I need to check on another patient, but I can come back in a few minutes. If he's awake when I get back, I'll see if I can explain things to him."

I stood up and thanked him, then watched as he disappeared back into the cold bowels of the hospital, not bothering this time with the spritz by the door.

Conflicted and confused, I returned to the chair by Dan's bed. The last thing I wanted was to be part of whatever drama might ensue once the doctor returned. Unfortunately, I felt like I had no choice, so I stayed put.

With Dan's groans now increasing in volume and his eyes flickering with the onset of consciousness, I took a series of slow deep breaths and tried to channel my mother. Closing my eyes, I visualized her face, hoping to soothe my jangled nerves, but my anxiety remained high, exacerbated by the increasing intensity of Dan's moans. And there was that smell—that horrible hospital smell that brought so many terrible memories. And the cold. *Why were hospitals always so cold*? I shivered, then opened my eyes and was suddenly looking at Dan struggling to raise his head.

"What's going on? What are you doing here?" he mumbled, blinking against the bright light of the room.

"You were in a car accident," I explained.

He squinted at his plastered arm. Upon realizing his other arm was tied, he began pulling on the restraint. "What the fuck is this?"

"Calm down," I said. "It's just there to stop you from yanking out your chest tube." I nodded down to where a hose filled with pink liquid terminated in a large plastic device that was out of Dan's range of vision. "You have a collapsed lung, so a tube in your side is connected to a machine down there."

"What?" he said, his mangled features buckling with confusion. He glanced down at himself, but most of his body was hidden under a white cotton blanket. Then he began, once again, trying to free his arm.

"Please, just relax," I said. "We can call a nurse and have that removed, but you have to stay still. Besides a chest tube, your arm is broken in two places and you have some broken ribs. You also have a catheter."

Dan laid his head back on his pillow and made a face as if he were in agony.

"You have a pretty serious head injury, too" I added, choosing to leave the tumor for the doctor to report.

"No shit," he said. "My head hurts like fuck. What the fuck happened to me?"

"You were in a car accident. You don't remember?"

He grimaced and shook his head. "I don't remember shit."

"Well," I said, "all I know is you were in an accident, and you were the only one hurt."

"Where's my truck?"

"I don't know anything about your truck," I said. "It's probably been hauled to some city lot somewhere, but judging by how you look, I'd say there's a good chance it's totaled."

Dan went quiet and appeared to be trying to think. Then, scowling and bewildered, he asked, "What happened to me?"

"I told you," I said. "You were in a car accident, but that's all I know."

As if hearing this for the first time, he said, "I was in an accident?" He struggled against the restraint on his left arm. "*What the fuck is this?*"

Dan had forgotten everything I'd just told him, so now we were back to square one.

I'd called for a nurse, and someone finally arrived to release Dan's hand from the rail. She also changed the bag attached to his catheter. Otherwise, the wait for Dr. Hashemi was an endless loop that might have been comical if not for the terrifying possibility it would never end.

By the time the doctor arrived back, I had explained to Dan no less than ten times about the accident, his injuries, and his truck. Almost to the word, he had responded each time with identical questions and phrases. In his diminished state, the whereabouts of his truck appeared to be his gravest concern. And I wasn't surprised. It was all he had left of his inheritance.

Much to my relief, after introducing himself to Dan, Dr. Hashemi assured us that Dan's memory would probably normalize over the next several days. Unfortunately, it was clear that while the doctor would be the first to deliver Dan the news about his tumor, he'd need to be reminded once he inevitably forgot.

I braced myself as Dr. Hashemi pulled a chair up to Dan's bed and leaned in close in an effort to hold Dan's attention. "There's something we've discovered in an MRI that I need to explain to you," he started.

Something, possibly the doctor's accent, caused Dan to have a bad reaction, expressed as a tensing of his already misshapen features.

"I don't want to scare you," the doctor continued, "so before I tell you what we found, I want to assure you that it's probably not life-threatening. Do you understand?"

Being so bruised and swollen, Dan's face was hard to read, but from where I stood, his expression appeared increasingly hostile.

"Do you understand what the doctor's saying?" I interjected. "He needs to tell you something, but he doesn't want you to worry."

Dan glared at me, his disposition no longer in question. "I need to get out of here!" he cried. "I can't stay here!" He abruptly tried to sit up, now fully back in the disruptive mode that had spurred the hospital to restrain him. "Let me the fuck out of here!"

"Please, Dan," I said. "You need to stay still. You're going to hurt yourself." I reached for his shoulder in an attempt to stop him from moving, but the instant I made contact he lashed out violently and struck me in the face.

"Get off me!" he screamed.

"Mr. Hayes!" Dr. Hashemi erupted, as though trying to jolt Dan back into his senses. "You can't possibly leave. Do you see all these things you're attached to? You have a chest tube, an IV…"

Before he could finish, Dan began to scream obscenities and struck out again with his free arm, forcing the doctor to physically restrain him.

"Go get a nurse!" the doctor shouted. "We need to sedate him before he hurts himself."

Following his order, I ran to the nurse's station. "Please!" I cried. "The doctor needs someone to come right now and sedate my brother!" I pointed to Dan's room, where now his shrieking was so loud that no explanation was needed. The nurse sprang instantly to action, calling a large male nurse who was nearby to come assist.

Panicked, I followed the two nurses back to Dan's room, where now Dr. Hashemi was the one yelling. *"He's seizing!"* he shouted to the nurses. *"Help me get him onto his side!"*

I watched as Dan lurched and jolted, his eyes rolled back in their swollen sockets. Waved out, I exited the room as Dr. Hashemi and the two nurses attempted to hold Dan down while struggling with the various tubes that were affixed to his body.

Feeling sick, I fled to the hallway overlooking the parking lot. When I got there, it was already occupied by a gangly man pacing with a cigarette. "I'm pretty sure smoking isn't allowed," I said without thinking. He stamped out the cigarette and left, and I immediately felt terrible. For all I knew, his wife was dying.

When I eventually arrived back at Dan's room, all was quiet, and he was harnessed and hooked-up as though nothing had happened. I was tempted to run, but decided to whisper his name to make sure he was asleep before leaving. To my surprise, his eyes opened to slits and he immediately began muttering. I doubted he knew who I was, but the words suddenly issuing from his mouth caught my attention, compelling me to sit down and listen.

"You think you're better than me?" was the first sentence I managed to discern, although it came out like, *"Youthickyrbrthnme?"* What followed was a slurred, *"Imafuckinshowyou."* The rest was impossible to make out, but the picture that emerged was both hostile and sad, making me wonder if removing his tumor might, by some miracle, make him more palatable. All I could do was hope.

CHAPTER TWENTY-ONE

IT WAS AFTER NINE-THIRTY when Nate finally knocked on my door. It was just as well that he arrived late, because it gave me time to decompress. I had a lot to think about, but instead of dwelling on the madness surrounding my brother, I'd trained my thoughts on Nate and Isaiah, wanting to shore up a life with them before facing what I feared would blow it all up.

I'd already briefed Nate on what was going on—focusing primarily on Dan's condition and the seizure—so when I pulled open the door to receive him, we had no need for words. He simply stepped inside and took me in his arms. Given all that had happened, I don't think he arrived with the expectation we'd be sexual, but the instant we touched, raw emotions combined with our well-established chemistry combusted to create a desire that propelled us almost immediately upstairs.

"You sure you're in the mood for this?" Nate asked, as we entered my room.

"Definitely," I whispered, pulling the spread off my bed to expose the sheets. I started to undress, and the look in Nate's eyes as he watched me was as much of a rush as the feel of his hands when he pulled me close for a kiss. When I eventually watched Nate remove his clothes, I marveled, as always, at the silkiness of his skin and stunning contrast of our bodies reflected in the mirror by my bed. Even scarred and burned as he was, Nate's body had a luster that took my breath away. As we stood, both unclothed and swaying in the warm interior of my room, I consciously banned thoughts of anything but the two of us, intent on losing myself in the ecstasy of my senses, which were aroused to a fever pitch.

ଔ

Lying in Nate's arms in the aftermath of another exquisite round of lovemaking, I felt an escalating desire to say things I feared were premature. I suspected he felt the same but feared the circumstances surrounding Dan might give him pause—and I still hadn't told him what I'd learned from Craig. I was running my hand over his bicep, contemplating how to express my feelings without sounding over the top, when he spoke up first.

"I hope you know by now that I love you, and whatever happens with your brother, I'll be here for you."

Filled with joy and relief, I raised my head from his chest and looked into his eyes. "I love you so much," I said. "I've been terrified that all my complications might scare you away."

"I'm not scared," he said. "Are you scared?"

"I'm not scared," I said, mimicking the lilt in his voice. I rolled over on top of him and broke into a grin that was reflected back in a look of affection more beautiful than anything I'd ever seen. I could read it on his face. He loved me.

ଔ

It wasn't until the next morning, after a magical night and deep, satisfying sleep, that Dan slipped back into my consciousness. Like always, Nate had risen and departed early, though not before leaving me with more sweet words and kisses to sustain me until we could be together again.

I looked at the clock on my bedside table. It read 8:05. Surely I could bask for at least another hour before facing whatever music the day had in store. I ran a bath, then spent the next forty minutes in the tub, rerunning the tape of the previous night. Waves shot through me each time I thought about some of the things we'd done, and especially the words we'd spoken to one another.

When I was finally up and dressed, it was nine-fifteen, and I couldn't avoid thinking about Dan any longer. I located my phone, which I'd left in my purse in the kitchen, and discovered I'd missed two calls from the hospital, both in the middle of the night. Something bad had obviously happened.

Taking a deep breath, I played the first voicemail: "This message is for Rachel Hayes. Please call Long Beach Medical Center as soon as you can regarding your brother." The second message was similar but also hinted something had happened during the night or early morning.

With a feeling of dread, I called the hospital and asked to be connected to the nurse's station for wherever Dan was at the moment. After being put on hold, being disconnected, then put on hold again, I finally reached someone who informed me that Dan had required emergency surgery in the middle of the night to relieve pressure on his brain. He was currently in a recovery room but was expected to be moved to another room within the hour.

Hanging up the phone, I felt rattled. I wasn't about to rush to Dan's bedside to be there when he woke up, but I knew I needed to go. I was out on the patio with a bowl of granola, trying to work up an appetite for the trip back, when I had a memory that stopped me breathing.

I was recalling one summer when I was charged with entertaining a couple of William's young nieces, and I suddenly knew, with near certainty, what Dan had been doing in the cottage. Both the downstairs bedroom and the loft had sizable window seats that my mother had requested as areas for storage when the cottage was being built. I was going to hide in one of them that summer during a game of hide and seek, but I discovered Dan had been using it as a hiding place of his own—for Playboy and Hustler magazines, bottles of alcohol, and switchblade knives. I hadn't told anyone what I'd found. I'd kept Dan's secret. But now—now I had a feeling he had a secret I couldn't keep.

Hoping I was wrong, but feeling an almost preternatural certainty I wasn't, I entered the cottage, remembering how a small trace of dirt had pointed to the loft. I climbed the stairs, then stared at the window seat for a good thirty seconds before finding the courage to lift the lid. Finally, I took in a long breath, said, "Okay," and opened it up.

I had thought I was more or less prepared for the worst, but the reality that now stared me in the face was so vivid and so extreme, I was momentarily stunned. I was no expert on weapons, but I knew enough to know that the guns I was suddenly gazing at were as lethal as they come. And Craig was right. They looked like military guns and assault rifles. I didn't want to touch anything, but I could see, lower in the pile, that there were also some smaller ones in the mix—some hand guns and a weird-looking thing I guessed was an Uzi. There were also boxes of bullets and stacks of what I recognized as metal clips of ammunition.

Confronted with what looked like a stockpile of pure evil, my mind flooded with scenes of mass murder—of carnage in churches and synagogues, massacres at concerts and movie theaters, psychotic attacks on school children... I wondered, with horror, what had been in my brother's mind. Had he been planning some terrible act? Was he part of some group itching for a race war? My head buzzed with fear and confusion, but there was one thing about which I was certain: I needed to get every speck of this madness out of my house.

cs

With my heart racing, I went back outside, locking the cottage door behind me. It occurred to me that I needed to check the other window seat, but I decided to do it later. For now, I had to figure out what to do.

I contemplated calling Craig. He'd said he'd be hard to reach for a couple of days, but I could at least leave him a message. It was the obvious thing to do, but I was hesitant to make a move of such magnitude. Once I got Craig involved, there would be no turning back. Dan was already fighting for his life. Did I really want to bring this down on him as well? I wasn't sure.

My mother's voice pleaded for mercy. William had a different view, but I foolishly shut him down, at least until I could think. But it was impossible to think with so much fear and anger surging through my veins. In my agitated state, even locking the cottage door had been a challenge.

I considered calling Nate, but he was heading into finals, and I didn't want to do anything to derail his studies. I was confused about a lot of things but not this: I could not screw up Nate's exams. If that happened, I'd never forgive myself.

Now on the patio, I plopped down on a chaise lounge and closed my eyes, determined to bring myself back to some kind of equilibrium. The air was warm and fragrant and, after several minutes, I did manage to achieve some semblance of calm, but nothing could alter the reality I was facing.

I opened my eyes, sprang up, then impulsively stripped down to my underwear and dove into the pool. At first, the cold water was a shock, but I began swimming laps, and soon I entered a zone that was both physically and mentally soothing. I had no goggles, but I didn't need them. I'd spent much of my early life in the pool, so even with my eyes closed, I knew instinctively when to turn, push off, then shoot back underwater before rising for the next breath. It had been years since I'd done any serious swimming, but now, flying through the water, I was reminded of its primordial appeal.

Finally exhausted, I was just reaching for the side of the pool when I was almost startled to death by a figure above me that seemed to appear out of nowhere. I let out a scream and, afterwards, because my vision was blurry and the sun was bright, it took me a few seconds to realize the figure was Arturo.

"I'm sorry, I didn't mean to scare you," he pleaded, obviously as unnerved by my scream as I was by his sudden appearance.

Relieved, but also disappointed at having lost whatever composure I'd gained, I reassured him. "It's okay, I just didn't expect to see you today." A moment later, I remembered I was in my underwear. I crouched, hoping the water offered some cover. Standing over me, continuing to nervously apologize, Arturo was oblivious.

"I'm fine. Really," I said, hoping he'd take the hint and leave so I could escape into the house. When he didn't budge, I added, "Is there something you want to talk to me about?"

"Yes, there is something," he said, and a sadness in his eyes signaled more than simply regret for having scared me. Something was wrong.

"Can you give me a minute?" I said. "I'd like to go in and put some clothes on first."

"Oh, yes, sorry," he said, now stepping away from the pool and gesturing toward the gate. "I'll be in front. In my truck."

cs

Now clothed, but stressed at having one more thing to deal with, I opened the front door and saw Arturo sitting in his truck, a troubled look on his face. As I walked up to his open window, he nodded, then hesitated a moment before speaking up. "I'm sorry," he said, "but I have to tell you I can't work here anymore."

This was so far from anything I'd expected that I was shocked. "Why not? What's wrong?"

He frowned, and I could see he was upset.

"What is it, Arturo?"

"You know I always liked working here. It's been so many years..." His eyes glistened beneath bushy eyebrows. "*Senor* William, your mother, the garden, those crazy squirrels..." He smiled and shook his head.

"What is it, then? What's happened? I hope it's not something with your family."

"No," he said. "It's nothing like that."

Arturo and I had known each other for years. He'd started working for my parents long before I inherited the house, and though I wouldn't say we were close, there was something almost familial between us. I simply couldn't fathom that he'd suddenly disappear. I searched his face for some sign of what might be wrong. "Just tell me Arturo. What's going on?"

He sighed. "I never told you, because you never asked, but I'm an illegal."

This didn't surprise me, and I knew *he knew* I didn't care. But now I was afraid for him. "What's happened?"

He leaned over and opened his glove compartment, then pulled out a rumpled piece of paper. "The other day I found this," he said, handing it over. "On my windshield."

"Someone put this on your windshield when you were parked here?"

He nodded.

I looked down at the paper, and large block letters written with a black Sharpie read: "**Watch out amigo. ICE is coming for you.**"

I couldn't be sure, but I suspected the printing was Dan's. "This was probably my brother," I said. "He's the one who's been prowling around the backyard."

My anger at Dan was now fully reignited. "I don't think he'd warn you if he were really going to do something. This is probably intended to hurt me, not you. But he's in the hospital now—he was in a pretty terrible car accident—so I don't think you need to worry. But I understand how you must feel, and I'm *so* sorry."

I could see by a twitching in Arturo's jaw how distressed he was. "I'm sorry, too," he said, "but I can't take a chance. I can't get sent back to Mexico."

"You don't have to explain," I said. "I understand. It's a big risk for you."

"*Si*, a big risk," he said. "My family, they see what's happening and they're afraid." His brow was furrowed and the wrinkles around his eyes had deepened into dark grooves. "My wife, she has a green card, and my children are citizens, but I don't have nothing." He glanced at the paper in my hand, then looked up at me with a pained expression.

Holding his gaze, I had no words—only a deep sympathy for a type of fear I could only imagine. Suddenly calling Craig didn't seem like such a bad idea. With Dan so intent on ruining my life, and now possibly Arturo's, why should I hesitate to bring the hammer down on his?

After hugging Arturo the best I could through the open window of his truck, I watched him drive off slowly down the street, anger rising inside of me. It was starting to get late, and I had a lot to figure out, but I was in such a state of turmoil, it was impossible to think clearly. I went inside and collapsed onto the living room couch, the same spot where Nate and I had first held one another. I was tempted to lie down and curl up, but I stayed upright, intent on keeping myself together. I remained there, thinking, until I knew what I had to do.

Soon I was back in the cottage, staring at the top of the window seat in the downstairs bedroom. When I finally found the nerve to pull it open, I realized, in an instant, that I might never go back to the hospital. As before, the vision that materialized was like a still life of madness. My brother could die for all I cared.

CHAPTER TWENTY-TWO

STARING DOWN AT A second cache of extremely lethal-looking weapons—some in a partially open duffel bag and some just loose—I knew I had to call Craig. This was too much to deal with on my own.

I closed the lid and looked in the closet. To my relief, apart from a couple of boxes of Christmas ornaments, it was empty. On impulse, I got down on the floor and looked under the bed. There, I found two empty duffel bags, a garbage bag filled with sweat clothes, and a small backpack. I pulled out the backpack, and it was so light, at first I thought it was empty. Upon closer inspection, I discovered an assortment of toiletry items in the central compartment. But something else that looked vaguely familiar also caught my eye. I pulled it out and recognized a cloth-bound diary my mother had given Dan one year for Christmas—I think at the recommendation of a therapist. Although it was decades ago, this was the first indication I'd seen that he'd actually used it. And he'd used it all right. It was filled with page upon page of Dan's handwriting.

Curious, and also fearful, I climbed onto the bed. I knew that what I was going to do was beyond the normal bounds of decency. Ordinarily, I'd never read someone else's diary. But this situation was anything but normal, so

I made myself comfortable and opened the book, praying that, whatever I found, it wouldn't be too terrible.

Before perusing the most recent entries for mention of his guns or anything else that stood out (my biggest fear was some kind of sick *manifesto*), I decided to take a look at the first page, curious to see when he'd started. The handwriting there was much neater than the scrawling toward the end, so I figured it probably went back quite a few years. As soon as I started reading, I knew he'd begun as a teenager. The very first line read: Mom thinks there's something wrong with me, but the only thing wrong is I'm being treated like a second-class citizen in my own home.

It was classic Dan, so emblematic of his character that I might have predicted every word. Equally predictable was the vitriol that followed. Mostly targeting William, it ranged from patently unfair to downright ugly, even going so far as to suggest my mother and William had "started up" before our father died, which was preposterous.

Flipping through pages, I found some of his complaints to be pretty garden variety for a teenage boy—like being forced to do his homework and having to "mow the fucking back forty." But the tone of it all was chilling, describing a home life I found utterly unrecognizable. William— or *William Big and Ugly*, as he was charmingly characterized—was the primary focus of Dan's animus, but he was not much kinder to my mother and me. He called my mother a *disingenuous bitch*, among other things. (I had to hand it to him for the vocabulary word, but he misspelled *disingenuous* as *disgenius*.) I was referred to variously as a *fucking brat*, *spoiled brat*, and *everybody's little favorite*. All in all, the picture that emerged was not surprising, but it was jarring to see his alienation expressed with so much earnestness.

Still afraid to see what the end might reveal, I turned to the middle, where the handwriting was sloppier and there were names I didn't recognize. Scanning pages filled with expletives, I could see that Dan used the diary as an outlet for his emotions, which, I supposed, was its intended purpose. In any case, thumbing through his most intimate thoughts and darkest moments was wrenching. Here, in his own scrawling hand, his expressions of pain and alienation were so raw, I found myself surprisingly moved. It was clear that Dan's outward-directed hostility was more than matched by self-hatred. One passage stood out for the care he'd taken to write it legibly. In block letters he had written: WHY CAN'T I BE NORMAL AND HAVE WHAT EVERYONE ELSE HAS? I FUCKING HATE MYSELF.

When I finally examined his last entries, most of what I could make out was over-the-top political nonsense. I found nothing about guns, or belonging to any groups, or criminal activity of any kind—although some of his handwriting was so terrible, it could have said practically anything for all I could tell. I did manage to decipher some pretty bitter venting about his Home Depot job and coworkers he hated. I learned he'd been fired and not quit, which was no big surprise. I also flipped back and found some entries around the time our mother died. This sentence stood out as particularly sad: At least if she dies I won't have to deal with her disappointment anymore.

This passage was also painful: *I can't stand the way Rachel looks down on me, like she's so fucking superior. The truth is, I have nothing and no one.*

My name cropped up elsewhere, but the handwriting was mostly unintelligible, and I didn't feel especially motivated to absorb his enmity, so I ignored anything about me and tried to see if I could discover how he'd lost his money. Unfortunately, nothing I read solved the mystery. When I'd finally had enough, I was eye-strained and dispirited, but I was relieved to have at least seen no indication that he was plotting a mass murder.

Soon I found myself back at the window seat contemplating Dan's armory. Staring at the vile assemblage of weapons, I wanted them gone. Immediately.

I knew, without a shred of doubt, that the only smart thing to do was pass the ball to Craig. But, for some reason, I couldn't do it. Maybe it was my mother's voice pleading with me. Maybe it was the pathetic self-loathing I'd read in Dan's diary, or the cancer attacking his brain. It was probably all of it, but the bottom line was I didn't know if I could live with myself if I had Dan arrested when he was already in such a terrible state. Craig had suggested he might be able to strike some kind of deal, but there was no way of knowing for sure what would happen if I got the authorities involved. But what was the alternative?

I started having crazy thoughts. I pictured myself throwing duffel bags off a bridge, or a boat. But this raised the problem of which bridge, what boat? And what if someone were to find them? I had to make sure that wherever the guns ended up, they weren't recoverable. I considered taking them up to the woods and burying them, but this presented other issues. I finally decided to shelve the problem until I had more time to mull it over. In the meantime, I would go back to the hospital after all. After reading Dan's diary, I didn't have it in me to abandon him. Whether I liked it or not, I really was all he had left.

CHAPTER TWENTY-THREE

I WAS PREPARING TO leave for the hospital when I was stopped short by an idea. I had a storage space that I'd rented after my divorce and hadn't yet cleared out. Close to where my space was located, there was a huge bank of trash dumpsters. What if I threw Dan's stash into one of those dumpsters and then made an anonymous call to the police from a pay phone? I was pretty sure there was a phone booth in the gas station just across the street. It was perfect. I could watch from there and make sure the police showed up. This would get rid of the guns without implicating Dan, and there would be no risk of the guns falling into the wrong hands.

I thought about the *falling into the wrong hands* possibility and decided that if the police didn't arrive, I'd keep calling until they did. I'd even call Craig, if necessary. It seemed like an ideal solution, so instead of heading for the hospital, I went back to the cottage.

Less ideal, as it turned out, was the prospect of physically removing the guns from their lair. Besides having a visceral fear of handling such lethal-looking objects, I worried that some of them might be loaded. There was also the question of fingerprints, so before doing anything, I'd need to find some gloves. I had both gardening gloves and rubber gloves I used for doing dishes. I also had surgical gloves that were a hold-over from when William and my mother had required care. I decided to use the surgical gloves, so I went back to the house and retrieved a pair.

Now back in the downstairs bedroom of the cottage, I used latex-covered hands to pull the two empty duffel bags from under the bed. Next, I opened the window seat and carefully pulled out the third partially-filled bag and placed it gingerly on the floor. Beneath where the duffel bag had been, I found two large handguns, three larger automatic or semi-automatic rifles of some kind, and a spine-chilling volume of bullets and clips.

It occurred to me, mid-spine-chill, that besides worrying about my own fingerprints, I needed to consider Dan's. The last thing I wanted was to handle anything more than I had to, but did I need to wipe Dan's prints? *"Fuck!"* I screamed in frustration, understanding the absurdity of what I was doing. Why should I protect Dan?

After probably five solid minutes of being frozen with doubt, I decided to grab a pillowcase and give at least a cursory wipe to every surface that seemed likely to hold a print. I did it more to protect myself than anything, because it occurred to me that if Dan's prints were found, the question of how the guns got into the dumpster would almost certainly lead to me.

When it was time to fill the duffel bags, I cautiously manipulated the weapons and ammunition like puzzle pieces to get everything to fit. Even so, I ended up having to retrieve the backpack with Dan's toiletries and fill that, too. When it came time to zip up the bags, I broke into a cold sweat, fearful that the associated tightening might set something off. As I slowly slid the zipper pull across each bag, holding my breath as I went, I experienced a sense of unreality, as though this were a scene from a movie and not real life. Only this was real life. As unbelievable as it was, this was really happening.

ભ

By the time I finished filling the bags in both bedrooms, it was approaching two o'clock. Part of me knew that what I was doing was insane, but I ignored that voice and pushed ahead, determined to follow through with what I'd started.

I was on my way to the storage place, feeling strangely confident, when I got a call from Nate. Since I was driving and not anxious to explain what I was up to, I was going to let it go to voicemail. But, then, inexplicably, I picked up after the fourth ring. I'm not sure what I was thinking when I answered, but when I did, I knew instantly by the timbre of Nate's voice that something was wrong. "Rachel," he said. "I hate to bother you, but I'm wondering if you can help me out."

"Of course," I said. "What's going on?"

"I just got a call from the lady who runs the little summer program where Isaiah is today, and she wants someone to come pick him up. There's been some kind of shooting or something right near her place. There are a lot of sirens and police cars everywhere. She feels it's upsetting to the kids. Unfortunately, my mom has my car because hers is in the shop, and she doesn't have her cell phone. She just *refuses* to use her phone." He sighed with exasperation.

"On top of everything, I'm working on a really important final paper I need to upload by five o'clock."

I could hear that he was under a lot of pressure. "I hate to ask," he said, "but do you think you could go get him? Wanda—that's the lady who runs the place—she says there isn't any more shooting going on. Just a lot of commotion with the police and ambulances and all that. I'd call my sister, but…"

"It's okay," I interrupted. "Really. Just give me the address and I'll pick him up. But are you sure she'll let me take him?"

"I'll let her know you're coming," he said. "And since Isaiah knows you, it'll be fine. But are you sure? I don't want to make you do anything…."

"I'm sure," I said. "Just text me the address. And don't forget to give me your address, too, so I can bring him to you."

"You seriously don't mind?"

"I don't mind at all," I said, trying to sound natural, although I was already worrying about doing so much driving with my trunk full of guns.

"I owe you big time. Thank you," Nate said, and there was both affection and relief in his voice. A few moments later he texted me the addresses, two hearts, and an emoji blowing kisses.

ೞ

After pulling over to type the first address into my Google Maps, I was on my way to Isaiah. According to my phone, I would be there in twenty-nine minutes under current traffic conditions. This gave me twenty-nine minutes to convince myself that there was no way the contents of my trunk could have any bearing on the task at hand. "In all the years I've been driving," I told myself out loud, "no one has ever pulled me over and looked in my trunk."

William was suddenly in the car with me. *"What are you doing?"* His voice was not velvety, not soothing. He was mad. *"Why are you trying to protect your brother? Was he protecting you by bringing those weapons into your house? Your home? I don't think so."*

I could picture him perfectly—arms crossed, eyes narrowed to a squint. *"If you were smart, you'd call the police right now and have them meet you somewhere and come get these guns. I mean it. Right now. Forget the storage dumpster baloney. Turn Dan's nonsense over to the authorities and be done with it."*

Realizing William was probably right, I mulled things over in my head. What if I did call Craig? He might not be in town, but if he answered, he could at least tell me what to do. If I couldn't reach him, I'd call the police. Or maybe drive to a police station.

In the end, I decided to forget the dumpster idea, but, no matter what, I had to take care of Isaiah first. I was convinced that everything would be fine if I could just stay cool. William was shaking his head, but I ignored him.

CHAPTER TWENTY-FOUR

IN ALL THE MENTAL tumult associated with the contents of my trunk, I hadn't thought about how it might feel to make my first venture into Compton. According to my GPS, I was just a couple of minutes away, but I guessed I was getting close by the increasingly worn-down appearance of surrounding homes and businesses.

I'd spent a lifetime battling the discomfort that was part and parcel of the white psyche where minority neighborhoods were concerned. Yet, despite everything, the struggle persisted, as evidenced by the quickening of my pulse as my phone directed me deeper into streets with fortified homes and storefronts, walls with razor wire and graffiti, and an atmosphere that spoke of economic distress. But soon my anxiety abated, and I realized that my nervousness was less a fear of my surroundings than of myself and what my reaction said about me. Compton wasn't Beverly Hills, but neither was it much different from neighborhoods through which I'd traveled all my life. I relaxed and admonished myself for my foolishness.

I stopped at a red light, and a silver Toyota pulled up next to me, music with a pulsating bass issuing from its open window. I looked over, and the young black man in the driver's seat met my gaze with a flirtatious smile. I smiled back and felt a rush of shame for having entered his domain with trepidation.

When I was almost to the street where I needed to collect Isaiah, my anxiety about the neighborhood was gone, but my trunk fears returned to fill the void. They heightened when, upon turning a final corner, I was met with a crime-scene that I had massively underestimated, complete with yellow tape, glaring lights of every hue, throngs of onlookers, and more police cars than I could count. I was fretting over where on earth I could possibly park when my phone rang. In my nervousness, I reached for it, then dropped it down the narrow space to the right of my seat.

"*Fuck!*" I screamed, understanding the hassle it would be to retrieve it. I probably appeared unhinged to anyone who might have been looking on, but I didn't care. I added a loud, "*Shit!*"

My phone kept ringing, but I had to ignore it and focus on finding a place to park. After probably no less than eight rings, it finally stopped. Then, like a miracle, a car pulled out of a spot just ahead of me.

I parked, turned off the car, and sat in a stupor for a few moments before looking around at street numbers to figure out how far I'd need to walk to get to Isaiah. As it turned out, it wasn't far at all, which explained why it was so important to pick him up. He was in the dead center of everything.

Unfortunately, before I could do anything, I had to retrieve my phone so I could double-check the address. Given the mechanics of my car, this required feats of physical agility I was hardly in the mood for.

After no small amount of effort, I finally got it. Then, keeping my head down, I made my way through a frenetic obstacle course of police activity, flashing lights, and gawkers, until I came to a low brick building with a meticulously-painted sign identifying it as a "Daycare & Learning Center."

Passing through a gate in a low cyclone fence, I arrived at a door with a small bar-covered window that matched windows to its left and right. I knocked, then was almost immediately face-to-face with an attractive black woman who met me with a worried smile, then quickly ushered me inside. In contrast with the chaos outside, the room I entered was warm and welcoming, with rainbow colors and children's art and learning materials adorning all the walls. But there were no children in sight. "I'm Rachel," I said, meeting the woman's smile with one of my own. "I'm here to pick up Isaiah."

"I'm Wanda," she replied. "All the kids are in the back watching a video." She nodded to a hallway leading to another part of the building. "I've been trying to keep 'em occupied, but they know something's going on."

She shook her head and frowned. "It's been crazy. They've got dogs out there and everything. Ambulances, fire trucks, about a million police—it's insane. This is normally a quiet neighborhood."

"Do you have any idea what happened?" I asked.

"I assume it was a drive-by, but I can't say for sure. All I know is we heard some pops. You know, like gunfire. *A lot of gunfire.* And then there was screaming, and tires screeching, and pretty soon a lot of sirens. After that, the police and all the rest arrived. It's been like a circus out there ever since." She sighed and cocked her head, which was impressively wound with hundreds of tiny braids. "How many people actually got shot, I don't know. I've just been trying to keep the kids in the back and away from everything."

She gestured to the hallway. "A door back there goes out to a little play yard. You'll be better off taking Isaiah out that way. There's a gate where you can get out, and you should be able to find your way back to where you parked pretty easily. If you go left, you'll come to an alley a couple of houses up that leads back to this street." She raised her eyebrows. "Did you manage to park nearby?"

"Yeah, I'm just up the street."

Isaiah suddenly materialized. Adorable as always, he was clad in blue shorts and a Superman t-shirt. I wanted to scoop him up in my arms but held back.

"Hey Isaiah," I said. "Your dad asked me to come pick you up and drive you home. Is that okay with you?"

He nodded.

I smiled, then turned to Wanda, who was looking at him with obvious affection. She sank to her knees and opened her arms. "Can I get a hug before you go?"

He beamed back a grin, then stepped into a big bear hug. When she released him, he looked up at me with a gleam in his eye and seemed to read my mind. "Do you want a hug, too?"

"I'd love one," I said. Then I knelt down and pulled him into a hug that I could have held onto forever.

CHAPTER TWENTY-FIVE

EXITING OUT THE BACK door, Isaiah and I crossed a small yard, passed though a gate, then turned in the direction of the alley Wanda had described. When we arrived at the alley, I was relieved to see that it provided a clear shot back to the street where my car was parked. Arriving at the end of the alley, we turned right, and I tried to be as inconspicuous as possible as we headed for my car.

The street was still crawling with police, and it may have been my imagination, but I felt as though a couple of them were watching me as I unlocked the car, then deposited Isaiah into the back seat. It occurred to me that he may legally have been required to be in a booster of some kind, but there was nothing I could do about that. I simply buckled him in as snugly as I could, then jumped into the front seat and typed Nate's address into my phone's Google Maps.

When that was set, I quickly checked to see who had called earlier. It was the hospital, but I didn't have time to think about Dan, so I started the car, put on my blinker, pulled out, and then did a careful U-turn before heading back in the direction from which I'd come.

Now blessedly clear of the drama and twelve minutes from Nate, I glanced at Isaiah and wondered how he was doing. He'd said very little since my arrival to pick him up.

I wasn't sure if I should engage him, or just leave him be. He seemed content to sit in silence, but I fretted over my uncertainty and inability to read him. I assumed he was affected by what he'd seen and heard. He'd heard *gun shots*, and we'd just walked through a crime scene that looked like something from a disaster movie, but I had no way of knowing how much he understood. I kept checking on him and wondering if I should say something, but he appeared to be fine, and nothing came to me, so I finally decided not to force it.

Now waiting at a red light next to a small storefront church and Jiffy-Lube, I looked in my rearview mirror and noticed a black and white police car a few cars back. I didn't think much of it, but it did strengthen my resolve to call Craig the instant I'd delivered Isaiah safely home.

When the light changed to green, I started across the intersection. Following the instructions of my GPS, I moved into the far right lane in preparation for taking the next right turn. After the turn, I was disturbed to see that the same police car was still behind me, now even closer than before.

Telling myself to relax—that it was ridiculous to imagine that the police were following me—I switched on the radio and pushed the button for smooth jazz, hoping to find some music that would be soothing. The song playing was perfect. *Smooth Operator.*

"I love Sade," I said, looking into the rearview at Isaiah. He'd nodded out, making me hopeful that his being relaxed enough to fall sleep meant he really was fine. I looked in my mirror again, this time to check traffic behind me, and the black and white was still there, like a shark in shallow water.

My GPS spoke up, telling me to take a left-hand turn in "one quarter mile." I turned on my blinker and moved into the left lane, assuring myself that, with the next turn, I'd finally lose the police and be able to relax. Taking some deep breaths, I focused on the soothing sound of Sade.

"Across the North and South to Key Largo, love for sale..."

By the time I arrived at the street where I needed to turn, the police had moved into position directly behind me, following me into the left lane and sending me into a state of terror and disbelief. *Why were they following me?* It didn't seem possible. And yet I couldn't see how, with so many turns, their staying behind me could be a coincidence.

Struggling against panic, I took the turn and wondered if I should pull over. If they were, in fact, following me, I didn't want to lead them to Nate's house. Just the thought sent my blood pressure through the roof.

I looked in my mirror at Isaiah, sound asleep with his head cocked to one side, and I didn't know what to do. I couldn't think straight. The GPS lady piped up again, telling me to take the next right turn. Feeling like I was on remote control, I turned the corner, then impulsively pulled over behind some trash cans placed at the curb for pickup.

I was now parked in a residential neighborhood of small homes. A Latino man working on a bicycle in the driveway just ahead glanced up as the police car pulled in behind me. I shot him a look of remorse—an apology for bringing whatever this was to his doorstep.

With a rising fear, I rolled down my window, then watched in my rearview mirror as two white uniformed officers readied themselves for whatever would happen next. One was talking on a radio and the other—a caricature with a heavy blond mustache and aviator sunglasses—was eyeballing the surroundings. After what felt like forever, the caricature removed his dark glasses, emerged from the car, and then slowly approached. Now my eyes turned to my side mirror, until he eventually arrived at my window and bent over to speak to me. By then, my heart was beating so hard and my face was so hot, there's no way I appeared normal, but I forced a smile.

"Ma'am," he said. He shot a quick glance at Isaiah, who was still asleep, then looked back to me.

"I noticed you were following me," I said, "but I'm not sure why. Do I have a tail light out or something?" My temples were pounding, and I could feel sweat rolling down both sides of my body.

"Can I see your driver's license and registration, please?"

"Sure," I said, trying, once again, to smile, and willing both my face and voice not to quiver. I pulled my wallet from my purse and removed my driver's license and handed it to him. "My registration is in the glove compartment," I said, wanting his approval before making any moves in that direction.

"Go ahead," he said, but he watched me like a hawk as I leaned over and slowly opened the glove box, then retrieved the envelope containing my registration. I felt like a criminal, and the vibe coming from the policeman was chilling. All the charm in the world was not going to work with this guy.

I handed the envelope over. "Can I ask you what this is about?" I attempted to sound friendly, but my cheeriness probably sounded phony, making it all the more apparent that I was nervous.

The officer nodded to Isaiah, who, thankfully, was still out. "Is this your child?"

"No," I answered. "He's the son of a friend of mine."

"Who is this friend?" he asked frostily, and the hostility suggested by his tone sent my fear skyrocketing. *What possible relevance could that have?* And yet I didn't want to behave as though I had something to hide—or worse, that Nate had something to hide—so I answered the question.

"His name is Nate," I said, trying desperately to quell my fear. "But can you tell me what this is about? I'm confused about why you were following me."

"Does this Nate live in this neighborhood?" he asked coldly.

This Nate, he'd said, as though Nate were someone sinister! Now I was so scared I could barely breathe. "Not too far from here," I answered. "But I don't understand what that has to do with anything."

"You're aware there was a shooting?"

"Yes, that's why I picked him up," I said, gesturing back to Isaiah. "But why would you be following *me*? You can't possibly think I had anything to do with it?"

"You seem nervous," the officer said.

"Of course I'm nervous," I said, battling back tears. "I went to pick up a child at a scene where there was a shooting, I've been followed by the police, and now you're asking me about someone who has nothing to do with anything. He's an engineering student in the middle of finals, which is why he asked me to pick up his son." I appealed with my eyes for sympathy. "Anyone would be nervous."

We were starting to attract the notice of people in the neighborhood, and the man with the bicycle, who had been watching intently, was now joined by a woman holding a baby. Another police car also arrived on the scene.

"Would you be surprised if I told you that while you were picking up the boy, your car was identified as suspicious by police dogs trained to detect firearms?" the officer asked.

"*Oh my God*," I said under my breath. I closed my eyes and bowed my head over the steering wheel. I could not believe this was happening.

"Okay, so now I understand," I said, straightening back up. I felt dizzy, and it was hot, because now that my car was off, I had no air conditioning. I glanced back at Isaiah, and he was visibly sweating, although, shockingly, he was still asleep.

I took some deep breaths and looked the officer straight in the eye. "I swear to God, I can explain all this," I said. "If you contact someone named Craig in the DA's office, he'll tell you. *It's my brother.* He hid these things in my house. I was on my way to turn it all over to the police when I got a call to pick up my friend's son because of the shooting."

I gave the policeman a pleading look, feeling suddenly ridiculous that I'd never gotten Craig's last name. I also thought about Craig being out of town and cursed my terrible luck. "I can give you his phone number," I said. "He's a Deputy DA. If you could *please* just call him, or let me call him. I swear to God, he'll be able to explain everything."

"I don't know about all that," the officer said curtly. "For now, I need you to step out of the car. And I'd like permission to search your trunk."

I was struggling with what to say or do next when Isaiah woke up and made a groggy squeak, compounding my stress. I gave the officer a look as if to beg him to give me a minute. "Hey Isaiah," I said as normally as I could. "We've just stopped for a sec, but we're almost to your house. I'll have you back to your dad in just a few minutes."

The policeman began shaking his head. "We'll need to call DCFS to come get the boy."

"DCFS?"

"Department of Child and Family Services."

"What are you talking about?" I blurted in a panic. "We're probably two blocks from his house."

"I need you to step out of the car," the officer said, this time more insistent.

Isaiah was now looking more alert, and I had no idea what to tell him. I tried to give him a reassuring smile, then slowly got out of the car, looking into the officer's eyes as I stood up. *"Please,"* I whispered. "Just let me take him home. I promise I can explain everything if you give me a chance, but let me take him home. He's been through enough trauma already."

The officer was unmoved. I could see it in his eyes; he'd heard it all.

Another police car drove up. A couple of moments later, a female officer got out and spoke to the officer in the car directly behind me. There were now three black and whites and an increasing number of onlookers on the street. The woman officer walked up to where I was now standing, terrified and weak-kneed. "We got a warrant," she said, handing a paper to the policeman next to me.

Feeling sick to my stomach, I appealed to the woman cop, hoping she'd be more understanding. "Can I please explain something to you?"

"Explanation or not, we've got a warrant to search the car," she said. Her tone was not harsh, but neither was it sympathetic. She was strictly business.

"I understand," I said, trying to tamp down the urge to cry, "but if I could just explain to you about what you're going to find." She ignored me. Didn't even acknowledge that I'd spoken. "Please," I said.

She gave me a blank look, then turned to the policeman who'd ordered me out of the car. "Go ahead and pop the trunk."

Pushing me aside, he leaned in over the driver's seat and pulled a lever under my dashboard, making a distinctive *FOOMP* that I remember like the starting signal of the nightmare that unfolded next.

CHAPTER TWENTY-SIX

MIRANDIZED AND HANDCUFFED IN the back of a squad car with Isaiah buckled in next to me, I was on my way to Nate's house. The police had finally agreed to drive us there, but they wouldn't let me call Craig, or even take his number. They also refused to let me call Nate.

I had hoped we'd be placed in the car with the lady cop, who, despite her reserve, seemed the most likely to listen to me. Unfortunately, we were with the original two, neither of whom wanted to hear about Craig or my brother. Each time I opened my mouth, they immediately shut me down, so I eventually kept quiet. I wasn't too worried about being under arrest. I figured, with Craig's help, I could get myself mostly out of trouble. But I was terrified of Nate's reaction at having Isaiah delivered home by the police, then learning that I'd gone to pick him up with a load of guns in my car. I was also horrified by the trauma I was inflicting on Isaiah. I wanted desperately to pull him into my lap or say something reassuring, but my hands were bound in metal behind my back, and I had *no idea* what to say, making me feel both inadequate and ashamed. I had quietly begged the police not to cuff me, arguing that it would scare Isaiah, but, as always, I was conspicuously ignored.

Staring at metal and Plexiglas in a back seat smelling vaguely of Clorox and vomit, I shook my head in disgust. I'd been fantasizing about becoming Isaiah's mother and look where I'd landed him. *How could I have been so stupid?* And, yet, gun-sniffing dogs? I could never have imagined such a thing. Nevertheless, I'd created the situation, and I knew there would be a serious price to pay, both with the police and with Nate. I just prayed there would be no lasting harm to Isaiah, with his sweet little Superman t-shirt and skinny legs sticking out across the seat of the police car. I tried to catch his eye and give him a comforting look, but his gaze was cast down. He had to be terrified, but he was eerily still. When they'd first taken him from my car, he'd whined about *wanting to go home, wanting his daddy,* but otherwise he'd been quiet, making me wonder if he might be in some kind of shock.

Despite all my guilt and fear, I tried my best to appear unafraid, though my heart was pounding out of control and I was inwardly in a panic. I wanted to stay strong for Isaiah, to minimize his fear by seeming fearless myself. But I wasn't strong, or fearless. I was petrified. *Some lawyer I'd be,* I thought bitterly. *And some mother.*

ଔ

I don't know how to explain it, but it never occurred to me until we pulled up in front of Nate's house that Nate himself might be in trouble. *Why would he be? He had no connection to the car.* But the instant we arrived—and three other police cars arrived—I was hit, like a hard slap in the face, with the realization that Nate was in grave danger.

As soon as I saw the other black and whites, I spoke up, trying to use a tone that wouldn't alarm Isaiah, who, blessedly, was too short to see the posturing taking shape outside the car window. "The person who lives here has nothing to do with what you found in my trunk," I called to the officers, who were still in the front seat.

Not even bothering to look at me, they abruptly exited the car and appeared to ready themselves for action, sending my fear into the stratosphere. Nate had not yet appeared, but his car was parked out front, indicating that his mother was now home. Suppressing a desire to scream, and with a rising terror, I suddenly had visions of innocent black men shot dead by police scrolling through my head. I cursed myself for my stupidity, for bringing this nightmare to Nate, for traumatizing poor Isaiah, who was now craning his neck, trying to see out the window.

Although he couldn't see what was going on, he seemed to intuit the danger, no doubt partly from reading me. I was trying mightily to hold it together, but fear was probably emanating from me in waves, and it was hot in the car, so I was sweating and red in the face. My heart was also beating so hard that I actually wondered if he could hear it. I tried to comfort him with words I didn't believe and looks of reassurance, but I could tell by the look on his face that he was frightened, and soon he was repeating that he *wanted to go home, wanted to see his daddy.* Nate was the last thing I wanted to see, because I knew that the moment he appeared, anything might happen.

My thoughts became so dark that I felt dizzy. Isaiah began crying, but there was little I could do to comfort him. I was useless, and I knew that whatever was going to happen, it would be my fault, *my* doing. It occurred to me that fear on my part might be construed by the police as incriminating to Nate, so I tried as hard as I could to appear steady, despite my terror. But it probably didn't matter, because the police were now laser-focused on Nate's house, as though expecting the worst.

I began deep breathing, then the front door opened and Nate materialized, dressed in black shorts and a Lakers t-shirt. He stepped out onto a small porch and immediately raised both arms over his head, obviously knowing the importance of showing his hands. Thankfully, both were empty. There was no phone, or anything that could be mistaken for a gun. After a moment, the shape of a woman that I assumed was his mother appeared behind him in the doorway.

To my horror, more police arrived, some with guns drawn and bullet proof vests. There were so many of them, they looked like a SWAT team. Almost immediately, neighbors began appearing in their yards and congregating on the sidewalk, some already filming with their phones and tossing out hostile remarks. I understood how they felt but worried they might make an already terrible situation even worse.

Nate looked both frightened and confused, and it didn't take long before he spotted me, at which point he appeared even more agitated. He couldn't see Isaiah. "What's going on?" he called out, his arms still raised, "What's happened? Where's Isaiah? Where's my son?"

Although he looked to be shouting, I could barely hear him, because the car window was closed and his house was well back from the street. But between lip reading and straining to hear, I could pretty well understand what he was saying, and there was no mistaking the terror in his eyes.

He shot me a questioning look, and all I could do was shake my head and mouth the words, "I'm sorry." When I turned my attention back to Isaiah, he was looking up at me with trails of tears staining his face, whining that he wanted to go home.

If a heart could really break, mine would have shattered. I had *never* felt more terrible, more helpless—even after all I'd been through. "I promise, everything is going to be okay," I said, summoning as soothing a voice as I could muster. I tried to smile. I wanted so much to comfort him and take away his fear, but I doubt I was very convincing. Inside I was going crazy—horrified by the threatening posture of the police and sickened over my part in it. I'd given them Nate's address! All I'd been focused on was getting Isaiah home with as little trauma as possible. I shook my head at the pathetic irony of my stupidity. *How could I have been so naive?* The instant the police saw a black child in my car, they considered Nate a dangerous suspect. It was just that simple. Pointing the police to Nate had put him in mortal danger.

Adding to my despair, I suddenly wondered if they thought Nate might somehow be connected to the shooting. *But how could they?* I had no idea, but it was clear by the situation stacking up in front of me that almost anything was possible.

I gave Isaiah one more look of feigned optimism, told him again that everything would be fine, then looked back up at Nate, who was now talking to the policeman with the mustache. He and another policeman I didn't recognize had entered the yard, and mustache was gesturing in my direction, probably describing what they'd found in my trunk, and—I hoped—also explaining that Isaiah was safe in the back seat next to me.

The look on Nate's face shifted from terror to disbelief, then he looked in my direction with an expression of shock. I had no way of responding in any meaningful way. The best I could do was look back with remorse. I eventually lost my battle to resist crying. I knew it would scare Isaiah, but I couldn't hold back any longer. I didn't sob, but water all but flew from my eyes—partly for relief, because I was beginning to comprehend that there would be no violent take down or blazing guns. Nate was now talking to the police in what looked, thank God, like a deescalating situation.

Nevertheless, people from the neighborhood—a mixture of African Americans and Latinos—continued to congregate, phones out and recording. I tried, for the moment, to block out the possible consequences of that for Nate. Thankfully, there were no more hostile remarks being heaved at the police by the crowd, at least none that I could hear.

Another police car arrived, and I wondered why, if things were deescalating, more police kept showing up. I took some deep breaths and tried to steady my nerves, all the while keeping my eyes on Nate, who was alternately listening to the police and talking too quietly for me to hear. His arms were no longer raised, and he was gesturing with his hands, which was a good sign that he felt safer, and that things were calming down.

Every now and then he looked over at me, and his face expressed a range of different emotions, but the most distinct I could identify was confusion. What he was seeing and hearing just didn't compute.

After what seemed like an awful lot more talking—including points where Nate was visibly upset—his mother stepped out onto the porch and began pointing to the car, calling for Isaiah. When she looked over, I turned away like a coward. I wanted to communicate that I was sorry—that I could be counted on to clear Nate of any association with the mess I'd created—but I wasn't able to look at her. The shame I felt was crushing.

The policewoman I'd spoken to earlier finally came over and pulled Isaiah from the car. The instant he caught sight of Nate, he began to shriek and stretch his arms in his direction. When he got close to Nate, he tried to lunge for him, but he was handed, instead, to his grandmother, who carried him swiftly into the house. Moments later, Nate was frisked, then ushered into the back of one of the police cars. Before he disappeared inside, he glanced in my direction, his look seeming to demand, "Why is this happening?"

Feeling utterly helpless and crazy with remorse, I, once again, mouthed, "I'm sorry," then I bent forward and screamed into my lap. But as terrible and devastated as I felt, I was clear-headed enough to notice that Nate had *not* been handcuffed. That, at least, was something.

CHAPTER TWENTY-SEVEN

MUCH OF WHAT HAPPENED next played out like a scene from a movie I'd seen a hundred times. I was driven to a police station, asked some cursory questions, then left alone for hours in one of those colorless questioning rooms you see in every episode of *Law and Order*. It didn't have a two-way mirror, but there was a camera up in one corner, which made me wonder if I was being watched. It was a small room, brightly lit, and cold, with plain white walls, a gray metal table, and three straight-backed chairs, all chained to the floor.

I had been asked if I wanted a lawyer, but I declined for the time being, wanting as quickly as possible to simply talk to someone who could help me find Craig. I had finally been allowed to call him—twice—but both times the call went straight to voicemail. I left him a couple of pretty frantic messages. Now, all I could do was wait and hope he'd come to my rescue.

I simply could not believe my bad luck—both with Craig being out of reach and, especially, the dogs. But I was certain that once Craig got my messages, he'd straighten things out, both for me and for Nate.

I wanted more than anything to fix things for Nate, who might have been in the next room for all I knew. The police assured me that he'd only been brought in for questioning, and that he'd come voluntarily, but I couldn't stand not knowing what was happening to him, and I knew one thing for sure: this would screw up his finals, and possibly his graduation. I could only imagine his worry, never mind what he was thinking about me.

Sitting in that terrible room, trying to appear innocent in case I was being watched, every minute felt like an hour, and it became harder and harder to remain composed. I thought about poor Isaiah, with his tear-stained face. And Nate's mother—what she must think of me. And Nate. *Oh my God, Nate.* I wanted to put my head down and cry, but, instead, I sat pillar straight, trying to affect the posture of a lawyer in court.

By the time someone finally came in to talk to me, I was sick with worry and exhausted from hours of containing my emotions. The man who arrived was no one I'd seen before. Wearing a suit and not a police uniform, he was on the young side. Probably in his mid-thirties. He was also Asian, which gave me a certain sense of comfort, although when he introduced himself as Special Agent Ed Tanaka from the "Bureau of Alcohol, Tobacco, Firearms, and Explosives, Los Angeles Field Division," it was an abrupt reminder of the seriousness of what I was facing. My stomach did a summersault.

"You've got some explaining to do, Ms. Hayes," he said, settling into a chair across from me. Nice looking, and with noticeably perfect teeth, he smelled subtly of a cologne that reminded me of my ex-husband.

He placed a number of items on the table, including a manila folder from which he pulled a stack of photographs. Before he spread them out in front of me, I already knew what they contained.

Barely glancing at the weapons in the pictures, I said, with a knot in my throat, "I really can explain."

"I'm listening," the agent said. "And be advised that this interview is being audio and video recorded." To my great relief, I detected a hint of sympathy in his voice. He had a gentle demeanor and kind eyes.

Trying to remain calm and think straight, I explained about my estrangement from Dan, and about his accident, and the tumor. I described meeting Craig, the weird coincidence, and what he'd revealed to me at the hospital. I told him about the shock of finding Dan's guns, and how I'd devised a plan to turn them over to the police, explaining that Dan's medical condition, and also reading his diary, had raised my sympathies and clouded my judgment. When I got to the part about Nate's phone call, I finally broke down, explaining that he'd had nothing to do with any of it. *"It was all me,"* I said, *"I swear to God."*

I went on to tell him about Nate's finals, and how hard he'd been working to pull his life together after being injured in Afghanistan and then losing his wife.

I pleaded with the man sitting silently across from me to believe me. "I know it was a horrible decision to pick up Isaiah with the guns in my trunk, but please don't punish Nate for my stupidity."

I shook my head and looked straight into Tanaka's eyes. "In my wildest dreams, I could never have imagined those dogs. If it hadn't been for those dogs, I'd have turned the guns over and none of this would have happened." I laughed pitifully. "I'm a bleeding heart liberal. I *despise* guns. I just wanted them out of my house."

I took some deep breaths and attempted a weary smile. "I know I need to answer for my bad judgment, but please let Nate get back to his finals. He's a totally innocent bystander."

Before he could respond the door opened and a black woman, also in plain clothes, signaled for him to come out and speak to her. He nodded to her before giving me a reassuring look. "I'll be back," he said, then he collected everything from the table, stood up, and exited the room, leaving nothing behind but the faint scent of his cologne.

When he returned about ten minutes later, a laptop was a noticeable addition to the items in his possession, and he was wearing a discernible frown. He deposited the laptop and other items on the table, then sat down.

"What is it?" I asked.

"We've spoken to the hospital and it appears your brother died earlier today." After a beat he added, "I'm sorry."

I was stunned, but I can't honestly say that I felt any real sadness for Dan. I was too busy trying to work out if his dying was something that worked in my favor, or against it. It wasn't initially clear, but I had a feeling it probably wasn't good.

"So, what does this mean?" I asked. "Do you believe me?"

"I'd like to," he said, "but I'm afraid we're going to need more than your word for it."

He opened the laptop. "We're doing some fingerprint analysis on the guns. In the meantime, I'd like to see if we can identify this Craig. We've cross-checked the phone number you gave us, and it doesn't appear anywhere in our database." He pressed a couple of keys on the laptop. "There are close to a thousand Deputy DAs in the Los Angeles DA's office. We've identified seven with the first name *Craig*."

He turned the laptop around to face me, wanting me to see if I could pick Craig from the list. For the moment, I was stuck on the fingerprint analysis. I simply couldn't believe that I may have wiped off the only physical evidence connecting my brother to the guns. I considered telling Tanaka what I'd done, but decided to keep my mouth shut. In my reticence to handle the weapons, I'd done a pretty slap-dash job. Maybe I'd get lucky and there would be one or two prints I missed.

"Ms. Hayes," Tanaka said, nudging me back to the present. "Can you please take a look."

"I'm sorry," I said.

Now turning my attention to the laptop, I was suddenly looking at a database table, each row containing a small photograph and details on someone named Craig. Unfortunately, after little more than a glance, and with a growing queasiness in my stomach, I could see he wasn't there. "I don't see him," I said, trying not to panic.

"Are you sure?" Tanaka said. "These could be old pictures. Look again."

I took a deep breath and looked again, this time taking my time on each candidate, but none looked even remotely like Craig, even accounting for a possible change in age, weight, facial hair, or anything.

"I'm sorry," I said, "but he's not there."

I sat back in my chair, confused and frustrated. "He has to be in your database somewhere. Are there maybe some special departments or something that are kept separate? He said he was involved in monitoring hate groups. Is there a special division like that that you could check?"

"If he's not in this database, he's not in the DA's office," Tanaka said. "And I can assure you that if he were involved in the types of things you say he is, I'd know him."

I thought for a few moments. "Maybe his name isn't really Craig," I said. "Or maybe it's his middle name, or a pseudonym he uses for dating. I can understand someone doing that, especially someone like him. Can I look at all the Deputy DAs? I bet that's it." I looked at Tanaka eagerly, convinced this was the answer.

He nodded. "Okay. We can do that."

Ten minutes later, I began scrolling through page after page of Deputy DAs, carefully scrutinizing anyone who was even marginally in the ballpark. But no matter how hard I willed Craig to be there, he wasn't. When I finally came to the end, I sat shaking my head in disbelief. "I don't understand how this is possible," I said to Tanaka, who'd sat patiently while I meticulously worked my way through the list.

I turned my gaze up to the camera above the door, fighting back tears. "Can we try calling him again?" I said, looking back at Tanaka. "He's got to answer eventually."

"We'll continue trying the number," he said. "But, in the meantime, we need to consider the possibility— assuming you're telling the truth—that he's not who he claims to be."

"I *am* telling the truth," I insisted. "But why would he do that? I mean, I can see someone lying about their profession on a dating site, but he went *way* beyond that. All that stuff he told me about my brother. He has to be who he says he is. There's no other explanation."

"I think we need to consider the possibility that he could be involved with your brother. Or was involved."

That seemed absurd. "*No*. That can't be it," I said.

"Think about it," Tanaka said.

I shook my head and tried to think, but it didn't make sense.

Tanaka raised his eyebrows. "If your brother really was a member of some white nationalist group, odds are, he's a member of the same group. And he may also be associated with the weapons."

"*Oh my God*," I said, remembering how close I'd come to sleeping with him. I thought about it some more. "It just can't be," I said. "It has to be something else. I don't believe it."

Tanaka gave me a look that seemed to say, *Believe it,* and it occurred to me in that instant that everything had changed. I no longer felt like a suspect. I sat back in my chair and a feeling of relief washed over me. "Am I still under arrest?"

Tanaka sighed, seeming to want to weigh his words carefully. "For the moment, we're not charging you with anything. *For the moment.* But that could easily change."

"And what about Nate?" I asked. "Is he still here? Because all of this has totally screwed him over."

"We've already released him," Tanaka said. "He cooperated completely, and his story checked out, so we saw no reason to hold him. I don't think you need to be too concerned."

"Are you kidding me?" I erupted. "Five police cars showed up at his house with guns drawn. It was terrifying. He could have been killed. Then he was hauled off in front of his mother and five-year-old son, and all his neighbors."

"That was unfortunate, but I'm afraid you're going to have to share some responsibility for that."

"I'm the first to admit that I was stupid," I said, "but the police were totally over the top. There's no way, if that had been a white neighborhood, that they'd have been so heavy-handed. It was ridiculous."

"Be that as it may, for the moment, you're better off focusing on your own problems. For starters, we need to search your house."

I closed my eyes and took some deep breaths, trying to slow my heart, which was now shot full of adrenaline and racing.

When I opened my eyes, Tanaka was staring at me. "You were discovered with serious illegal weapons," he reminded me. "Now, given what you've told us, and what we now know, we may not charge you—or, if we do, you might get off with a misdemeanor. But before we move forward, we need to go through a process, and part of that process is searching your home. We've already obtained a warrant."

"I get it," I mumbled, missing my parents so much in that moment that I felt like buckling completely. But, then I was struck with a thought that perked me up. I nodded at the laptop. "Would it be possible for me to use that to access Match.com?"

Tanaka paused to think, then picked up the laptop, closed it, and headed for the door. "Hold on a moment," he said, "I'll be right back."

CB

A few minutes later, Tanaka returned and placed a different laptop in front of me. The Match.com website was already pulled up. "Go ahead and find him," he said.

I logged in, and it took me less than thirty seconds to determine that Craig had vanished from the site without a trace. "He's gone," I said to Tanaka, who was, once again, seated across from me. "He's taken down his profile and all our communications are gone, too."

I began shaking my head, marveling bitterly at my seemingly endless stream of bad luck.

Exhibiting neither surprise nor disappointment, Tanaka opened a folder and pulled out a stack of papers, each filled with a checkerboard of faces—all men and all white, from what I could see. "Take a look at these," he said, pushing the papers to my side of the table. "See if you can find him here."

He leaned back in his chair and crossed his legs, his posture seeming to say, *take your time.* I fanned the papers out in front of me. Some of the photos were mug shots and some looked like they'd been cropped from pictures you might see on Instagram or Facebook. "Who are these people?" I asked.

"Just look," Tanaka said. "And look carefully. Remember, things like facial hair and glasses can make a difference."

"Okay," I said. I looked down at the pictures and, once again, began slowly perusing faces, taking extra time on those with beards, glasses, or any other characteristics that might be appearance-altering. After I'd eliminated all the men on the first page, I glanced up at Tanaka and he motioned for me to keep looking. I turned my attention to the second page, then methodically worked my way through the stack.

On maybe the fifth or sixth page, a mug shot unexpectedly jumped out at me. I put my finger on it and looked up at Tanaka. "I've seen this guy," I said. It was the man I'd seen smoking in the hallway at the hospital. I was sure of it. What looked like a serial number of some kind was written in small type below the picture.

Tanaka pulled the page to his side of the table and turned it around.

"Do you know him?" I asked.

"No," Tanaka said. "You say you saw him? When was this, and where?"

I stopped to think. "Yesterday," I said. "He was at the hospital before Dan died. I saw him in a hallway."

"Are you sure?"

"Yes," I said. "He was a little more clean shaven, but it was definitely him."

I nodded at the papers on the table. "Why are you showing me these men? Who are they?"

Tanaka rubbed his chin, seeming to measure me before answering. "This is pretty much a *Who's Who* of white supremacists in California," he said finally.

I swept my eyes over the collection of faces. Some definitely fit the stereotype, but others appeared alarmingly normal. "I guess I shouldn't be surprised," I said, "but it's hard to believe there are still so many people out there like this."

"We've been seeing a big resurgence," Tanaka said. He frowned, unable or uninterested in disguising his disapproval. "You can thank the internet and right-wing news media for a lot of it."

He paused, and I studied his boyish face, its smoothness disrupted only by a light mustache shadowing his upper lip. When he continued, his voice was lowered. "Not surprisingly, a lot of them are focused on the border, and immigration. Some are like a modern-day KKK, energized by Black Lives Matter. Others appear to be more anti-Semitic than anything else." He lowered his voice even further. "All of them are hyped up on extremist politics and some, like your brother possibly, are involved in paramilitary activities. Meaning they're heavily armed and anticipating some kind of violent confrontation, or race war. The group we believe your brother may have been involved with, based on the weapons we found, has training camps both here in California and in Idaho."

I inwardly grimaced, remembering how hard I'd tried to sell Dan on Idaho. Glancing down at the man I'd seen at the hospital, I wondered what he was doing there. The more I learned, the more surreal everything became.

Tanaka pointed to the pages. "Keep going."

Trying to put the smoking man out of my mind, I continued looking, taking my time on each and every face. I didn't see Craig. Until, suddenly, maybe I did.

On the very last page, a grainy photograph in the third row caught my attention. Unfortunately, the man had a short beard and his eyes were shadowed under a baseball cap. I studied the picture for a good twenty seconds, then looked up at Tanaka, who had been watching me intently. "Here's one that *might* be him," I said. "But it's not a very clear picture and the guy I know is clean shaven." I flipped the page around and pointed.

Tanaka examined the photo. "Look again," he said. "See if you can be sure."

I turned the page back around and focused hard on the image, but the hat and beard made it impossible to be certain. I studied his nose but became less sure the longer I looked. I shook my head. "I don't know. It *kind of* looks like him, but it could just be someone who resembles him."

Tanaka was frowning.

"Do you know him?" I asked.

"No," he said.

I picked up the paper and studied the face some more, trying to see Craig, but the more I looked, the more doubt I had. "I'm sorry," I said, "it's probably not him."

I finished the remainder of the page, then tossed it on the table. "The more I think about Craig, the more it doesn't make any sense. He was like the exact opposite of these guys. He was very convincing." I shook my head in confusion. "You're absolutely positive he can't be with the DA's office?"

"Positive," Tanaka said. "And if what you've been telling me is true, it's almost certain he's a member of the group connected to the weapons."

He placed the palms of his hands on the table and stood up. "I wish I could tell you something more specific. Unfortunately, I can't. But whoever this guy is, I'm guessing you won't hear from him again."

"What makes you think that?"

"Experience."

I tilted my head back and closed my eyes, unable to wrap my brain around any of the craziness that had transpired over the last ten hours. When I looked up again, Tanaka was preparing to leave.

"I'll make arrangements for the search, and for you to be taken home," he said. "There's no reason you can't be there while it's conducted. Also, I'll have someone bring you your phone. You should get your car back in a day or two."

He placed a business card in front of me, then gave me a penetrating look. "Assuming we don't find anything in the search that changes our minds, I'm guessing we won't be charging you. If you have any problems, call me. And don't leave town."

"Wait," I said, feeling panicked. "What if I do hear from Craig? *I left him messages.* What should I say if he calls me back? Do I pretend I still think he's with the DA's office?"

"I believe we can assume he knows you've discovered he isn't," Tanaka said. "But I doubt he'll contact you again." He looked me in the eye and his expression softened. "Think about it. Why would he?" He smiled reassuringly. "Trust me. He'll make himself scarce."

I wanted to believe him, but I wasn't convinced.

Tanaka read the distress on my face. "If he does contact you, tell him you've turned the guns over, everything has been straightened out, and keep the conversation as simple as possible."

He nodded to his card on the table. "If you have any problems, call me. And if you feel you're in any immediate danger, call 911."

CHAPTER TWENTY-EIGHT

HEADING HOME IN THE back of another police car, I stared at my phone. The calls I'd missed from the hospital were urgent pleas for me to call them, no doubt to inform me of Dan's death. I still hadn't really processed his passing. Despite all my anger, I couldn't help feeling some measure of guilt for not having tried harder to reach whatever parts of him might have been salvageable. And I wondered about the tumor. Could it have contributed to his craziness?

I'd received no calls or messages back from Craig, which, under the circumstances, was a relief. I'd also gotten nothing from Nate, which seemed like a bad sign. I felt physically sick when I contemplated the possible repercussions of what I'd done. Was Isaiah traumatized? Had I jeopardized Nate's graduation? Would he ever forgive me for what I'd put his family through? I was desperate to find out.

I wasn't about to call him from the back of a squad car, but I considered sending him a text. To apologize. To explain. To beg his forgiveness. I looked at my phone and wondered what would come back if I sent him just a few simple words. Would he answer me back with anger? With sympathy? With a cold rebuke and demand never to contact him again?

I imagined him being understanding, being worried about me, forgiving me. But the sad truth was I had no idea what would come back. All I had was blind hope and the withering suspicion I'd ruined everything.

When we were nearing my house, I finally found the courage to send him a text. Because of the impending search, it seemed like a bad time to invite a conversation, so I decided to establish contact but kick the can in terms of actually talking. My message was this, and I sent it with a galloping heart: "Nate, please forgive me. I'm so sorry. My brother died today. Guns were his. Will call tomorrow to explain. On my way home now with police to search my house. I hope you and Isaiah are OK. ILYSM..."

Afterwards, I held my breath, both hoping for and dreading the buzz of an instant reply. But no reply came. Not instantly, and not by the time I arrived home and was escorted inside by the officer who had driven me (with whom I had not exchanged a single word).

Shortly after I closed the front door, two more policemen showed up and they began their search. As I watched them methodically comb through closets, cupboards, and drawers—first in my house, and then in the cottage—I held fast to my phone, hoping to hear back from Nate. But nothing came. For the time being, it seemed, he was going to leave me wondering.

When the police finally left almost two hours later, I was too exhausted to deal with the shambles they'd made of my house and too keyed up to sleep, so I poured a glass of wine, filled the tub, and took to my traditional refuge, all the while clinging to the hope that I might get some kind of message from Nate.

Soaking in the dark with the door open just enough to provide a sliver of light, I closed my eyes and tried to calm my jagged nerves. The police hadn't found any more weapons, thank God, nor had they uncovered anything else of particular interest—although they did make a conspicuous show of discovering my marijuana. I was tempted to point out that it had been given to my mother when she was dying, but I let it go. After all their rummaging, the only things they ended up taking were my laptop, which they said would be returned *"in due time,"* and Dan's diary, which I'd volunteered practically the moment they entered the house.

It was painful thinking about Dan. Besides agonizing over what he might have been up to, I was worried about how to deal with the hospital, his body, his truck, and God only knew what other belongings and personal matters he'd left behind in a mess. Were all the loose ends of his life now my problem, or could I simply walk away? I had no idea.

I still hadn't talked to the hospital and gotten the details of what happened. All I knew, so far, was that he had died. I tried not to be glad. I wanted to feel something resembling sadness, but it was hard, under the circumstances, to work up much in the way of grief. What I mostly felt was anger. And—if I'm being honest—relief. Now, finally, I would be able to live my life in peace. But, of course, the life I'd visualized with Nate might be gone. Destroyed by Dan's insanity and my stupidity.

Tilting towards despondency, I shook my head in the dusky light, then slipped under the water and held my breath for a good ten seconds. When I sat back up, I finally let myself break down. I'd never felt more alone.

I cried until I felt spent, then reheated the water and stewed in the steamy darkness until my wine was gone and I knew I needed to try to sleep. Tomorrow would come soon, and whatever happened, I would have to face it.

ℭ

When I woke up the next morning, the first thing I did was check my phone for messages. I was relieved to see nothing from Craig, but upon seeing a text from Nate, I became so nervous I dropped my phone on the bathroom floor. It was a miracle it didn't shatter on the tile. When I read the text, I was the one who shattered. Nate's words were devastating: "Can't deal with you now. Two finals, plus fallout from yesterday. Might lose custody of Isaiah. I don't know what all that was about, but I can't believe you put my family at risk."

Overcome with panic and shame, and with my heart beating out of control, I stumbled to my bedroom and collapsed onto my bed. I cried for the better part of an hour, and all I could think about was Nate losing Isaiah. How could I possibly live with that? How could *he* live with that? The mere thought was excruciating.

I desperately wanted to talk to Nate. To hear him tell me everything would be okay. With Isaiah. With his finals. *With us.* But I knew if I called him, he wouldn't tell me any of those things. His message was clear. He wanted me to leave him alone.

But I couldn't do nothing, I had to at least send him another text, so I wrote back: "Please talk to me and let me explain. And please forgive me. I would never deliberately hurt you or Isaiah. I love you both so much."

William tried to prop me up. *"Give him some time. He'll eventually talk to you. In the meantime, be easier on yourself. I know you're scared and feeling like you committed some terrible crime, but all you did was make a mistake. If this man is as good as you think he is, he'll come around. Yesterday you made a bad decision and had some really bad luck, but you know who you are, and I think he does too. Just be patient and have some faith."*

I appreciated his sentiment, but he was missing one crucial point. If Nate lost Isaiah, he'd never forgive me, and I would never *ever* forgive myself.

CHAPTER TWENTY-NINE

WHEN I FINALLY CALLED the hospital, I learned that Dan had died from complications associated with another seizure. To my great relief, I also learned that I bore no responsibility with respect to his bill. However, as next of kin, decisions regarding the disposition of his body fell to me. Not surprisingly, Dan's driver's license indicated he was *not* an organ donor. I was wondering about the whereabouts of his truck when I got a call from Tanaka.

"Have you heard anything from your friend?" he asked almost immediately, referring to Craig.

"Nope, nothing," I reported, then I mentioned the truck.

"We're searching it now," Tanaka said. "We're also looking at his phone records and doing some other follow up, including fingerprint analysis on the guns, searching social media, and checking out his diary. Thank you for that, by the way. Also, we've finished with your car, so we'll be getting that back to you soon."

"What about my laptop?" I asked. "I need that."

"It might be another day or two," he said. "In the meantime, we appreciate your cooperation."

I thanked him for calling, then hung up and commenced berating myself for wiping the fingerprints. My thoughts were interrupted when the doorbell rang. Thinking it might be Nate, and with my heart in my throat, I headed for the door and looked through the peephole. To my surprise, what I saw was a badge.

I felt a flash of anger. Had Tanaka deliberately misled me? Was I going to be arrested again? Then it occurred to me that the police might be returning my car. The doorbell rang again, followed by knocking. I pulled open the door and was suddenly face-to-face with Craig.

"I apologize for not phoning first," he uttered immediately. "And I'm sorry I wasn't able to answer your calls yesterday."

I must have appeared terrified, because when he stopped talking, he didn't move but just looked at me like he was studying me. I knew I needed to say something, but I was frozen with panic.

"Can I come in?" he said. "I need to talk to you."

There was no sign now of a badge. I figured it was a ploy to get me to open the door. And it had worked. But now I was unsure what to do. In a gray suit and handsome under a canopy of green leaves, he didn't *look* threatening, but I didn't want to make another stupid mistake. Unfortunately, I was so unnerved I couldn't think straight.

Craig glanced at the phone in my hand, then nodded in the direction of the living room. "Can we go in there?" His voice was friendly. "I know what you might be thinking, but I promise you, you have nothing to be afraid of. I'll explain everything if you give me a chance." He looked into my eyes and smiled. "I promise."

I thought about slamming the door and calling 911, but, for some reason, I was more fearful of doing that than letting him in. I nodded reluctantly, then followed him into the living room, where *water world* was just starting to get underway. "That's interesting," Craig said, gesturing upwards to the reflections on the ceiling.

I said nothing and sat down on the couch, motioning for him to take a chair on the other side of the coffee table. "I'm sorry to just show up like this," he said after getting settled, "but I wanted to talk to you as soon as possible. I'm guessing the police told you I'm not with the DA's office, and you've been wondering who the hell I am. *Right?*"

The abruptness of the question put me off balance, and I didn't say anything at first. Finally, after a few moments of silence, I demanded, "So, who are you?"

"I'm sorry if I scared you."

"Yeah, you scared me," I said, trying to control my breathing and slow my heart.

He bowed his head, seeming to think how to begin. I started to ask him about the badge, but he started up at the same time. I nodded for him to go ahead.

He smiled, then heaved a long sigh. "I've been trying to think what to do," he said, "and I've decided to take a risk and tell you some things I shouldn't." He stopped and suddenly looked very serious. "I'm trusting you, and I hope after we talk, you'll feel like you can trust me, too."

"Please don't tell me anything that'll make me complicit in something illegal," I said. "I don't want to lie to the police, and as far as I'm concerned, the less I know the better."

"Here's the thing..." he started. He reached into his back pocket, pulled out his wallet, and tossed it across the table.

I picked it up and opened it, and there, staring me in the face, was a gold eagle-topped badge emblazoned, in all caps, with *Federal Bureau of Investigation, US Department of Justice.* An ID card identified him as Special Agent, David C. Bryant.

"David," I said. "And you're in the FBI?"

"The *C* is for *Craig*," he said. "And I'm sorry I lied to you, but I'm guessing it's not as bad as what you've been thinking."

"What the hell is going on?" I asked, studying his badge and ID. They definitely appeared authentic.

"I'm going to explain everything to you," he said. "At least to an extent." He hesitated, then stood up, reached over, and took his wallet back.

"Look," he said, sitting back down. "The work I do is undercover, and some of what I'm investigating involves the LAPD, which means it's *really* important that you keep what I'm going to tell you confidential. Can you do that?"

"I can do that," I said tentatively, my fear starting to give way to curiosity.

"You sure? It's critical. There's a lot on the line."

Taking and then exhaling a long, slow breath, I began to relax. "Go ahead," I said. "I'm listening."

He sat in silence for a few moments, and I wasn't sure if he was having second thoughts, or just trying to collect his thoughts. "Do you want a cup of coffee or some water or something?" I asked, figuring he might need some time.

"I'll take a glass of water," he said. "Thanks."

I stood up and went into the kitchen. While I was pulling glasses from a cupboard, I hollered to the other room. "Speaking of the police, I might be off the hook as far as the guns are concerned."

"Glad to hear it," Craig called back.

"If I were poor or black, I'm sure it would be a whole different story," I said, now returning with the water. I placed the glasses on the coffee table, then settled back on the couch and looked at Craig for a reaction. He didn't show any. He just reached for a glass, took a drink, then placed the water back on the table.

"Getting back to what I was saying," he said, now leaning back, "let me first apologize for not being honest with you. It's one of the difficult parts of my job."

"But our dates and all that, that wasn't you being an FBI guy. Your connection to Dan was a coincidence, right?"

He made a face signaling regret.

"Wow," I said. "Are you kidding?"

"I'm afraid not," he said. "I'm sorry."

I thought for a moment, then my understanding of the situation devolved into confusion. I don't know what Craig read on my face, but he must have seen I felt blindsided.

"Please understand," he said. "I did what I did to protect you. That's what I'm here to explain."

"What about trying to get me into bed?" I demanded, my voice rising in anger. "Was that part of your under-cover operation?"

He winced. "You have every right to be mad about that, but can we put it aside for the moment?" His eyes ex-pressed remorse. "Please."

"I'm listening," I said, still bristling but wanting him to go on. His mention of the LAPD, in particular, had piqued my interest.

He sighed. "Again, I'm going to caution you that you *have* to keep this confidential."

"I get it. Go ahead."

He took another drink of water, then replaced the glass on the table and crossed one leg over the other, casting an eye to the light playing across the ceiling before commenc-ing. "Your brother hit my radar about a month and a half ago," he said. "I'm working undercover on a case that in-volves members of the LAPD and a particularly nasty group of white supremacists. They're essentially a criminal gang, but their *theme*, you might say, is white nationalism."

"Policemen are in this gang?"

"Yes. Exactly." His demeanor seemed suddenly grave. "I can't talk about anything specific, but I can say that there appears to be a nationwide effort on the part of white na-tionalist groups to infiltrate both the military and police departments. The particular group I'm investigating is in-volved in illegal gun trafficking, which is how your brother got involved with them. He was buying guns, and also showing interest in joining the group—although some of the members were leery of him. He was pretty out there, even for them.

"What do you mean *out there*?"

"Unstable. Unpredictable. Maybe someone who could put their organization in jeopardy."

"After I saw you in the hospital, I found out he had a brain tumor," I said. "The doctor asked me if I'd noticed any mood swings or weird behavior, so now I'm wondering if some of his stuff was the tumor."

"Could be," Craig said. "But you can take it from me that there are plenty of dangerous people out there who don't have brain tumors. Anyway," he went on, "for several months now, I've been posing as a member of this group as part of a sting operation that, like I said, involves the LAPD. Your brother hooked up with them a little over a month ago, bought some guns, then got wind of the fact they're trying to buy some land where they can go out and play war games. I'm sure you've seen stories about this type of thing on the news. They call themselves *militias*."

He hesitated, then looked at me with an expression so grim, it was clear that whatever was coming next was bad. "When your brother heard about them wanting to buy land, he started saying he could get his hands on a million dollars. At first, no one paid any attention. They figured he was all talk, and kind of a nut. But eventually they started listening."

Craig went quiet and something about the way he was looking at me was unsettling. I got a sick feeling in my stomach. "You think it was my house."

Craig nodded. "That's what I think."

His face was dead serious, and there was no need for him to say more. There was no scenario in which Dan would have the house if I were still breathing.

ඞ

I took a drink of water and tried to clear my head. "So, explain about contacting me on Match?" I said. For the moment, I didn't want to deal with the bomb he'd just dropped.

Craig sighed, then leaned forward and clasped his hands between his legs. "I don't know anything about a brain tumor, but I do know your brother was an asshole." His features assembled into a look of disgust. "One day he was at a house where I happened to be, and he pulled up your picture on Match and started passing it around. Said he'd give a hundred bucks to anyone who could get a date with you."

My cheeks heated up. "I'm guessing not just a date."

Craig answered with his eyebrows, then added, "It was pretty crude."

"So you took up the challenge?"

"Look," he said, squeezing his hands so hard his knuckles turned white. "By then your brother had started up with the money thing, so it seemed like a good opportunity. Perfect, really. I'd already done some digging, so I knew it was just the two of you, and about your inheritance. I also learned from one of the guys in the group that he'd lost his share, which set off alarm bells." He tightened his lips into a line. "I figured the Match thing would be a good chance to assess what kind of danger you might really be in, and take steps, if necessary. Trying to get you into bed was never part of the plan. It just...happened. I don't know what else I can really say except I'm sorry. But, believe me, my only motivation in contacting you was to keep you safe."

I put my face in my hands and squeezed my eyes shut. After a few moments, determined to keep it together, I straightened up. "Did you happen to learn how Dan lost the money?"

Craig shook his head. "Sorry."

"So, okay, let's hear the rest," I said. "Tell me everything."

"All right," he said. "But, again, I need to caution you that, for now at least, this *has* to remain between us. It's crucial."

"I understand," I said.

He leaned back in his chair. "So, as I explained, these guys your brother was involved with want to buy land. A lot of land. So they got interested when he started talking about bringing big money to the table."

"A million dollars."

"Right. And when I started looking into it, which included making contact with you, it became pretty clear you might be in danger, so we set up special surveillance on your brother."

"Wow," I said. "Meaning what?"

"Meaning we tapped his phone, put a tail on him, and also put a listening device in his truck. He's a loner, but he mutters to himself a lot, so we figured if we bugged his truck, we might hear some interesting stuff—which we did. Some of it quite disturbing."

"So, you actually heard him talking to himself about killing me to get the house?"

"We heard enough to be concerned," Craig said. "We also believe he was originally planning something completely different—which was why he started purchasing guns and ammunition in the first place."

"Like what?"

He hesitated, then sighed. "We think he was gonna kill a whole lot of people."

I felt the blood drain from my face.

"You may know he was fired from his job."

"Oh my God," I said. "You think he was planning some kind of massacre at Home Depot?"

"We think so," Craig said. "And I'm afraid you may have been in the crosshairs at that point, too."

A swell of nausea was rising inside of me and I could feel my pulse pounding in my temples.

"I'm sorry," Craig said. "I know this is an awful lot to process."

I focused on composing myself, worried I might be sick. "You know that night we ate duck and he was here when I got home? I knew then that he had a stockpile of guns. He'd bragged about it to me. I *saw* one of them. I should have called the police right then. I knew he was unstable. If he'd killed a bunch of people, it would have been partly my fault."

I tried to picture the scenario Craig described, but it didn't make sense. "So, you're saying he was going to murder me, shoot up Home Depot, and then he expected to inherit the house?"

"No," Craig said. "I think his *original* plan, the one that included Home Depot, was going to end in suicide. After he started thinking about the land, I think he changed his mind about Home Depot. He figured he'd get rid of you, sell the house, go in on the land, and then go off in the woods and play war games with his white nationalist buddies."

"He really thought he could get away with all that and no one would be suspicious?" I shook my head in disbelief.

"This is where his talking to himself was helpful," Craig said. "Based on some things we heard him say in his truck, we believe he was planning to make it look like... I gather you've been seeing someone. What's his name?"

"*Oh my God,*" I said, understanding what he was suggesting. "You think he was going to make it look like Nate killed me?"

"We think that was his plan. Yes. He got the idea after seeing him in your backyard." He paused and winced. "We're pretty sure he was planning to act the morning he got in the accident."

I put my head down and took some deep breaths, trying to dampen the churning in my stomach.

When I looked back up, Craig was staring at me with intensity. "He'd never have gotten away with it," he said. "He was obviously delusional. Unfortunately, his worst impulses were being fueled by the company he was keeping. Company we'll hopefully be arresting very soon."

"Could you get into trouble for telling me this?" I asked.

He chuckled nervously. "Oh, yes."

"Then why are you?"

Craig's body language and everything about the way he was looking at me softened. "I wish I could say it's because I like you," he said. "And, believe me, I do. But it's critical that you *not* identify me to the police. We're close, now, to handing down some really important indictments, and some of them will be LAPD."

"You're taking a pretty big chance trusting me like this," I said.

"I am," he said. "But I think I'm a pretty good judge of character. And, frankly, it just didn't sit right. You worrying about me on top of everything else."

I tried to muster a look of gratitude, but I was so overwhelmed, I probably just looked shell shocked.

"By the way," he said, "I brought something to show you in case you still have any doubts." He pulled his phone out of his pocket, fiddled with it, and then handed it over. "See if you recognize this guy."

I flipped the phone around and was suddenly looking at a much younger looking Craig. He was standing between a man and woman that I guessed were his parents, and next to them was a brick-encased sign that read, *FBI Academy, Quantico, VA.*

"That was right after I graduated," he said. "I still have that suit."

"How many years ago was this?"

He took a few seconds to do the math. "Fifteen, I guess it's been."

I glanced once more at the picture, then handed the phone back to him. "This does help. Thanks."

Emotionally wasted, I collapsed back onto the couch and tried to visualize the horror story Dan had been planning. "Do you know how he was going to do it?" I asked.

Craig shook his head. "Not specifically. All I can tell you is we believe he was on his way to do it the morning of the accident."

"So, if you knew, you weren't going to just let him walk in and murder me, right? You were going to stop him." With the question hovering between us, Craig remained eerily silent, but he was staring at me with a strange look in his eyes. "Oh my God," I said. "Did you cause the accident?"

He said nothing, but his jaw twitched, and I detected the merest hint of a smile. He looked at his watch and stood up. "I'm sorry," he said, "but I have to go."

Seeing he was done, I got to my feet and tried to remain composed. "What do I do now?" I asked.

"You don't do anything," he said. "Just sit tight. You're in no danger as far as I can tell. If the police ask you any more questions, stick with what you've been saying. If they push you to try to identify me—for example, if they ask you to work with a sketch artist or something like that—

please hold off doing anything that'll blow my cover." He smiled. "If they press it, say I have a huge nose, or a unibrow."

I laughed and assured him I'd keep quiet.

He headed for the front door and I followed him. "We'll be making arrests very soon," he said. "Hopefully, in the next few days. After that, if they decide to prosecute you on the guns, I'll step in and see what I can do. But my gut tells me it won't be necessary."

He reached into his shirt pocket and pulled out a small piece of paper. "If you need me in the meantime, call me at this number. The one you had before won't work anymore." He handed me the paper and offered one more reassuring smile. Then he turned, opened the door, and disappeared into the checkered sunlight.

CHAPTER THIRTY

ALONE WITH SO MUCH to ponder, I felt crushing sadness and searing pain—so much so that, in the interest of keeping myself buoyant, I threw myself into straightening up the various messes created by the police. When I was finished, I moved on to chores like vacuuming, cleaning my bathrooms. I even cleaned out my refrigerator—anything I could think of to keep myself from a darkness that was pulling me like a magnetic force. When I finally collapsed, exhausted, onto the back patio, all the revelations about Dan, my fears about the police, my worries about Nate and Isaiah—all of it came crashing down on me, and what weighed heaviest was Nate.

William piped in unexpectedly. *"Forget about all the stuff you can't do anything about,"* he said. *"Concentrate on what you can do. If you want that man and little boy in your life, don't give up. Do whatever it takes to make things right."*

Lying on my back with my eyes closed, I hadn't seen him sidle up next to me. I despaired at my reliance, for solace, on a ghost, but I also welcomed his presence. And I knew he was right. I needed to focus on looking forward and not backward. But thinking about Nate losing Isaiah was excruciating.

"I don't think any judge is going to take that boy away from such a good father," William said, reading my mind. *"Start thinking positive. You'll get through this."*

I wiped tears from my face and whispered, "I love you, William."

"I love you too, sweet girl," he said.

I took in a long deep breath, and with William's spirit all around me—and feeling my mother's presence now, too—I began to have an inkling of hope that maybe, just maybe, everything might turn out all right.

☙

Notwithstanding my buoyed hope, I held off sending any more messages to Nate. I'd used my phone to write multiple versions of an email—explaining everything and begging him to forgive me—but I could never hit Send. I was too afraid of some final devastating pronouncement coming back. So I waited, praying he'd reach out to me first.

Days passed, and sadness settled inside of me like cement. I had to force myself to eat, and I had a terrible time sleeping. When I did manage to sleep, I had nightmares about my brother. More than once I woke up screaming in the wake of some violent bloody scene. I thought about calling friends—I even considered calling my ex-husband—but I couldn't bring myself to talk to anyone. I mostly listened to audio books and watched movies, trying to keep my mind occupied and away from painful thoughts. I also spoke to William. I don't know what I would have done without William.

When I finally got my laptop and car back from the police, I was told by Tanaka that a search of Dan's truck and diary had produced some "actionable evidence," although he was tight-lipped as to what, exactly, they'd found, or who might be in the police cross-hairs as a result. I wondered how all of it jibed with Craig's investigation, but there was no telling, and, in any case, I wanted to stay out of it.

The same day I talked to Tanaka, I broke down and called Nate. For good or for bad, I simply had to do it. I couldn't take the silence anymore. It was early afternoon, and I went out to the patio and stared at my phone for a good thirty minutes before I dialed. I wanted to slow my heart before calling, but no amount of deep breathing seemed to work, so I finally just gave up and went ahead. When he answered, I became immediately undone.

"Rachel?" he said, hearing little more than distressed breathing from my side.

"How are you?" I finally managed, my throat so constricted, I barely recognized my own voice. "I've been so desperate to talk to you. I haven't been able to eat, or sleep..."

I tried to hold back crying, not wanting to seem manipulative—an accusation I'd sometimes heard from my husband—but hot tears were suddenly flowing from my eyes. "Are you going to lose Isaiah?"

"I'm sorry I haven't called you," Nate said. "I've just had so much crazy stuff going on."

"But what about the custody thing?" I pressed. "I've been so worried."

I heard Isaiah's voice in the background, then a woman that I guessed was Nate's mother saying something that sounded like, *"Is that her?"* I heard other voices, too, but they were too muffled to understand.

"Hold on a sec," Nate said, then the phone went silent. When he came back a few seconds later, he sounded mildly agitated. "I'm sorry, but can I call you back? Maybe tomorrow, or in a couple of days? I really can't talk right now."

"All right," I said. "But can you at least tell me if everything's okay with Isaiah, and with your finals?"

"I don't know about Isaiah yet," he said. "I'm working on it. I didn't turn a paper in on time, so I'm going to fail that class and won't be able to graduate."

My heart began pounding out of control and I felt like I was going to be sick. "The paper you were working on when you asked me to pick up Isaiah?"

"That's right," he said. "But it's my fault. I shouldn't have put it off till the last minute."

"It's not your fault, it's *my* fault," I said in a panic. "Did you explain to the professor what happened?"

"He doesn't care what happened. I didn't get it in. That's all he cares about."

"What if I talked to him?" I pleaded.

"Rachel, look..." he said, and I could hear he was trying to contain his temper. "I don't need you, or my mother, or anyone else to make excuses for me. It's done. That's all."

"Oh my God, Nate, *I'm so sorry.*"

"I'm sorry, too," he said, "but I can't talk about this now. I'll call you soon, I promise. In the meantime, eat something."

Before I could say anything else, he hung up, leaving me staring at my phone and devastated. A pair of squirrels eventually drew my attention across the pool and onto the roof, but looking at the cottage now, all I could see was a pile of guns and a brother capable of mass murder. Of killing his own sister.

I hated Dan, I hated myself, and I simply could not believe the mess I'd made of Nate's life.

CHAPTER THIRTY-ONE

I DID EAT SOMETHING, although I still had no appetite. Afterwards, I retreated to my bedroom and tried to detect Nate's scent on my pillow as I recalled, in vivid detail, both erotic and tender scenes that had played out just days earlier. I simply couldn't accept how radically things had changed since Nate and I had explored one another's bodies in candlelight, whispered words of love. I had meant every word and touch, every loving gesture. Replaying images of our last lovemaking, I wondered if Nate were inclined to revisit these scenes—if he'd somehow find his way back to my bed. I doubted it, but was engaging in fantasies along those lines when I finally fell asleep.

Hours later, I was walking with Nate and Isaiah in a lush green landscape when I was awakened by my phone. Hoping it was Nate, I picked it up immediately, my consciousness still half-planted in the dream. But the voice on the other end was not Nate's, it was Craig's. "Turn on the local news," he said.

"I was sleeping," I said, trying to wake up and clear my head. "What's going on?" I sat up and surveyed my room, looking for the remote control. Not seeing it, I began rummaging through the drawer of my bedside table, still holding the phone to my ear.

"There was a raid on the group I told you about," Craig said, "and a shoot-out. There's a press conference going on about it right now. Because of the evidence you brought to the table, it ended up being a joint operation between the LAPD and FBI."

"Oh my God," I said. "Were you there? Was anyone killed?"

"Two people were killed and three wounded," he said, "but none on our side. I was there, but with the joint team, and only on the sidelines because I didn't want to blow my cover. Things happened pretty fast after we last spoke, and, believe it or not, your trunk shenanigans played a major role. Probably saved lives."

"What are you talking about?"

"After doing fingerprint analysis on your brother's guns, the police ended up questioning one of the LAPD guys I told you about. His thumb print turned up on something, and when they pulled him in for questioning, he talked. He made some kind of deal, which is unfortunate, but, among other things, he told them about something really major the group was planning. Something I wasn't aware of—which is also unfortunate, but that's another discussion. The point is, if your brother's guns hadn't led to this information coming out, something really terrible might have happened."

"What do you mean *something terrible?* What, exactly, were they planning to do?"

"I can't talk about the details. I don't think that information's going to be released. I *can* tell you that hundreds of people might have been killed. Maybe thousands. If you turn on your TV, you'll hear about it, and you may get a call from the police. But, again, I'm going to have to ask you not to mention you've talked to me. I'm sorry, but it's a can of worms I can't open."

"I understand."

"I have to run," Craig said, "but turn on the press conference. The Chief of Police is speaking now."

"I will," I said. "And thanks."

After we hung up, I found the remote and turned on the news. The Chief of Police was still speaking, and Tanaka, in full dress uniform, was among a small group of men standing to his right and left, all with the same somber expression and hands folded in front of them.

Craig had not exaggerated. According to what I learned, if not for the brave men and women of the LAPD and FBI, Los Angeles might have been the scene of one the bloodiest home-grown terrorist bombings in U.S. history.

CHAPTER THIRTY-TWO

TANAKA CALLED ME ABOUT an hour after the dissolution of the press conference. By this time, footage of the violent confrontation had played on all the news stations, and it was the main story on CNN.

As promised, I played innocent with respect to what I'd already learned from Craig, but everything Tanaka told me about the raid and subsequent shoot-out more or less matched what Craig had described, including my own unwitting role in thwarting what might have been a catastrophic act of terror. He didn't mention the fingerprint connection to the LAPD, but that didn't surprise me.

"There's something else I need to talk to you about," Tanaka said toward the end of the call, and I detected a change in his demeanor.

"All right," I said, wondering what was coming.

"We found some troubling items in your brother's truck when we searched it."

"I'm almost afraid to ask, but what did you find?" I braced myself for the worst.

He hesitated, seeming reluctant to tell me whatever it was. "There was a large locked trunk in the back of the truck," he said finally. "Like a big tool chest. Inside, we found two automatic rifles, a hand gun, and hundreds of rounds of ammunition. We also found a letter in his glove compartment. Something he obviously intended to be read in the event he was killed by the police, or possibly by suicide."

I had been standing by my bedroom window, but hit with a swell of revulsion, I moved to my bed and sat down.

"It appears he was planning to murder some of his old coworkers at the Home Depot where he was recently fired," Tanaka said. "Of course, we can't be certain he'd have gone through with it, but according to what he wrote, he intended to shoot up their daily staff meeting."

"Oh my God," I said, pretending I was hearing this for the first time. "What did the letter say, exactly?"

"It was mostly about his boss and other people he felt had *'disrespected'* him. There was also some paranoid political rambling. Nothing that would probably surprise you, given what you've told me about him." He sighed. "Under the circumstances, I'd have to say his accident was probably a blessing. He might have killed quite a few people."

I felt an overpowering dread. "Is this going to be on the news?"

"I can't say for sure, but I don't think so," Tanaka said. "The folks at Home Depot would like us to keep it quiet, and I don't see any reason why it has to come out. I'm telling you because I think you have a right to know. But I suggest you not talk about it unless you want to see news trucks out in front of your house."

"Believe me, I'm not going to talk about it," I said.

"Still no word from your friend?" Tanaka asked, referring to Craig.

"Not so far."

"Okay. Well, I need to cut this short. There's a lot going on right now, as you can imagine. I'll be back in touch at some point. In the meantime, you know how to reach me if you need to."

After we hung up, I tried to feel lucky, or at least something resembling relieved, but what I mostly felt was sick. The carnage Dan and his lunatic friends might have caused was just too much, too terrible. I felt more rage than relief. I also felt desperate, and I knew I'd stay that way until I heard back from Nate.

∞

The next couple of days were an agonizing blur. I tried to distract myself with activities that at least got me out of bed, but the truth is, I was a wreck. When things felt darkest, I called on William for solace, but until I talked to Nate, the best I could do was tread water. And all that kept me afloat was hope.

On the third day after the police shootout and news conference, I still hadn't achieved anything resembling equilibrium, but I was beginning to accept that I'd lost Nate. I figured I could survive it. I'd survived so much already. What I couldn't deal with, or accept, was the damage I may have done to him. I supposed that if the worst happened and he lost Isaiah, I would simply have to live with it, but, in the meantime, not knowing what was happening was eating me alive.

Nate finally called in the early afternoon of that third day. When I heard his voice, it took all my willpower not to become unglued.

"I'm sorry I didn't call sooner," he said. "I know you have to be messed up over everything."

"I'm the one who's sorry," I managed. "How's Isaiah? I've been so worried about him."

"He's doing okay," Nate said. "He didn't actually see too much, and we've downplayed everything, so I think he'll be all right. But we're keeping an eye on him."

Relief swept over me. "What about the custody thing?"

I held my breath.

"Nothing's carved in stone yet, but it looks like that'll be all right, too. With the police at the house and all that, my in-laws kind of went crazy, but they're starting to back off. A friend of mine is a lawyer, and she doesn't think I need to worry. She sent 'em a letter saying that if they push it and lose, they'll have to pay my court costs, and I might not let 'em see Isaiah at all. I hated to threaten that, but I kinda had to. I also have some good job prospects, and that helps."

"Oh my God, what a relief," I said, and that was an un- derstatement. I felt like a spike had been pulled from my heart. "And what are the job prospects? Are you getting offers even though you aren't graduating?"

"Turns out I will graduate," Nate said. "My professor called me a couple days ago. He got worried when I didn't turn in my paper. I explained everything, and he ended up accepting the paper late."

Upon hearing this, I broke down sobbing, and it was a good two minutes before I was able to stop.

"I'm so sorry," Nate repeated as I cried. "I should have called you sooner. I've just been in the middle of so much chaos and confusion. Please forgive me."

"It's okay," I said when I could finally talk. "I'm just so relieved, and so happy." I took some long deep breaths, then walked to the bathroom to get some tissue. I blew my nose, then looked at my face in the mirror. It was blotchy and swollen, but I felt like a thousand pounds had been lifted from my shoulders.

"So, what are these job prospects?" I asked.

"Well, I have two interviews set up for next week—one with an aerospace company you've never heard of and the other with SpaceX, believe it or not. I've also got a recruiter lining up some other stuff, so things are looking pretty good, and I haven't even officially graduated yet. Oh, and here's something else you'll like. Turns out my mom knew William. She's actually been to your house."

"What? *Really?*" I made a face in the mirror and actually wondered if I were dreaming.

"I know. It's crazy," Nate said.

"How was she at my house?"

"Both William and my dad were members of the African American Chamber of Commerce. I think William may have been on the Board. They called him Big William, right?"

"Right." I couldn't believe what I was hearing.

"I guess quite a few years ago, he threw some kind of big barbecue in your backyard, and my parents were there. My mom remembers the yard and pool, the little house back there—the whole thing. And she definitely remembers William."

"Wow," I said, casting my mind back over all the parties and fundraisers my parents had thrown over the years.

"She remembers you, too," he went on. "The barbecue was like a family thing—with kids, and horseshoes, and swimming. She remembers you playing with the kids in the pool."

I suddenly knew exactly the party he was talking about. It was the summer after my junior year in high school. William had paid me fifty dollars to be a lifeguard and organize games for the kids.

"What a bizarre coincidence," I said.

"It is pretty weird. We were having an argument—you know, about you and everything that happened—and somehow I mentioned the big and tall thing. She was really upset, but once she connected you with William, she kinda lightened up. And, like I said, she remembered you, too. Oh, and that reminds me. She told me to ask you if you ever wear a jean jacket and purple scarf."

"I do," I said, wondering what was coming next.

"She's seen you out in front of your building giving food and money to the homeless guy who camps out in the bus stop."

I hadn't recognized her from the back of the police car, but now I could picture her with clarity. "I know who she is, now," I said. "When she's not scared shitless, she has a nice smile."

"I really am sorry I didn't call you sooner," Nate said, his voice gentle with remorse. "I'm not going to lie. I was pretty angry. But I shoulda called sooner. I hope you'll forgive me."

"Of course, I forgive you. And I don't blame you for being mad. I can't even imagine what you must have been thinking. You must have thought I was crazy."

I'd been sitting on the edge of my bathtub, but now I stood up, turned off the bathroom light, and went to my bedroom. "Speaking of crazy, there's something pretty unbelievable I need to tell you, too," I said. "You know the white supremacists they've been going on and on about on CNN? That shoot-out and the whole thing happened because of the guns they found in my trunk."

"What? Are you serious?"

"Swear to God. It was a fingerprint on one of my brother's guns that led the police to find out about whatever it was they were planning. If they hadn't pulled me over, those lunatics might have killed hundreds of people."

"Oh my God..."

"I know," I said.

I went on to tell him about the letter the police found in Dan's truck. I did *not* tell him about the 'Plan B' I'd learned about from Craig. I decided to keep that one to myself, at least for the moment.

When I was finished explaining everything, Nate's shock and horror were summed up in a single passionately-delivered syllable. *"Damn."*

After a short silence he followed up with a question that brought me, once again, to tears. "When can I see you?"

CHAPTER THIRTY-THREE

ANTICIPATING NATE'S ARRIVAL, I was pacing around like a crazy person, but when I opened the door to the vision of Isaiah in his arms, all my nervousness melted away. "I didn't know you were going to bring Isaiah," I said. "What a great surprise."

Isaiah greeted me with a sweet smile, and I marveled at the resilience of children. The last time we'd been together was in the back of a police car.

Nate set Isaiah down, then looked at me for a long moment before reaching out and taking my hand.

Isaiah gazed up and tugged on Nate's shorts. "Can we go see now?"

"He wants to see inside the house in the back," Nate explained. "I think it reminds him of something he's seen in a story."

I smiled down at Isaiah. "Is that what has you so interested?"

He suppressed a grin and shrugged his shoulders. "I just wanna see."

"We can take a look if your dad says it's okay."

"Okay by me," Nate said.

"Well, let's go then," I said, giving Isaiah an encouraging nod toward the living room.

He shot Nate a satisfied look, then sped off toward the doors to the patio. Nate and I followed, but only after a long embrace that made me weak in the knees. "Thank you so much for bringing him," I whispered as we headed outside.

Nate squeezed my hand. "You've always known we're a twofer."

The day that unfolded from there was one of the happiest of my life. After exploring the cottage and determining that neither Santa Claus, nor a witch, nor a gnome or mythical character of any kind was living in my little house, we all jumped in the pool and I gave Isaiah a swimming lesson.

Clad in snazzy Spiderman underpants, he was soon a champ at submerging his face in the water, blowing bubbles, and holding his breath. Once he was comfortable, and with Nate observing happily from the sidelines, I pulled him slowly through the shallow end while he gleefully kicked his legs. I eventually set him loose with a pair of red water-wings that went perfectly with his "tighty Spidies." He and Nate then splashed and played together so joyously, I wanted to simply sit back and watch. When we finally retreated to the patio, Isaiah immediately zonked out on a chaise lounge. The look on his face was so angelic, it gave me goose bumps.

With my eyes glued to Isaiah, I sat down on Nate's lap and wrapped my arms around his neck. His skin was warm and smelled vaguely of chlorine. "I'm almost afraid to feel this happy," I said.

"Don't be afraid," he said. He touched my face with his fingertips and turned it gently in his direction. Water sparkled in his hair like tiny diamonds, and his expression was dead serious. "Really," he said. "Why be afraid? I say let's go for it."

He ran a hand over my leg and up my arm, all the while looking into my eyes. "Why shouldn't we be happy? We don't have to trip on things that happened that we can't change." Anguish crept into his voice. "I've seen how that goes. People getting bitter, never letting anything go. I don't want any of that. I've had enough of that." He exhaled and shook his head. "I just want a life that makes some sense. And I don't need all of this," he said, gesturing to the house and yard. "It's about you, and me, and Isaiah. That's it."

He smiled, then kissed me. "Don't be afraid to be happy. I'm *going* for happy."

CB

Later, while Isaiah snoozed on the patio, Nate and I took another swim. This one veered in the direction of an X rating, although we were careful not to go too far, understanding that Isaiah might perk back up at any moment. But wearing so little clothing, and with the warm sun and shimmering water enveloping us, it was impossible not to come together like magnets. With my legs around Nate's waist and arms around his neck, our kisses had never been sweeter. I understood lust, but I also understood love, and with the touches and smiles and moments of tenderness that passed between us, I knew, without a doubt, that this was love.

When Isaiah finally awoke, he raised his sleepy head, looked around, then lit up when he spotted us in the pool. "Can I come in, too?"

"Grab your wings," Nate said, pointing to where he'd shed the water wings at the edge of the lawn.

Isaiah got up, put his wings back on, and soon was leaping into Nate's outstretched arms. While the two of them resumed merrily where they'd left off, I got out, wrapped myself in a towel, and headed for the kitchen. There, I poured drinks and prepared a plate of finger food, drunk on love and giddy with optimism.

CHAPTER THIRTY-FOUR

THAT EVENING NATE HAD intended to take Isaiah home, but, with very little resistance, I convinced him to stay. Now that I had him and Isaiah back, I didn't want to let them go. Isaiah helped me pick vegetables from the garden, then the two of us made a salad while Nate grilled chicken out on the patio. After dinner, we spent another sublime session reading, starting with *Frog and Toad*, and ending with *The Velveteen Rabbit*—although, by the third page, Isaiah was asleep.

When Nate and I were finally alone, I think we both entered my bedroom with as much nervousness as relish. We'd made it to the other side of something terrible, but there was still a lot we hadn't talked about. When we found ourselves in bed, we bypassed a night of lovemaking for a simple closeness that made me feel, at times, like we were the same person, although saying it out loud sounds ridiculous. But that's how it felt, lying in Nate's arms, hearing his heartbeat combined with my own heart thumping in my ears.

That night we shared parts of ourselves that seemed to recognize no boundaries between us. It was vastly more intimate than any physical act I'd ever experienced. I told him about the agony of carrying, then burying a baby boy. Nate talked about his father's suicide and its devastating impact on his family. He confessed to feeling like he'd abandoned them when he joined the Army. "I'll never forgive myself for that," he told me. "I needed to step up, and, instead, I bailed." I tried to comfort him, but he wasn't interested in absolution. He said he'd done the wrong thing and would simply have to live with it.

Later, we kissed and caressed on what felt like a whole new emotional plane. Afterwards, before we drifted off to sleep, Nate finally told me about his experience with the police. Up to that point, I think he was avoiding the subject because he'd decided to forgive me, and didn't want to stir things back up. I finally point blank asked him about it.

"I was prepared for the worst," he said. "And I'm not gonna lie, I was scared to death. I didn't know *what* was going on, or what was gonna happen. And, trust me, I was, like, 'Yes sir, No sir' right down the line. All I could think was just, 'Don't say or do anything to make things go sideways.'"

"What happened at the police station?" I asked, my pulse kicking up at the memory of seeing him hauled off and being helpless to stop it.

"It was what you probably imagined," Nate said. "They put me in a room and a couple of guys started asking me questions about you, and what I knew about guns you were supposedly driving around with in your trunk. I was, like, '*I don't know anything about any guns,*' and I just tried to calmly explain about you picking up Isaiah, and my finals and everything. I emphasized being in school, and getting my degree, and also that I'd been in the Army. Turned out one of the cops questioning me had spent time in Bagram, which is where I was stationed. That was a huge stroke of luck. I hate to admit it, but I played up getting a couple of medals—a Purple Heart and one other. After that, things got less tense. I also think that whatever you were saying probably helped. Our stories obviously matched up. So even though things started out bad, it all eventually smoothed out."

"What was the other medal?" I asked.

"It's no big deal. I only mentioned it to the police because I was trying to make out like I'm some kinda boy scout or something."

"I understand, but I'm curious. What was it?"

He hesitated, then said, "It was for pulling a couple of guys out of the Humvee after we got hit."

"So it was like a Medal of Valor or something like that?"

"Bronze Star. But, like I said, it's not a big deal. I did what anyone would have done. And it wasn't what you might think."

"I don't know what you think I might think, but you were hurt pretty badly yourself, right?"

"Yeah, well, you'd be surprised what you can do when you're shot full of adrenaline."

I had placed some candles around the room, and Nate's face looked somber in the flickering light. "None of us died," he said, "but we all got burned. Two guys *much* worse than me." He shook his head. "I pulled 'em out, but for what kind of life? I don't know if I'd want to live like that."

He was stroking my arm with the tips of his fingers, and I could feel him vibrating with emotion. "You hear about survivor's guilt, but until it happens to you, you don't get it. I'm always thinking, 'What if I'd got in there sooner?' or 'Why them and not me?'"

When he spoke up again there was a tremor in his voice. "Honestly, I don't want any of this stuff in my head anymore. I just want a simple life, and to raise Isaiah in a way that makes some sense. And I don't ever want him going to war, or being involved in violence or craziness of any kind."

He was silent for a few moments, then let out a heavy sigh. "I guess it's why you showing up with the police like that hit me so hard. I just want some peace."

CHAPTER THIRTY-FIVE

LATE THE NEXT MORNING, the aroma of pancakes and bacon was thick in the air. I was cooking, Isaiah sat coloring at the island counter, and Nate was upstairs in the shower. "Can I go see the squirrels?" Isaiah said, pointing to the window by the kitchen table.

I turned and gave him a look. "You'll keep away from the pool?"

He nodded, then raised his arms as a gesture for me to help him down from the stool. I lifted him down, then opened the side door, reminding him, as he ran out, to stay on the lawn.

Minutes later Nate materialized and kissed me on the back of the neck. "Where's Isaiah?"

"I let him go out in the backyard," I said. "I hope that's okay. I told him to stay on the lawn."

"He should be fine," Nate said, "but I'll go out and keep an eye on him." He surveyed the pancakes and nodded at a pile of bacon by the stove. "Okay if I take a piece?"

"Go ahead. I'll bring the rest out in a second. Everything's almost done."

He plucked a strip from the plate and took a bite. "You're spoiling us."

"That's the idea," I said, pulling him into a kiss. It wasn't the first we'd shared that morning.

Just as I was letting him go, we were shaken by an ear-splitting blast from the backyard. It sounded like a gunshot. I froze. "Could that be a car backfire?"

Not taking time to answer, Nate sprinted for the door. I followed him out and watched him disappear around the side of the house, calling "*Isaiah!*" as he ran. A moment later my heart almost stopped when I heard him yell, "*Oh no! Isaiah!*"

Afraid to look, I fell to my knees and put my face in my hands, crying, "*Oh my God, please no...please, please, no...*" After a few seconds, I jumped back to my feet and ran to where Nate was now holding Isaiah in his arms, tears streaming down his face.

Near his feet, my mother's gnome was on its side and a large handgun lay on the grass. I struggled to make sense of the scene, but I was unable to process the horror in front of me. Nate hollered for me to call 911, but I was paralyzed. Isaiah was bleeding, maybe dead, but I couldn't move.

ᙍ

"Rachel."

"*Rachel.*" This time more insistent.

I was shaking. No, someone was shaking me. "Wake up." It was Nate's voice. "You're having a nightmare."

My heart was pounding like a jackhammer, and I was confused. My eyes were open, and I understood that I was in bed, but my terror was still so real, I couldn't detach from the scene I'd just witnessed. Nate said my name again, and it slowly sunk in that I'd been dreaming. When it fully hit me that Isaiah was safe, I experienced the moment as an overwhelming physical rush. "*Oh my God,*" I managed, awash in relief, "I was dreaming something terrible happened to Isaiah."

"Nothing's happened to Isaiah," Nate whispered. The sun was starting to come up, and I could see his face in the dusky light.

"He'd been shot," I explained. "He'd gone into the backyard, and we heard a shot, and..."

"*Shhh,*" Nate said, pulling me into his arms. "It was just a dream."

It was a good ten minutes before my heart finally stopped racing. I squeezed Nate. "Can you go get him?"

"You want me bring him into bed with us?"

"Could you please?"

"Of course," Nate said. He gently moved me over, then lifted the sheet and got out of bed. When he returned, Isaiah was in his arms, still fast asleep. Seconds later, he was snuggled in between us, a soft glow of morning sun lighting his face, which wore a smile even as he slept.

With nightmare images now fading from my mind, the swell of love I felt for the child lying next to me was more powerful than I could ever describe. Breathing him in, and eventually hearing the steady breathing of Nate sleeping beside him, I made a concerted effort to stay awake—to enjoy every sweet second of what felt, in the dawn of a new day, like a miracle.

CHAPTER THIRTY-SIX

BY THE END OF that summer, Isaiah was swimming like a fish, Nate had a great job with an aerospace company, and I was studying to retake the LSAT. We were also living under the same roof. We'd considered selling my house and moving to a new place all our own but decided, at least for the short term, to live in my house, with Nate's mother in the cottage, where she could take it easy and help with Isaiah once I was in law school.

I had been nervous about living with Nate's mother, but her association with William had greased the wheels of our relationship so completely, she and I got along right from the start. At least mostly. She was initially territorial where Isaiah was concerned, but we eventually worked things out. By the third week of her moving in, she and I fit each other so well, it was hard to imagine a more perfect situation.

Nate and I joked about our *"Hallmark ending,"* and it was pretty close to the truth. It took me a while to trust the happiness that I felt like a renewed blessing each day I woke up next to Nate—with Isaiah not infrequently nestled between us. But soon I began to relax, and before I knew it, we were talking about get married in a quiet ceremony at City Hall, which was exactly what both of us wanted.

Just as I'd imagined, Isaiah started first grade in the little school up the street, and life became an almost picture-perfect facsimile of the one I'd dreamed of. Nate still had some issues to iron out with his former in-laws, but after a couple of sit-downs and a barbecue that would have made William proud, they eventually agreed to quit the custody threats and be satisfied with a traditional role as grandparents.

I still occasionally commiserated with William, and I felt the spirit of my mother each time the living room lit up with the afternoon sun, but my reliance on the two of them for support took on a more normal hue. I tried to remember Dan with more pity than anger, but I dealt with him mostly by putting him out of my mind. Thinking about him was just too painful.

As for all the stuff with the police, there were news stories and ultimately criminal convictions associated with the white nationalists Dan had been involved with, but connections to the LAPD were never publicly aired, at least not to my knowledge. I never heard another word from Craig. I tried calling him once at the number he'd given me, but the number was "not in service."

I did hear back from Tanaka. We spoke on several occasions, and I was eventually brought in for a deposition, but that was it. I was never called to testify in court.

Notwithstanding all the sadness and trauma we'd both been through—and recognizing a mutual tendency toward pessimism where some things were concerned—Nate and I made a pact to stay positive and regard our happiness as a gift. I intended to practice law in some form or fashion that would make William proud, but I was equally determined to make my new family good, and strong, and healthy. Nate's single-minded goal was to give Isaiah a happy childhood, unencumbered by the weight of history, or expectations of any kind beyond simply getting a good education and becoming a kind and thoughtful human being.

Nothing would have made me happier than to support that one simple goal. Or so I thought until I was diagnosed with a baby I'd been told was impossible. Nate was so elated by our miracle pregnancy that he began referring to my expanding belly as "Our Little Hallmark Baby." He joked about the names *Mark* for a boy, or *Holly* for a girl. Isaiah, who was hoping for a boy, lobbied for *Gus*, after his class guinea pig. In the end, Isaiah got his brother, and we decided to call him William. William Markus Matthews. Under the circumstances, I put off law school for a while longer and, instead, stayed home with the baby and worked on a novel.

A year later, Nate and I were married, Isaiah and William were thriving, Nate had been promoted twice, and his mother had bonded with Arturo around the garden. I was enrolled in Pacific Coast Law School and had finished the first draft of a novel. I initially titled it *The Sins of My Brother*, but eventually settled on *The House*.

CHAPTER THIRTY-SEVEN

LATE ONE AFTERNOON, FOLLOWING a class on torts, I was invited to meet some people in a nearby restaurant for a drink. I was anxious, as always, to get home, but I'd been wanting to make some law school friends, so I called Nate's mother to see if she'd mind if I got home a little late. "Take your time," she told me. "The kids are fine."

I had just arrived at the restaurant and was passing through the bar on my way to the bathroom when my attention was drawn to a TV tuned to CNN. The volume was turned down, so I couldn't hear what the commentator was saying, but the picture for the story stopped me in my tracks. It was Craig.

When my eyes eventually moved down to the news crawl, my legs went rubbery and I had to sit down at the bar to steady myself. I glanced at the bartender, and he could see that I was having a reaction to whatever was happening on the television. He turned and looked up at it. "Can you turn it up?" I asked.

He shrugged, then picked up a remote and adjusted the volume as I stared, in disbelief, at the words crossing the bottom of the screen: *Self-described white separatist Richard Cruikshank found dead after shooting incident at his Lake Elsinore home.*

Barely able to breathe, I listened as an attractive brunette reported that a member of a Southern California white nationalist group had been shot in his home, where automatic weapons, thousands of rounds of ammunition, and bomb-making materials were later discovered by the police.

By the time I absorbed this basic information, my heart was beating so hard that I could barely process what I was hearing—although I did manage to glean that he'd apparently been shot by another member of his group.

My friends eventually found me sitting frozen at the bar, looking sick. Not wanting to explain, I apologized, said I needed to beg off, then went out to the parking lot and sat in my car until I felt normal enough to drive. When I was finally on the freeway and heading home, my head was spinning with horrifying "what ifs," the most serious being, *What if, because of my silence, Craig had pulled off some horrible act of terror?*

Thinking back, I tried to make sense of all my interactions with him, starting with our initial date and progressing through all our meetings. What had he wanted from me? I thought about him sitting in my kitchen, speculating on how much my house was worth. Was he conspiring with Dan to kill me for the house? Did he fabricate the story about Dan's dare, or was it true, and he really had been trying to collect? I cringed at how close he'd come. And had Dan really plotted to kill me at all?

The more I reflected, the more confused I became. What had Craig been after when he'd met me at the hospital? Dan's guns? Had he known they were in my cottage and wanted me to turn them over to him? *I nearly had.* And what about his FBI badge, and the Quantico picture? Had he really gone to the FBI Academy? I had so many questions and no way of getting any answers.

I wondered if I should call Tanaka and tell him that I'd seen the news and recognized Cruikshank as Craig. I wouldn't have to mention our last meeting at my house. I thought about this at length and decided that I *would* call him, but only after I'd had more time to process everything, and possibly learn more about Cruikshank as the story unfolded.

Putting that aside, I once again considered how many lives might have been lost because I'd kept quiet about his last visit. I felt both ashamed and sick.

William was suddenly talking to me, and his voice was so welcome, I nearly broke down. *"Don't do this to yourself,"* he said. *"There's no point in torturing yourself with questions you can't answer. That band of hate mongers, with their poison and their ignorance—Dan brought that ugly world to your doorstep, you didn't ask for it. Forget Craig, or Richard, or whatever his name was. And, I'm sorry, but forget Dan, too. Who cares what he was up to? Go home, love Nate and those beautiful kids, and let all that other stuff go."*

"You don't think I need to tell Tanaka about Craig?"

"I don't think you need to tell anyone anything if you don't want to. What could possibly be gained?"

I pondered this question for the rest of the ride home.

By the time I arrived at the house, I was both calm and determined. I would talk to Tanaka and Nate about Craig at some point. Maybe. But later. For now, I would put him out of my mind and concentrate on my family.

When I walked in the front door, Isaiah rushed to meet me and immediately began chattering about Legos, which were his latest passion. Following him into the living room, I was greeted by Nate's mother, who was sitting on the couch with William on her lap. When he saw me, he raised his arms in my direction, his face brightening into a dimpled grin. I picked him up and breathed in the sweet smell of his curly hair.

A moment later, Nate appeared. "Hey, look who's home," he said cheerily. With a flourish, he swept Isaiah up over his shoulder, then crossed the room and planted a kiss first on William, then on me.

In the warmth of Nate's gaze, I nuzzled William and channeled my father. "Ain't *no* place I'd rather be."

***

AUTHOR'S NOTE

Deep feelings about race and inequality are baked into me. I was born in 1957 and raised by parents who talked openly and often about the demonstrations for equal rights that we watched in black and white on the evening news. In 1964, my Southern grandfather disowned my family after fighting with my parents over Civil Rights. Thus, I knew at an early age that an epic struggle was taking place, and there was no question as to whose side we were on.

I went to integrated junior high and high schools, and benefited not only from having black classmates, but also from seeing, up close, how some lives were shaped by a history of racial discrimination. In college, my interest in race and social justice intensified, and, from there, it has never abated. My novel, *Arkansas Summer*, was my first attempt at using fiction to express my feelings about these things. Set in Jim Crow Arkansas, it shines a spotlight on the white supremacy and racist violence of the segregated South. Parts of the plot were inspired by the extreme bigotry of my paternal grandfather. The love story was inspired by my own experience with interracial love. *House of Fragile Dreams* is a further expression of my interest in race and social justice.

Sadly, between the time I started *Arkansas Summer* and finished *House of Fragile Dreams*, unabashed Jim Crow-style racism has seen a shocking revival. This took me by surprise. I never imagined Americans capable of such a dramatic backslide. I pray that by the time my *next* book is finished, we will have seen another dramatic shift—this one in the right direction.

— Anne Moose

ACKNOWLEDGEMENTS

Some writers keep early pages of their work to themselves, preferring to wait until they have at least a finished first draft before seeking advice or criticism. I like feedback all along the way. It keeps me going if I have cheering from the sidelines, or arms waving me back on course if I veer off into the woods. This being the case, those friends and family members who were willing to read as I wrote have a special place in my heart. For this novel, the saintly readers who read pages that sometimes arrived daily were Beth Moose, Katy Culver, David Silva, and Sue Grether. My late parents, Jim and Virginia Moose, were also faithful readers. I dearly wish they'd lived to see the finished product.

I also roped in quite a few others along the way, all of whom provided valuable feedback at different times. This list includes my husband, Peter Dingus, Pamela Schneider, Ara Gregorian, Excetral Caldwell, Pamela Shepherd, Paula Berggren, Julie Didion, Robert Egan, Ruth Mary Lovitt, Yvonne Sheer, Martha Casey, Teresa Laughlin, Randy Goodwin, Nancy Klann-Moren, Baron Birtcher, Kay Marshall, Richard Turner, Rosie de Guzman, Sarah Maclay, Charlie Maclay, Russ Thompston, Jim Eberle, Tami Sheikh, Susi Allison, and Cathy Boggs. A gigantic *thank you* to all of you for your wonderful support and advice.

Finally, to my sons Paul Dingus and John Dingus, my daughter-in-law, Olivia Weeks, and all my other friends and relatives who've embraced and encouraged me as a writer (including Maddie Margarita, Larry Porricelli, and other members of the Southern California Writers Association), thank you from the depths of my heart. Your steady love and support mean more to me than I could ever adequately express.

ABOUT THE AUTHOR

Anne Moose was raised in Sacramento, California and received a BA in Social/Cultural Anthropology from U.C. Berkeley. She authored her first book, *Berkeley USA*, in 1981, and her second, *Arkansas Summer*, in 2017. Thirty-plus years of writing and editing happened in between, mostly in small publishing and the software industry. *House of Fragile Dreams* is her second novel. She has two grown sons and lives in Mission Viejo, California with her husband, Peter Dingus.

Made in the USA
Las Vegas, NV
28 October 2022

58306854R00173